Fergus Hume

The Sacred Herb

Fergus Hume

The Sacred Herb

1st Edition | ISBN: 978-3-75235-231-3

Place of Publication: Frankfurt am Main, Germany

Year of Publication: 2020

Outlook Verlag GmbH, Germany.

The Sacred Herb

BY

FERGUS HUME

CHAPTER I.

THE LATEST SENSATION

Lord Prelice felt desperately bored. Like Xeres, he longed for some new pleasure, yet knew not where to look for one. This was the result of being surfeited with the sweets of extraordinary good fortune. Born to a title, endowed with passable good looks, gifted with abilities above the average, and possessed of admirable health, he should have been the happiest of men; the more especially as his income ran well into five figures, and he had the whole wide world to play with. Certainly he had played with it and with life, up to his present age of thirty-five years. Perhaps this was the reason of his acute boredom. If all work and no play makes Jack dull; all play and no work must necessarily make him *blase*.

Therefore, in spite of the excellent breakfast spread before him on this bright summer morning, when London was looking at its best, the young man was ungratefully wondering what he could do to render life endurable. He ate from habit and not because he enjoyed his food; he read the morning papers, since it was necessary to be abreast of the times, for conversational purposes, although very little was new therein and still less was true. By the time he arrived at the marmalade stage of the meal he was again considering the possibilities of the next four and twenty hours. In this discontented frame of mind he was discovered by his aunt.

Lady Sophia Haken bustled into the pleasant room exasperatingly cheerful, and very pleased with life in general and with herself in particular. She was an elderly woman of a somewhat masculine type who lived a simple out-of-door existence, and who proclaimed loudly that it was necessary for humanity to return to the Stone Age for true enjoyment. Having been riding in the Row for the last two hours, she entered in her habit, filled with the egotism of the early riser. As a near relative, she could not do less than scold Prelice for lingering over a late breakfast, and told him,—also as a near relative—that she scolded him for his good. She had done so very often before without result, and, but that she loved to lay down the law, would have long since given over the attempt to improve her nephew. Nevertheless, anxious to achieve the impossible, she attacked him with pristine vigor, as though aware for the first time of his bad habits.

"Nine o'clock and still at breakfast," said Lady Sophia significantly, and slapped her skirts with a whip which she would have dearly liked to lay across her lazy nephew's broad shoulders.

2

Prelice looked indolently at the clock, then at the table, and finally at his fuming aunt. "I cannot deny it," he said, with a yawn.

"Is that all you have to say?" she asked, much disgusted.

Prelice heaved a sigh. It was necessary to say something, if only to stem the coming tide of verbose speech. "How well you are looking."

"Because I have been up since six o'clock."

"How unwise; you will probably sleep all the afternoon."

Lady Sophia snapped, tartly: "I shall do nothing of the sort."

"Oh, very well," he assented, "you will do nothing of the sort. Anything for a quiet life, even agreement with the improbable."

His aunt grasped her whip dangerously. "How exasperating you are!"

"I was just thinking the same about you," confessed Prelice, good-humouredly; "it is so disagreeable for a late riser to be reminded of the time." And having folded his napkin, he lighted a cigarette.

"How long is this going on?" demanded Lady Sophia fiercely. His imperturbability made her long to shake him thoroughly.

"How long is what going on?" asked Prelice provokingly.

"This idle, idiotic, insane, sensual, foolish, wicked, dilatory existence!"

"Seven adjectives," murmured the young man, opening his eyes. "Waste, waste—oh, what waste!"

"How long is this going on?" inquired his relative again, and whipped her skirts—instead of Prelice's back—with renewed vigour.

He was forced to answer. "As long as I do, no doubt. What else is to be done, I should like to know?"

"You shall know. Serve your country."

"What! And be abused in the penny press? No, thank you."

"You can surely help your brother-man."

"Surely—only to learn how much ingratitude exists in the world."

Lady Sophia stamped, bit her lip, and looked like a ruffled cockatoo in a bad temper. She wanted to quarrel, and it annoyed her that Prelice would not meet her half way, by supplying a reason. She had to invent the quarrel, and bring about the quarrel, and carry on the quarrel, and finish the quarrel without assistance. "Marry!" was the one word which suggested itself, and she hoped that it would be like a red rag to a bull.

"Oh, Jerusalem!" Prelice shook his closely cropped fair head. "I would much rather serve brother-man than marry sister-woman. You offer me a choice of unoriginal evils."

"You never will face the truth," declared Lady Sophia irrelevantly; and forthwith—according to an old-established custom—she proceeded to recount the family history—that is, she picked out the worst traits of Prelice's ancestors and debited them to his account. He smoked through two cigarettes, and nodded at intervals, not very much interested, since he had heard the same oration at least a dozen times. Lady Sophia having worked her way from the reign of Elizabeth down to that of Edward VII., ended with a lurid, penny-sensational picture of what would befall her listener in the near future, unless he worked like a nigger.

"Such a bad illustration," interposed Prelice placidly; "niggers don't work. As I have just returned from the West Indies, I ought to know." Lady Sophia snorted down the interruption, and seeing that he was still unimpressed, tried to goad him into industry by mentioning several of his school-fellows who had attained to comparative fame and fortune, while Prelice—as she scathingly put it—had been grovelling in the mud. "Even young Shepworth," ended Lady Sophia, somewhat out of breath, "and *he* was never clever—even *he* is Counsel for the Defence this very day in an important murder case."

"I'm deuced sorry for his client," murmured Prelice indolently.

"Why should you be?" demanded his aunt aggressively.

"You said that he wasn't clever."

"He must be." Lady Sophia contradicted herself with feminine calmness. "If he wasn't he certainly would not be talking this very day at the New Bailey. Go and hear him, Prelice, and be ashamed that a fool—yes, a superlative fool —should succeed where you fail."

"What *do* you mean?" inquired her nephew, with great curiosity. "First you say that Ned isn't clever——"

"Ned! Ned. I never mentioned Ned. Who is Ned?"

"Shepworth. Edward Shepworth—Ned for short. We were great chums at Eton, you know. But you say that he isn't clever, then you insist that he is, and wind up by calling him a fool."

"You know quite well what I mean," said Lady Sophia with dignity.

"I really don't," confessed her nephew artlessly, "you describe such a complex character. However, as I have nothing to do to-day——"

"And never have anything to do—idler."

"I shall go to the New Bailey, and listen to Ned hanging his client!"

"So brilliant a barrister as Mr. Shepworth will certainly get her off," said Lady Sophia decisively.

Prelice passed over this new contradiction. "It's a woman?"

"Yes. Mona Chent. You know her."

"I'm sure I don't. The criminal classes don't attract me."

"She is not a criminal, but a lady," said his aunt, as though the two things were incompatible; "and you *do* know her. Mona Chent, the niece of old Sir Oliver Lanwin."

Prelice reflected with bent brows. "I never heard the name before, I assure you, Aunt Sophia," he said at length. "Remember that I have been travelling round the world for the last seven years and know very little of the latest London sensation."

"You ought to stay at home, and make yourself acquainted with people, Prelice."

"Including this murderess?"

"She is not a murderess," cried Lady Sophia energetically. "I always did think that she was a sweet girl, and if she did kill her uncle, it was no more than he deserved. I never liked him."

"Therefore he ought to be murdered," said Prelice, rising and stretching himself before the empty grate. "So Sir Oliver was the victim. I have heard of him. He used to send Ned shells and barbaric things from the South Seas. And now Ned is repaying him by defending his murderess."

"I tell you Mona did not murder the man. I know her. I have received her. Would I receive a murderess?"

"It might be a draw to some of your parties," said Prelice politely, and with a recollection of several dull entertainments. "But I cannot quite gather from your clear explanation if she is guilty or not."

"Half London thinks that she is, and half asserts her innocence."

"What does Shepworth think?"

"He naturally believes her to be innocent."

"Because he defends her?"

"Because she is his future wife."

Prelice looked startled. "Oh, Jerusalem! And if he proves her innocence he'll marry her, I suppose."

"As she is her uncle's heiress, and Mr. Shepworth is poor, I presume he will. Ten thousand a year is not to be despised."

"But a wife with such a past," protested the young man. "Ugh! Did Miss Chent murder her uncle to get the money?"

"She didn't murder him at all. Look at the facts of the case——"

"I shall be delighted to, if you will place them before me."

"You ought to know all about them," said Lady Sophia, rising impatiently; "everyone has been talking about the case for the last month;—ever since Mona Chent was arrested, in fact."

"Ah, but you see I have only just arrived in London. I shall go to my club and get posted up in the latest scandal."

"The latest sensation," corrected his aunt. "Go to the New Bailey instead, and hear Mr. Shepworth place the case before the judge and jury. His eloquence will make you sorry for your lazy, useless life; he will be a K.C.," cried Lady Sophia, becoming prophetic, "and Attorney-General and Lord Chancellor, and——"

"King of Timbuctoo, no doubt. Loud cheers."

Lady Sophia looked indignantly at the scoffer, who beamed on her benignly with laughing blue eyes. "You *have* deteriorated since you left the Army."

"No doubt, the standard of morality in the Army being so high."

"Oh!" His aunt stamped, and flung open the door with a tragic air. "I have done with you. Your flippancy is disgusting. I repeat, Prelice, I have done with you." And she departed hastily, lest a reply from the scoffer should spoil her impressive exit.

Prelice laughed, knowing that Lady Sophia would never be done with him while she had a tongue to wag. Also he believed that she was truly fond of him, and knew that she had only too much reason to accuse him of wasting his life. He resolved to mend his ways, more as an experiment in self-denial than because he wanted to, and cast about for a model person to imitate. After Lady Sophia's conversation the name of Edward Shepworth naturally suggested itself, so Prelice arrayed himself in purple and fine linen, and ordered round his motor car. Within two hours he was driving out of Half-Moon Street, and was soon dodging the traffic of Piccadilly.

It was so delightful, manipulating the machine in the sunshine, and acting as a chauffeur so appealed to him that he was minded to turn the Mercedes in the direction of Richmond. But the hints about the murder being an unusual one kept him to his earlier determination; also a copy of *The Daily Mirror* assured him that the accused girl was exceedingly pretty; finally, he had always been

6

friendly with the Counsel for the Defence, and thought that he would renew the tie of old school-days. These things brought his smart Mercedes to the bran-new portals of the Criminal Court, and when he had handed over the steering-wheel to his chauffeur he sought out the arena, wherein Shepworth was fighting for the life of his promised wife.

Naturally the first person at whom the young man looked was the prisoner in the dock, and he mentally confessed that *The Daily Mirror* photograph had not done her justice. It could scarcely do so in mere black and white, as Miss Chent needed vivid tints to convey her peculiar charm. She was one of those rare blondes who embody sunshine in hair and eyes: a dragon-fly of humanity, all radiance and glow. Since she was on trial for her life, Prelice quite expected to see a white-faced, terrified creature, worn out with shame and suffering. But Miss Chent might have been in an opera-box, for all the emotion she displayed. Prelice had more experience of women than was good for him, but he never beheld so perfectly dressed, or so perfectly serene a girl. It would be absurd to say that so level-headed a young man fell in love with this attractive criminal at first sight; but he certainly felt drawn to her. She looked like a captive angel, and without knowing the rights or wrongs of the case, Prelice mentally pronounced her to be entirely innocent. Her calmness, if not her beauty, acquitted her, as his susceptible heart decided, for no woman with an unclean conscience could have faced judge and jury with such manifest confidence. Prelice thought of Joan of Arc on trial for sorcery; of Mary Stuart before a prejudiced tribunal; of Marie Antoinette; and of the Vestal, who proved her innocence by drawing Tiber water in a sieve. He might also have recalled the Marquise de Brinvilliers, likewise calm, beautiful, and—guilty. But he did not.

The Court was filled with more or less fashionable people, who came to make a Roman holiday of Sir Oliver Lanwin's violent death, and Miss Chent's position. Doubtless she had been well known in Society, and those who had been her friends were here to watch her in the new role of an accused criminal. Prelice was disgusted at the heartless conduct of some ladies, who whispered and tittered, and used opera-glasses to stare at the unfortunate girl. He internally commended his aunt for having had the good taste to remain absent, and then turned his eyes on the array of barristers to search for Ned Shepworth.

If the prisoner was serene in the consciousness of innocence, her counsel certainly was less composed. A strong will and the second nature of custom kept Shepworth sufficiently self-controlled to deceive those who had but a passing acquaintance with his personality. But Prelice, who had known the young barrister for years, noted that his usually ruddy complexion was whiter than usual, and that his eyes seemed to be sunken in his head by reason of the dark shadows beneath them. Shepworth was a slim, handsome man, brown-haired and brown-eyed, with a clean-shaven face and a resolute mouth. In his wig and gown he looked a very presentable son of Themis, if somewhat less composed than the traditionally unemotional lawyer should be. He was seated at the long table with two older men, who apparently were his coadjutors; and near the defence trio the Counsel for the Prosecution—appointed by the Public Prosecutor on behalf of the Crown—was chatting amiably with his colleague, a keen-faced young barrister. Behind sat many other lawyers wigged and gowned, who were taking the deepest interest in the proceedings. For the moment the Court was so still that the rustling of the briefs, as the barristers turned their pages, could be plainly heard.

"Are those two fellows assisting Mr. Shepworth in the defence?" Prelice whispered to a legal-looking bystander at his elbow.

"No," replied the man in a low voice; "the big fellow is Cudworth, K.C., and the other is young Arkers, who acts as Junior Counsel, Shepworth is not defending, as he was in the house when the crime was committed, and will be called as a witness."

So Lady Sophia was inaccurate as usual, and Prelice felt somewhat disappointed that he would not have an opportunity of hearing his old school-chum orating. However, he had little time to think, for at this moment the Prosecuting Counsel got on his legs to open the case. Prelice felt that the curtain had risen on a tragedy. He wondered what would be the scene when the curtain fell.

CHAPTER II.

THE TRIAL.

The Counsel, in a clear and deliberate voice, opened his speech with an unvarnished statement of the case; and a very remarkable story he unfolded. Prelice, as an experienced traveller, had always believed in the impossible; but it seemed to him that he had returned to prosaic England to hear a veritable fairy-tale. There was something extremely fantastic about the way in which the crime was said to have been committed. As set forth by the speaker, the event happened in this wise.

Sir Oliver Lanwin, the last male heir of an ancient Kentish family, whose seat was situated near Hythe, had found himself, some forty years previous to the trial, a pauper with a newly inherited title. Seeing no chance in England of rehabilitating his fortunes, he had taken what little money he possessed to

New Zealand, leaving his only sister well provided for, as the wife of an army officer named Chent. After making some money in various ways at Hokitika, Sir Oliver had purchased a fruit schooner to trade amongst the South Sea Islands. Being successful, he had bought other ships, and for more than thirty years he had been a kind of Polynesian merchant-prince, owing to his wealth and enterprise and keen business capacity. He had never married, because of an early disappointment, and ten years before, he had returned to England with a capital representing ten thousand a year. With this he had retired to his ancestral seat, near Hythe, and there proposed to end his days in comfort, after the fashion of Sinbad, the famous sailor of the Arabian Nights. He brought with him an old shell-back mariner, Steve Agstone by name, who was an important witness for the prosecution. Unfortunately, said the Counsel, the man had disappeared, immediately before the inquest, after hinting to the housekeeper, Mrs. Blexey, that he had actually witnessed the committal of the crime, for which the prisoner was being tried. In spite of all efforts made by the police, this witness could not be discovered, and it was impossible to say why he had disappeared. But Counsel hoped to produce other witnesses, who would prove beyond all shadow of a doubt that the prisoner was guilty.

After proceeding thus far, Counsel sipped a glass of water, hitched his gown more comfortably on to his shoulders, and continued his speech amidst the breathless silence of the listeners.

Being a bachelor, Sir Oliver felt somewhat lonely, since he was of a sociable disposition. For a few months he kept open house, but as his nature proved to be exacting and imperious, he did not get on well with his neighbours. Finally, he proclaimed that they were all idiots, and closing his doors, he became more or less of a recluse. It was then that Sir Oliver's widowed sister, Mrs. Chent, died suddenly, leaving her daughter Mona—the prisoner—to the care of her uncle. Sir Oliver became extremely fond of the young lady, who was of a lively and amiable disposition. Indeed, his attachment was so great that he made a will in her favour, by which she was to inherit ten thousand a year and the family-seat.

"And here," proceeded Counsel impressively, "I may mention a circumstance which, in the light of after events, has some bearing on the case. Mr. Oliver, while bathing at Samoa, had his leg taken off, from the knee, by a shark. He thus was unable to indulge in field sports, in games, or indeed in any kind of out-of-door life. He therefore took to reading, and of a somewhat unusual kind. Jacob Bohme, Paracelsus, and Eliphas Levi were his favourite authors, from which it can be judged that the dead man took a deep interest in psychic questions.

"He also consulted palmists, fortune-tellers, astrologers, and crystal-gazers, frequently asking them down to Lanwin Grange. In fact, at the very time when the crime was committed, Madame Marie Eppingrave, a well-known Bond Street interpreter of the future, was staying in the house. She will be called as a witness. But you can see, gentlemen of the jury, that the late baronet was an exceedingly superstitious man, although clear-headed in business and perfectly capable of managing his affairs."

It was at this point that Shepworth caught sight of Prelice, and he nodded in a friendly manner. Then he scribbled a note, and sent it by an usher to the young man. It proved to be a request that Prelice would wait for him at the door when the Court adjourned for luncheon. Prelice slipped the missive into his pocket, and nodded a reply. Shepworth seemed to be pleased with this prompt acceptance, and immediately resumed his attitude of attention, while Counsel continued to boom out facts with the drone of a bumble-bee.

As the narrative proceeded it appeared that, a few months before his death, Sir Oliver had received a South Sea visitor in the person of a young sailor called Captain Felix Jadby, whose father he had known at Tahiti. The baronet was extremely intimate with the visitor, and practically gave him the run of the house. Captain Jadby came and went at will, and Sir Oliver talked to him a great deal in connection with matters dealing with Polynesian trade. This was not to be wondered at, since the baronet, having been a trader himself, it was pleasant for him to converse with one who knew about such things.

Unfortunately, Captain Jadby fell in love with the prisoner, and wished to marry her. She refused to become his wife, on the plea that she loved Mr. Edward Shepworth, and was engaged to him. Sir Oliver was annoyed at the engagement, as he desired the marriage with Captain Jadby to take place. On the day of his death he quarrelled seriously with the prisoner, and, according to Madame Marie Eppingrave's evidence—since she was present during the quarrel—Sir Oliver stated that if the prisoner did not marry Captain Jadby he would disinherit her. Prisoner still refused, and retired to her room, saying that she would not reappear until Captain Jadby was out of the house. For the sake of peace Jadby went up to London that same day, with the intention of returning by the ten o'clock train. Then, if prisoner still remained obdurate, he intended to say good-bye to his host, and leave for the Colonies within the week.

"And now, gentlemen of the jury," continued Counsel, with another hitch of his gown, "we come to the most important part of the story. Previous to going to London, Captain Jadby had a wordy quarrel with Mr. Shepworth, and from words the quarrel came to blows. Mr. Shepworth's foot slipped and he slightly sprained his ankle, so that he was not able to leave Lanwin Grange, as he desired. His position was an unpleasant one, since Sir Oliver was not well disposed towards him on account of the engagement which existed with the prisoner. As Captain Jadby had left the Grange, Mr. Shepworth wished to go also, and would have gone, but that his sprained ankle prevented his removal, and he therefore remained in his room. Now, gentlemen, you can see the position of the several people connected with this matter at the time when the crime was committed. Captain Jadby was in London, intending to return at ten o'clock; Mr. Shepworth was in his room with a sprained ankle which prevented his leaving it; the prisoner was also in her room, and even though Captain Jadby had departed, for the time being, she declined to come down to dinner. Madame Marie Eppingrave and Sir Oliver dined alone, and then the baronet retired to his library, where until nine o'clock—according to Madame Marie's evidence—he chatted with her on occult subjects. Also, as Madame Marie will state, Sir Oliver expressed himself strongly on the subject of the prisoner's refusal of Jadby.

"As Sir Oliver was in the habit of retiring early to bed on account of his health, his factotum, Steve Agstone, entered the library at nine o'clock to bolt and bar the windows. There were no shutters; and this please remember, gentlemen, as it is an important point. The servants had already retired, and after making the library safe, Steve Agstone left the room with the intention of waiting up for Captain Jadby, who was expected back by the ten o'clock train, and who intended to walk to the Grange. Madame Marie lingered for a few minutes to say good-night, and then retired to her bedroom. She declares that it was five minutes after nine o'clock that she left the library. Sir Oliver— so she says—was seated at the table near the window reading and smoking.

"Here, gentlemen," pursued Counsel, taking up a plan, "is a drawing of the library." He passed it by an usher to the foreman of the jury. "You will see that there is only one door to the library, which leads out into the hall, and which is opposite to the fireplace. The inner walls of the room, on three sides, are covered with books, but the fourth wall—the outer wall, gentlemen—has in it three tall French windows, which lead on to a terrace over a lawn. The lawn extends for some distance, ending in flower-beds, these in their turn being encircled by shrubs, and farther back by the park trees. When Madame Marie left the room Sir Oliver was seated at his writing-table, marked 'X,' immediately before the middle window. As the night was chilly there was a fire burning in the grate. You understand, gentlemen? Good. Now we come to the discovery of the crime."

Counsel then went on to state that Captain Jadby returned, according to his promise, at ten o'clock—that is, his train arrived at the station, which was about half-a-mile from the Grange. He walked to Sir Oliver's house, as he had no luggage to carry, and the night was fine if somewhat cold. On emerging from the avenue on to the lawn he saw that there was a light in the library; and it was here that Counsel again drew the jury's attention to the fact that the windows had no shutters. Captain Jadby therefore thought that, as Sir Oliver had not retired to bed, he would knock at one of the windows, and enter the house that way, so as to avoid rousing the other inmates by ringing the bell. He advanced to the lighted windows, and looked through the middle one, which was veiled, as were the others, with curtains of Indian beadwork. To his surprise, he saw that Sir Oliver, seated at his desk, was lying forward on the writing-table. "I am precise to a fault here, gentlemen," said Counsel jocularly, "but it is absolutely to be even pedantic, so that you will understand.

"Sir Oliver," he continued, "was lying with his face on his outstretched hands, and in an armchair near the fireplace sat the prisoner, in a white dressing-gown with her hands on her lap. Captain Jadby could not see very distinctly, owing to the beadwork curtains, but he saw sufficient to guess that something was wrong, especially as his knocking produced no effect either on Sir Oliver or on the prisoner. He unconsciously pushed at the middle window, and, to his surprise, discovered that it was not locked. He therefore entered, and what he saw made him ring the bell at once, to summon the household.

"And what did he see, gentlemen of the jury? he saw that Sir Oliver was dead. He had been stabbed to the heart, under the left shoulder-blade, apparently while seated at his desk. The body had naturally fallen forward. The prisoner, seated in the armchair with her hands on her lap, was in an unconscious state, but her hands and the white dressing-gown were stained with blood—with the blood, gentlemen," said Counsel impressively, "of her uncle. Before anyone could enter the room she revived, and on seeing the body of her uncle, displayed great terror and horror. Steve Agstone, who had been waiting up for Captain Jadby, was the first person to enter, and on discovering the dead body of his master—to whom he was sincerely attached—he at once rushed out of the house for a doctor. By this time the servants were aroused by the noise, and with them came Madame Marie Eppingrave. Even Mr. Shepworth, lame as he was, managed to crawl down the stairs, so loud had been the clamour which had awakened him.

"And what did the prisoner say to all this? Gentlemen, she told a most ridiculous story to account for her presence in the library. According to her statement, which the inspector from Hythe took down in the presence of witnesses, prisoner said that she could not sleep on account of her quarrel with her uncle. She came down the stairs at a quarter to ten o'clock, and entered the library, with the intention of making friends with her uncle. When she entered—so she declares—the room was filled with pungent white smoke, through which she could dimly see Sir Oliver seated at the writing-table. The smoke made her senses reel, but by holding her handkerchief to her mouth she managed to stagger to the middle window. She had just managed to unfasten the catch when she fell unconscious. The next thing she remembers —according to her preposterous story—is the presence of Captain Jadby. She declares that she did not know when Sir Oliver was stabbed, and when she entered the library did not know why it should be filled with smoke. When Captain Jadby entered—as he will tell you—there was no smoke, and the fire had burned down to red cinders."

Again Counsel had to drink a sip of water, as he had been talking for some time, and there was a low murmur of conversation heard before he again began to speak. The story, which he alleged that Miss Chent had told, seemed ridiculous; and even Prelice, prejudiced as he was in her favour, thought that the defence was absurd. But Miss Chent never moved a muscle; she did not even change colour. Quiet, and without a word, she sat in the dock, waiting patiently for her innocence to be made manifest. And yet, as everyone thought, her tale was too ridiculous for words.

"And finally, gentlemen," said Counsel, taking up his brief, "I would draw your attention to the medical evidence. The doctor called in stated that Sir Oliver was murdered about ten o'clock—mark that, gentlemen—about the very time that the prisoner confesses she was in the library in a state of unconsciousness. Captain Jadby did not arrive until thirty minutes after ten, as he did not walk very quickly. And again, gentlemen, no weapon was found wherewith the wound—a wide, clean wound—could have been inflicted. But an Indian dagger with a jade handle, used by Sir Oliver as a paper-knife, is missing. With that I verily believe the deceased was stabbed. And remember, gentlemen, that the window was unfastened; and if we are to believe this foolish tale of a pungent smoke, prisoner unfastened it when she entered and immediately before she fainted. Gentlemen, she *did* faint, but not then. No! Can you not guess what took place? The prisoner came down the stairs to see her uncle; perhaps, as she declares, to make it up with him, since we may as well give her the benefit of the doubt. But in place of reconciliation, the quarrel grows more bitter. Impulsive and furious, the prisoner snatches the paper-knife—a dangerous weapon remember, gentlemen—and while Sir Oliver turns again to his book, stabs him in the back. She then opens the window, and buried the paper-knife, all bloody, in the garden. On re-entering, the sight of the dead body shows her what a terrible crime she has committed. Instead of refastening the window she staggers forward, with the intention of regaining her bedroom, and of playing the part of an innocent woman. But her nerves, which maintained her strength and consciousness so far, fail at the critical moment. She manages to reach the armchair, and falls into it unconscious, some time after ten o'clock. There she lies, with blood-stained hands and dress, until Captain Jadby arrives, when she recovers her senses to tell a wild and improbable story. Sir Oliver, as the medical evidence proves, was alive when she entered the library at a quarter to ten. He is dead, and his blood is smearing the prisoner's dressing-gown at half-past ten, when Captain Jadby arrives. And all that time prisoner says that she was unconscious. Quite so. She was, up to the moment of Captain Jadby's arrival, and from the moment, when she staggered into the room, after burying the knife in the garden. And now, gentlemen——" Here Counsel went on to state that in spite of all efforts the knife could not be found. He also detailed more explicitly the medical evidence, and gave the name of the witness whom he proposed to call, and ended with a damning indictment of the reasons which had led the prisoner to commit the crime. Amongst these was the fact that by Sir Oliver's death prisoner would inherit ten thousand a year at once, and would thus have been enabled to marry Edward Shepworth.

When his speech was finished Counsel sat down, wiping his brow, and a hum of conversation rose in the crowded Court. Mona's eyes wandered here and there, and rested finally on the pitying face of Lord Prelice. For a moment she remained calm, and then flushed deeply, the first sign of emotion she had given. A moment later and she was led away in charge of a warder, while the Court adjourned for luncheon.

CHAPTER III.

THE PAPER-CUTTER.

"I am delighted to see you, Dorry," said Shepworth, addressing Prelice by his Eton nickname, when the young man had been called "Dormouse," shortened as above, on account of his lethargic habits. "I want you very badly. Come and grub somewhere, and we can talk."

Prelice responded very cordially, as the two had been very close friends at the old school, and submitted to be led round the corner to a small hidden restaurant much affected by the gentlemen of the long robe. Here, when they were snugly ensconced in a corner, Shepworth ordered food for his friend, but contented himself with a cigarette, and a cup of strong coffee. "I can't eat a morsel," he protested when Prelice advised a meal. "I am too much bothered over this case. How the deuce did you come to the Court, Dorry?"

Prelice, who possessed a hearty appetite, tackled a plate of cold beef, and answered between mouthfuls. "My aunt Sophia bully-ragged me this morning as an idler, and advised me to hear you spouting. She wanted to make me ashamed of myself."

"And are you?" asked Shepworth aimlessly.

"Rats!" said his lordship inelegantly; "but I'm sorry, old man. This is a sinfully hard business for you. Why didn't you write me that you were engaged?"

"I didn't know where to find you, Dorry. Lady Sophia, whom I met once or twice, told me that you were scampering round the world. I *have* wanted you, Prelice, these last few months. Yes, and before that."

"Before the murder, do you mean?"

"Yes! I have never had a chum since I left school. Lots of friends, no doubt, good men all, but a chum," he laid his hand on Prelice's shoulder with a burst of emotion. "Oh, Dorry, what a mercy you are here, and that I have some safe person in whom to confide. I should have had to tell someone in the long run."

"Tell someone what?" asked Prelice soberly.

"About that poor girl."

"Miss Chent?"

"Yes! It is an awful position for her, and for me. No! Don't look at me like that, Dorry. I swear that I'm not thinking of myself. I'd give my right hand to save Mona."

"She is innocent, of course?" asked Prelice, pushing away his plate.

"Yes! I am certain that she is innocent, although——" He hesitated for a moment, then flung away his cigarette, leaned his arms on the marble-topped table, and looked earnestly at his friend. "You heard Belmain's speech?"

Prelice nodded. "You mean the prosecuting Counsel."

"Yes! He was fair enough in the beginning and in the middle, but he had no right to rub it into the jury about the knife and about Mona's guilt being so certain. That part should have been left to the time when he addressed the jury, and after the evidence on both sides had been heard."

"I thought it was rather prejudging the prisoner myself, Ned."

Shepworth shuddered. "Don't call Mona a prisoner," he expostulated. "Every time that infernal Belmain alluded to her so, I felt sick."

"It is rough on you undoubtedly," murmured Prelice; and not wanting any more food, for Shepworth's agitation had spoilt his appetite, he turned to the waiter and ordered coffee. Shepworth passed along his cigarette case. "Very rough on you, Ned."

"Oh, don't talk about me," rejoined the barrister, restlessly; "think of Mona, a young girl, gently born and bred, being accused of murder and being put into prison. It's horrible."

"She seemed to me to be the calmest person in Court."

"Because she knows that she is innocent. She's a religious girl too, and firmly believes that God will prove her innocence."

"Well, He will," said Prelice quietly. "I'm not a saint myself, but I know that God looks after us all."

"Yet innocent people have been hanged before now, Dorry!"

Prelice did not answer immediately. Lighting his cigarette, he meanwhile looked very straight at his friend. "You don't seem to have a good defence," he remarked suddenly.

"Yes and no," replied Shepworth, fidgeting. "Not only is there a very good reason why she should love her uncle, but a better one that she should wish him to have remained alive."

"What do you mean?"

"That will, you know, Dorry; the will made by Sir Oliver in favour of Mona?" Prelice nodded. "It has been destroyed," went on Shepworth; "bits of it were found in the grate. There was a fire burning in the library on that night, if you remember Belmain's speech. Well, the will had been torn up and thrown into the fire. A few bits fell under the grate, and these prove beyond all doubt that it is the will which Sir Oliver made in favour of Mona. Now, if guilty, why should she destroy a document which gave her ten thousand a year?"

"But I say," remarked Prelice thoughtfully, "towards the end of his speech Belmain distinctly stated that Miss Chent had killed her uncle so as to get the money. If he knows of the burning of the will——"

"Oh, the other side admit that a will was burnt, but deny that it was the one made in Mona's favour. They will try and prove that Sir Oliver was drawing up another will disinheriting her because she would stick to me, and that she burnt this will after killing the old man. We fight hard on that point, Dorry."

"Has the will in favour of Miss Chent been found?"

"No. The lawyers have not got it, as Sir Oliver kept it himself. It can't be found, and, of course, we say—that is, our side, Cudworth, Arkers, and myself—that the will was burnt."

"Presuming it is, who inherits?"

"Captain Jadby."

"What—the South Sea chap?"

Shepworth nodded. "It seems that Sir Oliver was a great friend of his father's at Tahiti, and made a will out there in favour of young Jadby. He brought it home with him, I believe. Of course, the will in Mona's favour invalidated the first document, so unless the second will had been destroyed, the first would not hold good."

"Which points to the fact," said Prelice quickly, "that Jadby had a reason to murder Sir Oliver."

"I say," Shepworth glanced around in alarm, "don't talk so loud. There isn't a shadow of evidence to connect Jadby with the crime. He was in London on that day, and only returned by the ten train. However, he claims the property, but until this trial is ended nothing will be done about that."

"Humph!" said Prelice reflectively. "I expect it was on account of the earlier will that Sir Oliver wished Miss Chent to marry Jadby."

Shepworth nodded. "He thought to kill two birds with one stone; to let them both have the money, and, so to speak, blend the two wills into one. Jadby loves Mona too, but she hates him."

"And, moreover, is engaged to you," mused Prelice, tipping the ash off his cigarette. "It's a queer case."

"Much queerer than you think, Dorry."

"Now what do you mean by that?" asked Prelice.

Shepworth glanced round again, and cautiously brought his lips to his friend's left ear. "I swear that Mona is innocent. She is a good, kind, religious girl, who would not hurt a fly, much less Sir Oliver, whom she loved in spite of that ridiculous quarrel. All the same——"

"Well, well, go on!" said Prelice impatiently.

"That knife," breathed Shepworth nervously.

"The jade-handled paper-cutter. Well?"

"She had it in her hand."

"When? Where?" Prelice could not grasp the true significance of this very serious statement.

"In the library, when she was unconscious in the chair."

"How on earth do you know, Ned?"

Shepworth looked round again, and wiped his face. "See here," he whispered. "I was in bed with that sprained ankle, as Belmain said. In our row I gave Jadby the worst of it, including a black eye, although he fought like a cat with nine lives. But I tripped, and hurt my foot, as Belmain said in his speech. It was swollen and painful, but not so much but what I could have got away to town."

"Why didn't you?"

"Because Mona asked me to stop and support her. She expected further trouble with her uncle. I lay awake, trying to bear the pain as best I could, for my ankle got worse when I lay down. About a quarter to ten I heard Mona pass my door and go down the stairs."

"How did you know that it was Miss Chent?"

"I would know her footstep amongst a hundred; and she admitted afterwards that she had gone down to the library at that hour. I wondered where she was going, but lay quiet, listening for her return. At length, some fifteen minutes or so after ten o'clock, I could bear the suspense no longer, and hobbled downstairs in my dressing-gown. I thought that she might have gone to the library to see her uncle, and that further trouble might be brewing. As I promised to stand by her, ankle or no ankle, it seemed right that I should learn what was going on."

"Very reasonable of you, Ned. Continue." Prelice was deeply interested.

"I opened the library door, and saw her seated in the armchair."

"Was there any sign of smoke?"

"No! But there was a peculiar smell in the room."

"What kind of a smell?"

Shepworth wrinkled his brows. "I can scarcely describe it," he said after some thought; "a sweetish, heavy, sickly scent—like a tuberose. That's as near as I can get. Mona told me afterwards that she also thought it resembled the thick perfume of a tuberose. It came from the smoke, of course—it must have come from the smoke."

"You believe in the smoke then?"

"Oh yes. Sir Oliver had evidently been trying some magical experiment."

Prelice looked doubtful. "Magic is all bosh," he remarked.

"I'm not so certain of that, Dorry. There are queer things done, even in this twentieth century."

"H'm! Then you believe Miss Chent's improbable story?"

"I do—because I saw her insensible in the chair."

His listener reflected. "Was Sir Oliver dead then?"

"Yes! Sitting in his chair and lying half on the desk. He had been stabbed in the back."

"Was the window, or one of the windows, open?"

"I never noticed. And remember, Jadby did not say that the middle window was ajar, but only that the latch had been unfastened."

"I remember that. What happened next?"

Shepworth explained. "I found Sir Oliver dead, and Mona unconscious."

"One moment, please." Prelice became quite like a cross-examining barrister himself. "Had she fainted?"

"It was more than a faint, Dorry. She was in a kind of trance—quite like a person seized with catalepsy. I know; I am sure; because I shook her, and pinched her, and tried my best to rouse her."

"You should have opened the window to admit the fresh air."

"I never thought of doing so. I was too agitated."

"Natural enough—natural enough," murmured the other absently, and cast his eyes round the restaurant idly while thinking of what next to say. His gaze fell on a slim, boyish-looking young man of medium height, who had just entered, and who was looking at the unconscious Shepworth with an undeniable scowl. "Who is that?" asked Prelice in a whisper. "He seems to know you."

Shepworth looked up and across the crowded room, whereat the man—he was dark and clean-shaven and somewhat Italian in his looks—scowled more than ever. "Jadby," said the barrister under his breath. "Captain Jadby!" And he stared hard at his enemy. On his part, the captain returned the stare with scowling interest, and dropped into a seat near the door, no great distance away.

"Looks like a half-caste," breathed Prelice, glancing furtively at the young man; "good-looking too, but with a bad temper I should say."

If expression went for anything, Jadby certainly did not possess a superlatively even temper. His mouth was hard, his eyes were filled with sombre fire, and he seemed to be an alert, wiry, impetuous man, who could hold his own excellently in a fight. Dressed in a well-cut frock-coat, with dark-stripped trousers, a white waistcoat, a highly-polished silk hat, and patent-leather boots with spotless spats, he looked a great dandy, quite of the Bond Street-Piccadilly-Pall-Mall type. All the same, there was a suggestion of the sea in the way he rolled in his gait and held his slim brown hands. "A dangerous man to have for an enemy," thought Prelice, looking furtively at the smooth, feline face and sullen eyes.

However, as Jadby busied himself in selecting a luncheon from the menu-card, Prelice, after taking in his picturesque personality, paid no further attention to him. Nor did Shepworth. He and the captain scowled grudging recognition of one another, and then ostentatiously looked in other directions. Lord Prelice lighted another cigarette, and resumed the conversation, which the episode of Jadby's entrance had interrupted. "You say that Miss Chent was holding the paper-cutter when you found her."

"Yes! It was a dangerous Indian dagger, and the blade and the hilt were stained with blood. Mona's hands and dress were also stained. I really believed for the moment that she had killed Sir Oliver, and my only thought was how to save her."

"A terrible situation," murmured Prelice, looking round again for Jadby, and then saw to his surprise that the man had disappeared. It was apparent that the captain, not liking to be in the same room with the barrister who had thrashed him, had gone out again. However, this was just as well, as Jadby could not listen. "So you removed the knife," said Prelice, eying his friend.

"Yes! It seemed the most reasonable thing to do. I took it away at once, seeing that I could not rouse her for an explanation. It was my intention to hide the knife in my bedroom, and then return to take Mona away. I ran upstairs with the knife, and concealed it in my mattress, and then cautiously came back to the library. When I reached the door, however, I heard someone moving in the room, so thought it best to go back. Don't think me a coward, Dorry. You must see that I was in as dangerous a position as Mona herself, after I hid the knife."

"I quite understand," replied Prelice swiftly. "I expect Captain Jadby was in the library."

"He was. I am certain he was, for just as I reached the first landing I heard the library bell ring. Remember that he said he rang it as soon as he found Mona insensible and Sir Oliver dead."

"What have you done with the knife?"

"It is concealed in my desk in my study in my flat. I dare not produce it, lest I should get into trouble. Besides, its production would do Mona harm, as would my evidence of finding it in her hand. I must hold my tongue, Dorry, and lie as best I am able. But now you can see how needful it was for me to hold my tongue and have you beside me. You must be silent and stand by me."

Prelice shook hands, and they rose to return to the Court. The action brought them round to face the door, and there—at the marble-topped table—they saw Jadby sipping coffee, as though he had never moved. "H'm!" said Prelice, rather puzzled. "The fellow comes and goes like a ghost. Just like a half-caste cat." And he stealthily glanced at the captain, who was ostentatiously reading a newspaper, and took no notice, even when the young men brushed past him to leave the restaurant.

"I say, Ned," remarked Prelice thoughtfully when they were outside, "do you think that Miss Chent will be proved guilty?"

"No. I suppress my evidence about the knife, remember; and then the destroyed will is in her favour. The sole chance for the prosecution to prove Mona's guilt is to find Steve Agstone. He declares that he was looking through the window, and saw Mona kill Sir Oliver."

"To whom did he say this?"

"To Mrs. Blexey, the housekeeper. She is a witness for the prosecution, and is nearly broken-hearted. She loves Mona, like everyone else."

"H'm! Do you believe Agstone's story?"

"No! The old man hated Mona for some reason or another, and besides, he was drunk when he confessed to Mrs. Blexey. I expect, when sober again, he found that he would be forced to prove his words, and knowing that he could not, made himself scarce. I hope that he won't be found, Dorry."

"What does it matter if he is telling lies?"

"I believe it is a lie, Dorry, and so do you; but will the judge and jury believe as we do, if Agstone appears and sticks to what he told Mrs. Blexey? No, hang him, I hope he'll not turn up."

"Who do you think murdered Sir Oliver?"

"I can't say. But remember that the middle window was unfastened. Anyone could have entered from the outside and stabbed him."

"You forget," said Prelice quickly, "Miss Chent herself confesses to having unfastened the window."

"Quite so; but recollect also that she did not know when she entered the library if her uncle was dead or alive. A quarter to ten that was."

"But he surely would have made some sign if——"

"No!" interrupted Shepworth decisively. "What of the thick white smoke at which everyone jeers? It probably rendered Sir Oliver insensible, as it did Mona."

"Can you explain the smoke?"

"I cannot, unless Sir Oliver was trying one of his infernal experiments in connection with the next world."

"What book was he reading when found dead?"

"There were several books open on the desk," explained Shepworth; "one was the first volume of Captain Cook's voyages; another Pierre Loti's 'Reflets sur la Sombre Route'; and the third 'Polly in Polynesia,' some silly book with a silly title by a silly feminine globe-trotter. I expect Sir Oliver had been refreshing his South Sea memory."

"Were the books open at pages dealing with any particular subject?" demanded Prelice after a pause.

Shepworth considered. "When examining Sir Oliver's body, I glanced down at the open pages, and saw something about Easter Island. I didn't take much notice, as you may guess; but an illustration of the Easter Island statues was displayed in Cook's voyages. But I'll tell you a queer thing, Dorry. Afterwards, when the murder was discovered, the three books were all closed."

"That is natural."

"I don't agree with you," rejoined Shepworth emphatically; "the desk should have been left in its original untidiness until the police came to take possession. But someone closed those books."

"What do you make of it?" demanded Prelice abruptly.

"Well, my theory is that someone—I can't say who—wished to prevent the police seeing that Sir Oliver had been reading about Easter Island. Why, I don't know; and perhaps I may be making a mountain out of a mole-hill."

"Mole-hills are important on occasions," said Prelice dryly; "witness the death of William III. Easter Island! Easter Island!" he went on in a musing way. "H'm! h'm! h'm! now what the dickens do I know about Easter Island in connection with this case?" But he asked this question in vain. His memory refused to supply information.

CHAPTER IV.

EVIDENCE FOR THE PROSECUTION.

The Court had reassembled rather late in the afternoon, so there was little chance of much evidence being taken. Prelice went back to his seat still wondering what thought hovered at the back of his brain about Easter Island. He had visited that lonely and little known spot during his travels in the company of a friend given to occult studies, who insisted that the dismal spot of land was one of the remaining portions of the great Continent of Lemuria, which was said to have stretched from New Zealand to Africa. They had seen the famous statues, and had fraternised with the somewhat dirty natives, who had welcomed them warmly, as might be expected, seeing how few visitors ever came to the desolate land. For one week Prelice and his friend, Dr. Horace by name, had dwelt with the savages, and during that time had seen much of their manners and customs, and even had witnessed religious rites in front of the gigantic statues. Prelice had an idea that there he had seen something, suggested anew by this murder case, but vainly attempted to recall what it was. His memory would not help him in the least.

Meanwhile Shepworth, looking much more cheerful now that he had unbosomed himself to his chum, was again beside Cudworth, K.C., and young Arker. Belmain called his first witness as soon as the judge took his seat, in the person of the medical man who had examined the body of the murdered baronet.

The medical evidence was very scanty. Dr. Quick stated that, to the best of his belief, the dead man had been stabbed somewhere about ten o'clock. The blow had been delivered straight and strong, and the blade of the weapon used had penetrated right to the heart. Death must have taken place instantaneously, and while Sir Oliver, suspecting no treachery, had been reading. Belmain in cross-examination deduced from this that the prisoner was guilty, since Sir Oliver would scarcely have turned to his reading again had a stranger been in the room. Also, had the person who committed the crime been one whom the dead man suspected of any such design, he would assuredly not have presented a defenceless back to such an assassin. No! It was evident that the prisoner, after quarrelling with her uncle, had waited until he again was buried in his books, and then had stabbed him with the paper-knife. The doctor stated that the wound had been caused by a broad, thin blade, which exactly described the jade-handled paper-knife which was missing.

Several of the Grange servants were called to prove that Sir Oliver had been heard quarrelling violently with his niece. He was, as the evidence proved, a very hot-tempered and imperious man, and used language of the worst. In fact, the coachman, called to prove an outburst of temper when driving his master, said the late baronet could outswear any navvy. It was also clearly proved that Sir Oliver and his niece were on the worst possible terms when the crime was committed. Several times Sir Oliver declared that he would disinherit her, unless she surrendered her will and married Captain Jadby. But prisoner, as her maid said, had as imperious a temper as her uncle, and was well able to hold her own. "I don't mean," said the witness, "that Miss Chent was ever unkind to me, for she always behaved with consideration. I only mean that Sir Oliver could not brow-beat her, as he did the rest of them."

"What do you mean by that?" asked Belmain. "Who did he brow-beat?"

"Captain Jadby for one, sir. He was fond of Captain Jadby, and used to walk arm in arm with him in the garden, using him as a crutch for his lameness, as it were, sir. But he stormed a good deal, and Captain Jadby didn't fight like Miss Chent."

"You imply then that Captain Jadby was frightened of Sir Oliver?"

Witness (evasively): "I don't know, sir. I'm sure that my master was a terrible man, and only liked those who gave way to him."

In cross-examination, Cudworth for the defence asked: "Do you believe that prisoner is capable of committing the alleged crime?"

"No, sir, no," declared the lady's maid fervently. "Miss Chent is as good and kind a young lady as ever breathed. I don't think for one moment that she killed the master, and no more does anyone else."

The other servants gave similar evidence, all pointing to Sir Oliver's ungovernable temper, and to Miss Chent's dexterous way of managing him by meeting like with like. With Sir Oliver she fought on every occasion, otherwise she would have been reduced to slavery; but with other people Miss Chent was always kind and even-tempered. Although the witnesses called were for the prosecution, not one of them would confess to a belief in the prisoner's guilt. Belmain was rather disconcerted by his unanimous approval of Miss Chent, and tried his best to bully the witnesses into blaming her. But he failed on every occasion, and even when Mrs. Blexey was hoisted into the box he could not induce her to run down the girl. This loyalty created a deep impression, and prisoner for the first time showed emotion.

Mrs. Blexey was very stout, and very red-faced, and very tall, and extremely frightened. She looked like an elephant, and certainly possessed the timid nature of a rabbit. The contrast between her gigantic appearance and her timid speech amused those present so greatly that a continuous tittering was heard until the judge threatened to clear the Court.

Belmain: "You are Emma Blexey, the late Sir Oliver's housekeeper?"

Mrs. Blexey: "Yes, my lord!" (with a curtsey).

Belmain (facetiously): "You need not give me a title before I have earned it, my good woman." (Laughter.)

Mrs. Blexey: "Oh no, my lord—I mean my dear sir." (Laughter.)

When the laughter over this second form of address had subsided, Mrs. Blexey stated that the prisoner was as attached to her uncle as he was to her. They had tiffs on occasions, as Sir Oliver's temper was none of the best, but Miss Chent was never in the wrong, and usually contrived to pacify the irascible baronet. He was as fractious as a child, said the housekeeper, and required similar management. But, on the whole, he and Miss Chent—Mrs. Blexey refused to call her young mistress "the prisoner"—got on extremely well. As to the phrase about disinheriting, that was a favourite threat of Sir Oliver's, which meant practically nothing. He used it on every occasion, sometimes in earnest, and often in fun. It meant nothing, she said again.

Belmain: "He meant it when the prisoner refused to marry Captain Jadby, no doubt."

Mrs. Blexey (wiping her red face): "The Lord knows what he meant, sir. He was a queer gentleman."

Then Belmain proceeded to question the housekeeper regarding the admission which Steve Agstone was said to have made to her. It would have been preferable to obtain the evidence of the old sailor first hand, but since he could not be discovered the Counsel got what he could out of Mrs. Blexey. And what she knew he had to drag out of her by persistent questioning, for her sympathies were entirely with the prisoner. She stated that Agstone drank a great deal, and was always in trouble with Sir Oliver on that account. But that he had been the baronet's factotum for many years he would have been dismissed dozens of times. A drunken, grumpy, sullen savage, was the description given by the housekeeper. "But he was good-natured enough when sober," she confessed, "and quite devoted to Sir Oliver."

Belmain: "A kind of loyal henchman, in fact. Well, and what statement did he make to you, and when did he make it?"

Mrs. Blexey: "On the morning after the murder, Agstone—or Steve as everyone called him—was drinking rum to drown his grief at the death of Sir Oliver. He sat for a long time in my room weeping, and said that he knew Miss Mona would do for her uncle. Those were his very words, and I told him that he was speaking rubbish."

Belmain: "What happened then?"

Mrs. Blexey: "He fired up, and declared that while waiting up on the previous night for Captain Jadby, he had gone down the avenue to see if he was coming. Not finding him, and seeing the light still in the library, he wondered if Captain Jadby had arrived and had gone in to say good-night to Sir Oliver. He therefore went to one of the windows, and saw Miss Chent stooping over the fire to burn something. Sir Oliver was leaning forward on the desk with his head on his outstretched arms. Miss Chent also had a knife in her hands. Steve said that he thought there had been a row, and that Sir Oliver was weeping, as he sometimes did, being old and feeble from much hardship. He said that, had he guessed that Miss Chent had just murdered his master, he would have given the alarm. As it was, afraid lest Sir Oliver should be angry at his spying, he stole back into the house by the front door, and went to his own room at the back of the house. There he waited for Captain Jadby, and rushed into the library when he heard the bell."

Belmain: "I understood that Agstone told you that he had actually seen the prisoner kill Sir Oliver."

Prelice, in the body of the Court, thought so too, as he remembered what Ned had said during the luncheon. But Mrs. Blexey emphatically denied such a story. "I mentioned the matter to Mr. Shepworth but I am sure that he said nothing. But Steve might have talked in his drunken way to others, and might have told a different story. I know that there is a prevailing impression that he saw the murder, but he did not say so to me."

So spoke Mrs. Blexey, and Belmain looked worried. "You are telling the truth?" he demanded, in vexed tones.

"I am here to tell the truth," retorted Mrs. Blexey, "and I am, so there." After this somewhat incoherent speech she was cross-examined by Cudworth, and expressed her belief that Agstone had scarcely measured his words. Being devoted to Sir Oliver himself, he had always been very jealous of the favour shown to Miss Chent, and fairly hated her. Undoubtedly his wild maunderings were intended to hurt Miss Chent, and to get her into trouble. But Agstone had disappeared before the inquest, where he would have had to give evidence on oath. Mrs. Blexey firmly believed that had he been put on his oath he could not have substantiated what he had said to her. "I never could bear that Steve," she cried; "he was a sneaking dog, saving your presence, and had no love for anyone except Sir Oliver."

"Do you know where he is now?" asked Belmain, returning to the attack.

"No, I don't, sir, and I don't want to."

"I quite believe that," rejoined Counsel dryly, "seeing that you are prejudiced in prisoner's favour."

As Mrs. Blexey had surmised that Steve might have told a story of actually seeing prisoner kill her uncle to the other servants, Belmain recalled several witnesses. But not one of them could state that the current report was true. Steve had certainly hinted to several that he could bring home the crime to Miss Chent; but he had supplied no details, and as his hints were given when he was drunk, no one paid much attention to them. On the afternoon of the day following the night of the murder Steve had gone out for his usual stroll in the direction of Sandgate, and had not returned. The evidence of a detective proved that he had taken the train to London, and had been traced as far as Charing-Cross Station. There he had disappeared, and in spite of all search, his whereabouts could not be discovered.

By this time it was growing late, and judge, jury, lawyers, and listeners all exhibited symptoms of weariness. Therefore the Court rose, with the intention of sitting at eleven o'clock on the following morning. It was the general opinion that, unless Steve Agstone could be placed in the witness-box, the prisoner would not be convicted. Also Miss Chent's calm demeanour, and the loyalty of the Grange servants, which had placed her character in so attractive a light, went far to enlist public sympathy in her favour. Those who left the Court had more belief in her innocence than when they had entered. Many insisted that she could not possibly be guilty; but others pointing to the fact— which had been forthcoming at the inquest—that she had burned a new will disinheriting her, declared that, without doubt, she had murdered her uncle so as not to lose the money. All the same, the majority favoured the prisoner, and many well-wishers hoped for her acquittal.

Shepworth was pleased and hopeful. "The tide is quite in Mona's favour, Dorry," he said to Prelice when the Court rose, "and unless Steve Agstone turns up, she must be set free for want of evidence."

"There is the question of the burnt will, you know, Ned."

"We can prove that it was the will made in Mona's favour which was burnt," said Shepworth decisively. "Sir Oliver made no new will, as he had not left the house for quite a month, and could not have altered his will before then. His lawyer never came down to the Grange to draw up a will, and if Sir

Oliver had drawn up a new one himself, he would have asked some of the servants to be his witnesses. We know that no one was asked to witness any document."

"Captain Jadby and Steve Agstone might have witnessed."

"No. There is a chance certainly that Agstone might have done so, but one signature would have been of no use. And had Jadby witnessed a new will, he would not have benefited under it. Besides, since he had the will made in the South Seas, and Sir Oliver assuredly wished him to have the money, along with Mona, all that had to be done was to destroy the will made in Mona's favour, and then Jadby, having the cash, could leave her penniless unless she married him. Which is just what has happened," ended Shepworth.

"Of course," said Prelice thoughtfully, "Miss Chent might have been trying, when seen by Steve, to rescue the will from the fire into which it had been thrown by Sir Oliver."

Shepworth wheeled round. "Do you believe that she is guilty?"

"Oh, no. But we must look on all sides. And Agstone——"

"Is a liar," interrupted the barrister quickly. "I don't believe that he saw Mona bending over the fire. She was insensible, by her own showing, from the moment she entered the room until Jadby woke her. And remember that I found her insensible."

"It would help her if you said so."

"I don't agree with you. Were I examined about my presence in the library, I might let slip that the knife——"

"Yes, yes," said Prelice hastily. "I see. It will be better for you to hold your tongue. I hope that Agstone will not appear."

"If he does not, Mona is safe," rejoined Ned, with a sigh of relief. "Oh, poor Mona. Think of her in prison, Dorry."

"She will soon be out of it," answered Prelice soothingly. "I am quite sure that she will be acquitted. Where are you going now?"

"Home to my flat. I am quite worn out. Come and look me up this evening about ten or eleven, when I have had a sleep. I live at Alexander Mansions, Kensington Gore. Number Forty."

"Alexander Mansions," repeated Prelice, surprised; "why, here is the long arm of coincidence, Ned. Mrs. Dolly Rover has asked me to a masked ball, which she is giving in her flat—a most unsuitable place for a *bal masque* I think."

"Oh, no," said Shepworth, with a flush of colour, though why he should show this emotion Prelice could not say; "the flat occupied by Mrs. Rover is above mine. She has, in fact, two flats furnished on a most palatial scale. Her husband is a rich little beast, you know."

"Why a little beast?" asked Prelice, rather perplexed.

Shepworth's colour grew deeper. "He is not worthy of his wife. She was Miss Newton, you know, very clever and very beautiful. Dolly—fancy a man being called Dolly——"

"Short for Adolphus. It is not an uncommon abbreviation."

"It is contemptible for a man—and he's a rat. Dolly Rover," added Shepworth contemptuously, "fooh! the effeminate monkey. Well, good-bye. I'll see you between ten and eleven."

When Ned jumped into a cab, Prelice walked home wondering why he should run down the dapper little stockbroker whom Miss Newton had married. Then he remembered that Shepworth had admired Miss Newton before she changed her name to Rover.

CHAPTER V.

MRS. ROVER'S MASKED BALL.

"It is a long lane that has no turning!" Lord Prelice began to believe that there might be some truth in the proverb, for the lengthy lane of idleness, down which he had sauntered for many years, seemed to be rounding the corner to open out into the road of industry. The chance observation of Lady Sophia, which had sent him to the New Bailey, had become a sign-post, as it were, showing him which way he was to go. In other words, he was now involved in Shepworth's troubles, out of sheer friendship. Ned had confessed that he required assistance, and had turned to his old school-chum for the same. Prelice was naturally willing to do what he could towards aiding Ned in extricating Miss Chent from her perilous position, and so found work for his idle brain to do. Of course, as he tried to believe, he could resume his former life when the service was duly rendered. The wedding-bells which rang for Mr. and Mrs. Shepworth would dismiss their best man once more to his sauntering.

But this, as Prelice began to think, was easier said than done, mainly owing to the looks of Miss Chent. He had not spoken to the girl, and knew her character solely through the evidence of the Grange servants, who had been placed in the witness-box. Also Ned, as he remembered, had said very little about his affianced wife, and Prelice knew none whom he could question as to the prisoner's qualities. Yet, for all his scanty knowledge, he felt strangely drawn towards the unhappy woman, and confessed inwardly that he would feel a pang on seeing her become Mrs. Shepworth. Without doubt Prelice was in love, although not head over ears, and he swore at himself for being so disloyal to his friend. Mona—the name slipped quite naturally into his mind —Mona would assuredly be acquitted, unless the missing Agstone appeared, which was extremely unlikely, and then she would as assuredly marry Ned, who had so manfully stood by her in this grave trouble. Therefore it behooved Prelice, as an honourable gentleman—and he was all that—to put her out of his mind, if he wished to continue meeting Shepworth's gaze squarely. And, after all, a peer worth twenty thousand a year could pick and choose almost any woman for his wife; it was hard on Ned that such a peer should play the part of David in the parable, and select the less fortunate commoner's one ewe-lamb.

The struggle between more than a liking for Mona, and a feeling of genuine friendship for Ned, made Prelice waver in determining his future behaviour. His first inclination, when aware of his feeling, was to cross the Channel for a prolonged stay abroad, and leave Shepworth to his own devices. Then it occurred to him that this course would be cowardly, and he resolved to remain and help. Nothing that the world could cavil at could ever take place, since Prelice, with his high sense of honour, never dreamed of paying marked attentions to Miss Chent. All the same, if he came often into Mona's company —and that seemed inevitable should he remain—his life's happiness would certainly be at stake. He would have his feelings to smother, and therefore— as he plainly saw—would be most unhappy. Prelice at this early stage of infatuation termed his feeling towards the girl "affection," but he knew very well that, given time and opportunity, affection of this sudden kind might easily increase to love. In that case, seeing how Miss Chent was engaged to be married, he would be vainly crying for the honeymoon.

His lordship, then, felt less happy in the evening than he had done in the morning. Then he had been heart-whole; now the sight of a beautiful woman in peril had aroused the deepest and most chivalrous feelings of which his nature was capable. Placed thus between the devil and the deep sea, Prelice compromised dangerously with his conscience. He resolved to crush down his newly born desire for Mona, and to help Ned as best he could. In this way did the young man mix fire and snow, in the vain hope that such hostile elements would blend. Common-sense should have told him otherwise.

Having so decided—although not over-pleased with his decision, and with good reason—Prelice dressed for dinner. He remembered that he had promised to partake of this agreeable meal at his aunt's. A solitary chop at his club would have been preferable, as he was disinclined for company. But, aware from experience that Lady Sophia would strongly object to an excusing telegram, Prelice smothered his unwillingness, and reached the abode of his relative shortly before eight o'clock.

Lady Sophia lived magnificently in Brummel Square. The fourth daughter of a pauper Duke, she had married a wealthy city man—that is, she had entered into a social partnership, as there was little genuine marital feeling about the union. Simon Haken was a dried-up, active atom of humanity with a bald head, a pair of piercing dark eyes, and an exasperating chuckle, which he used when getting the better of anyone. As he usually scored over less clever financiers, he chuckled very often, and this sardonic merriment imparted a somewhat cynical expression to his withered face.

His wife, large, and expansive, and fresh-coloured, looked like an elephant beside a grasshopper, when the two went into Society, and they were generally known as the Mountain and the Mouse. But Haken cared as little for the jest as did Lady Sophia. As husband and wife in its strictest sense they were failures, being two and not one; as partners they were admirably matched. Having no children, and plenty of money and excellent health, and no strong emotions, the two enjoyed life immensely. Possessed of a complacent husband, of a good position, ample cash, and absolute freedom, Lady Sophia even forgot to sigh for the delights of the Stone Age when she reflected upon the position in life to which it had pleased Providence to call her.

On this occasion Mr. Haken, as usual, had wired detention in the city on business, so Lady Sophia received her nephew in a solitary drawing-room, as handsomely furnished as she was dressed. "You are just in time for dinner," said she with emphasis, implying thereby that Prelice was usually late.

"I always am in time," answered the guest, smiling but preoccupied. "Dinner is a sacred feast which cannot be trifled with. I would as soon insult the King as the Cook." Then he sat and stared at the points of his patent-leather boots with the air of a misanthrope.

"You are out of spirits," declared Lady Sophia, rapping his knuckles with her lorgnette. "I prescribe a round of pleasure. To-night you shall escort me to two dances and four musical parties."

"But I haven't done anything to deserve such punishment."

"How absurdly you talk. These festivals——"

"I agree with the man who said that life would be endurable were it not for its festivals."

"Nonsense. He could not have been in Society."

"He just was, and so made a profoundly true observation. I renounce Society and all its play. Besides," added Prelice inconsequently, "I am going to a masked ball to-night at Mrs. Dolly Rover's."

"That woman!" cried Lady Sophia, with disdain.

Prelice looked up, surprised. "I thought you liked her?"

"As Constance Newton, not as Mrs. Rover," she informed him swiftly.

"They are one and the same," he urged.

"Not at all. Marriage changes a woman into something entirely different. Constance was a charming girl; Mrs. Rover is a flirting, fast-living, heartless, spendthrift, Society doll."

"Society Doll—y Rover," murmured Prelice, noting his aunt's usual waste of adjectives. "Will you come to this ball?"

"What!" Lady Sophia almost screamed, "a masked ball, and at my age? Oh, how can you be so ridiculous, Prelice? And at Mrs. Rover's too; a woman who neglects her husband, and squanders his money, and whips him like a poodle, I believe."

"He is something of a poodle, isn't he?"

"That is no reason why he should be whipped," she snapped heatedly; "and if you knew how she had treated your friend Mr. Shepworth, you would not go near her disreputable ball."

Prelice pricked up his ears, remembering the unnecessary blush of the barrister at midday. "How did she treat Shepworth?" he asked.

"How? Can you ask?"

"Of course, seeing that, as a newly returned traveller, I know nothing."

"Well then, she was almost engaged to him, and he was very much in love with her. She threw him over in a cold-blooded way, because Dolly Rover came along with a better-filled purse. He's a horrid little cad," added Lady Sophia candidly, "and his father was a chemist, or a draper—I forget which. All the same, he is too good for a jilt, who played blind hooky—don't raise your eyebrows, Prelice; it's vulgar, but expressive, and I shall use it—who played blind hooky with poor Mr. Shepworth."

"But are you sure, aunt? Ned is engaged to Miss Chent."

"Out of pique—out of pique," she assured him. "Mona is a nice girl, poor darling, even though she did murder her uncle, not that I believe she did. But Constance is the one love of Mr. Shepworth's life, and fifty Monas won't make up for the loss. Mona, if ever she does become Mrs. Shepworth, which I very much doubt, will only be a make-shift."

"Oh!" Prelice was almost too indignant to speak. That so peerless a girl should be talked of as a "make-shift" seemed positively wicked. "You must be mistaken. Ned would not behave so badly."

"Ask him then."

"I shall do this very night."

"Then you will go to that woman's?"

"Yes. I accepted, as I always liked Constance. Besides, I have to see Ned, who lives in these same mansions——"

"I know he does," burst out Lady Sophia; "quite indecent I call it."

"Oh, hang it, aunt, a man must live somewhere."

"Not next door to a woman who has jilted him."

"He doesn't live next door, but on the floor below."

"It would be more creditable if he lived in Timbuctoo. I believe that he loves her still, and she's quite capable of loving him back in spite of the marriage service, which I don't believe she listened to. As for her husband——" Lady Sophia was about to give her opinion of Mr. Dolly Rover, when the butler threw open the door, and announced dinner. At once she took her nephew's arm, and changed the conversation. "Tell me about the case," she chattered as they passed to the dining-room. "Have they hanged that poor girl?"

"Who? Miss Chent? No, and I don't believe they will."

"Ah!" Lady Sophia pulled off her gloves. "I always said that she was innocent."

"Of course, if Agstone turns up, she may be convicted."

"Agstone—oh yes; the man who declares that he saw her kill Sir Oliver."

Prelice corrected her, while taking his soup. "He only saw her bending over the fire with a knife in her hand."

"Burning the will after killing her uncle. What a horrid girl!"

"Aunt Sophia, will you tell me plainly if you believe Miss Chent to be innocent or guilty?"

"How can I judge when I haven't heard the evidence? You talk as though I were on the jury. I like Mona, and I'm sure she didn't kill him; but if she did, he deserved it, as he was a nasty old bully."

Prelice desisted in despair, and helped himself to fish. Lady Sophia seemed to change her mind every half minute, and never considered facts when she wanted to deliver an opinion. Besides, she preferred fiction, as it was less trouble to invent than to remember. All the same, her sympathies appeared to be with Mona, and Prelice felt pleased that it should be so. Should the girl be acquitted, her position would be extremely difficult, and she would require a staunch friend of her own sex. Why should not that friend be Lady Sophia, whose support could do much to efface the stain of a Criminal Court? But until the case was decided, Prelice did not dare to hint that such an idea had crossed his mind. As the servants were hovering round the table he could not talk confidentially to his aunt, so drifted into general conversation about mutual friends. He thus became posted up in the latest Mayfair gossip, and so was brought up to date in necessary knowledge. And Lady Sophia knew as much about London as Asmodeus did about Madrid, and like that delightful demon, she could unroof houses to some purpose. Luckily for the men and women about whom she talked, the presence of the butler and two footmen prevented entire candour.

As the food was excellent and the conversation interesting, not to say necessary—for Prelice as a newly returned traveller required much posting-up in recent scandals—nephew and aunt lingered for a considerable time at table. When the meal was ended Prelice preferred to accompany Lady Sophia to the drawing-room, instead of remaining solitary over Haken's famous port. They had half-an-hour left for coffee, and then Lady Sophia would have to start out on her round of festivals.

"You ought to come with me, Prelice," she said later, as he helped her on with her cloak; "everyone thinks that you are dead."

"Well, aunt, you would not have much pleasure in taking a corpse about with you. Besides, I promised to look up Ned this evening."

"No doubt, and he'll be at that woman's ball. Most indecent, seeing that poor Mona is in gaol."

"Ned isn't such a blighter," cried Prelice crossly.

"I never called him a blighter, whatever that may mean," retorted Lady Sophia with great dignity. "Mr. Shepworth is an estimable young man, whom you would do well to imitate."

"I intend to. He and I are going to save Miss Chent."

"How horrid; you'll be a kind of detective."

Prelice nodded. "It's something to do."

"As if you required anything to do with your rank and money."

"But I say, aunt, you advised me this morning——"

"Oh, I never remember anything I say in the morning," said Lady Sophia airily. "You are so stupid, Prelice, you always take one at the foot of the letter. You won't come with me. Oh, very well. Help me into the brougham, you horrid boy. I believe you'll fall in love with Mona, and give me a criminal for a niece."

This was Lady Sophia's parting shot, and when her motor-brougham spun towards the first turning out of the square, Prelice laughed long and loudly. His aunt was nearer the truth than she had been the whole evening, although she was far from suspecting it. It never entered her elderly head that a man of the world, such as her nephew certainly was, would fall in love on the spur of the moment. "And I should not have suspected myself of such lunacy either," thought his lordship as he turned in the direction of Half-Moon Street to procure domino and mask for the ball.

The street before Alexander Mansions was filled with carriages and motors and four-wheelers and hansoms, together with a crowd of onlookers, who passed remarks, complimentary and otherwise, on the many guests of Mrs. Rover. The mansions themselves were palatial and splendid, with a royal flight of broad marble steps to the main entrance. Prelice, shuffling on his domino and assuming his mask, climbed these, to find himself with other revellers in a vast hall, with two staircases ascending on either side at the farther end, and between them two lifts, the cages of which soared and sank with parties of pleasure-seekers. Prelice delivered his rainbow-hued ticket of invitation to a gorgeously uniformed commissionaire, and took his time in climbing the long stairs. Many other people did the same, instead of waiting for the lifts, but, as all were masked and cloaked, the young man could recognise no one.

As Shepworth had stated, Mr. and Mrs. Dolly Rover occupied the whole of the third floor—that is, they tenanted two flats which faced each other, and the outer doors of these, opening on to a spacious landing, had been removed from their hinges. Thus the guests could pass easily from one flat to the other, and the landing between was a nest of greenery and roses, like the hanging gardens of Babylon. The flats themselves had wide corridors, spacious rooms, and lofty ceilings, so they were capable of receiving a large number of guests.

On this occasion they were crowded, and it would seem as though Mrs. Rover had invited everyone on her visiting-list. And there may have been others, not set down on that list, since the masks and dominos prevented recognition.

Prelice looked about for his hostess, but found himself received by a tiny, pale-faced man with large, plaintive blue eyes set in a white expanse of absolutely colourless skin. He wore a domino over his smart evening-dress, but no mask, and was so clipped and curled, and brushed and washed, that Prelice easily guessed him to be the poodle mentioned by Lady Sophia. Pushing out a small tightly gloved hand, he murmured a nervous greeting to each new arrival; but after this ceremony was ended no one seemed to take any notice of him.

As all who came were masked, Prelice wondered how Mr. Rover could possibly know whom he was greeting. Of course, there was the rainbow-hued ticket given to the commissionaire below, which would guarantee the respectability of the presenter. But tickets of this sort could be stolen and forged, and as no further supervision was exercised to ensure the identity of the guests, Prelice considered that such a procedure was somewhat rash. His thoughts were confirmed by a dried-up little man who appeared without a mask, and who was rebuked by Mr. Rover for his originality.

"You shouldn't, you know," expostulated the host in a penny whistle kind of voice; "no one is to know anyone until the clock strikes twelve, when we all unmask for supper. Why, even my wife insisted that I should receive in her place. She would be spotted, you know, if she stopped here to shake hands, and she doesn't want to be found out until midnight. The whole fun of a masquerade lies in secrecy, so obey the rules, Haken, and put on your mask."

Prelice started when he heard the name, and twisted his neck to see if the new-comer really was his uncle-by-marriage. It was Simon Haken sure enough, for no one could mistake his looks let alone his celebrated chuckle. The young man laughed, and wondered what Haken—by no means a Society butterfly—was doing at the ball of a lady whom his wife openly disliked. And then he remembered that lying telegram from the city. Mr. Haken had his little secrets it would seem, and was more human, under the rose, than when posing as a money-making machine. His dutiful nephew determined, before the evening was out, to let his sly uncle know that his misdoings were discovered.

Meanwhile the little millionaire was chuckling and masking. "It is a risk, you know, Rover," he observed dryly. "You don't know who is here. Half the swell mobsmen of London may have come after diamonds."

"Oh, dear me, how can you talk so, Haken?" said the host fretfully; "the man below examines the tickets."

"As if anyone could not forge or steal one," retorted Haken, voicing his nephew's thoughts. "Well, in to-morrow's papers I shall look for a criminal scandal." And with his odious chuckle Haken brushed past Prelice towards the ballroom of the left-hand flat.

His lordship, tired of watching new arrivals, thought that he also would go and view the revellers. But he had hardly moved half-a-dozen paces when he unexpectedly began to think of Easter Island. A sweet, heavy perfume, as of tuberoses, was wafted in his nostrils. But why should such a familiar fragrance recall that desolate land, environed by leagues of ocean?

CHAPTER VI.

A STARTLING DISCOVERY.

Odour is one of the strongest aids which memory can have, and a chance whiff of a particular scent will recall to the most lethargic brain, circumstances both trivial and important of long-forgotten years. But the well-known fragrance of the tuberose usually brings funerals to mind, since that flower is so extensively woven into burial wreaths and mortuary crosses. It was strange indeed that it should conjure into an idle-thinking mind the vision of a heathen festival.

There were many people crowding the corridor, so that it was impossible for the young man to tell who wore the flowers which gave forth the magical scent—for magical it was in its effect. They might adorn a man's button-hole or a woman's bodice. He could not tell, since the evening-dress of both sexes was veiled by voluminous dominos. But as he leaned against the wall, the vision became clearer and more insistent. His body was in London—in Alexander Mansions, at a masked ball, as he well knew—but the scent of the tuberose had drawn his spirit across leagues of trackless sea to the uttermost parts of the earth. The present vanished, and he beheld the past.

Before him, as the interior vision opened, he saw colossal images of a vanished and forgotten race, rudely hewn into the semblance of human beings, each bearing a cylinder—according to Captain Cook's description— on its gigantic head. These reared themselves from vast platforms of

Cyclopean architecture, overgrown with tropical vegetation, and strewn with bleaching bones. And in the soft radiance of the southern moon Prelice beheld a kneeling crowd of bronze-hued worshippers, tattooed and painted, adoring the weird stone gods. An old priest, his face and body streaked with white pigment, murmured strange names over a rude stone altar, whereon blazed a clear fire. He invoked terrible deities incarnate in the giant idols—Kanaro! Gotomoara! Marapate! Areekee!—and cast upon the flames the yellow leaves of a sacred herb. A thick white cloud of smoke spread like a milky mist before the statues, veiling their grotesque looks and vast outlines, and the sickly scent of the tuberose grew powerful. Then did the priest become rigid as the dead, and his spirit blended with the spirits of those grim gods he worshipped. Finally, the fragrance which loaded the heavy air—whether of Easter Island or London Prelice could not tell—passed away, and with that odour passed the vision.

It could only have lasted a minute or so, but was so terribly vivid that Prelice could scarcely believe that his surroundings were real when the material asserted its sway. He had closed his eyes to behold the vision, which the scent had invoked, and opened them again, with a bewildered expression, to see the pushing, laughing, chattering throng of guests. Although a commonplace young man, and contemptuous, as a rule, of the unseen, he felt that the recollection had not been brought back for nothing. The dead man at Lanwin Grange had been reading about Easter Island when foully stabbed, and the accused girl had described to her lover the white smoke and sickly perfume, which also had to do with that isolated land. And Mona also—Prelice remembered faithfully what Shepworth had told him—had been in a state of catalepsy, like the priest of the vision. And, after all, although he chose to call what he had seen mentally a vision, it was simply a vivid recollection of what he and Dr. Horace had beheld a year or two before. But what had a fetish worship in Easter Island to do with a murder in Kent? That was a question which Prelice could not answer.

There was no time to invent possible explanations or to reason out answers. Being in Rome, the momentary dreamer had to do as the Romans did; and as Prelice was at a ball, he was compelled, out of courtesy to his hostess and host, to enjoy himself. He did not have far to go for an adventure, as a lady in a blue domino, and with a fringed mask to disguise her voice, stole to his side, and engaged him in airy conversation. Who she was the young man did not know, and probably she was equally ignorant of his identity. But on this especial night, Mrs. Rover's flat was Liberty Hall with a vengeance, for men and women, trusting in masks and dominos for concealment, flirted and danced and drank and laughed with one another in a most outrageous manner. There was no need of introductions, or of reticence, or of timidity; in that

Eden's Bower of flowers and ferns faces were hidden, but souls were revealed.

The blue domino proved to be a most charming companion, full of fun and flirtation, and a delightful dancer. Prelice found her extremely entertaining, and she appeared to reciprocate the feeling. After a particularly perfect waltz, and an inspiriting glass of champagne, his lordship did his best to lure the unknown into a corner where she might unmask. But the lady shook her head laughingly, and ran off to the ballroom with another man, whose stature of a life-guardsman had caught her roving eyes. Prelice solaced himself with another glass of wine, and looked about him for another female of man. It was then that a chuckle at his elbow made him turn.

"Now then, now then," said the gentleman who had chuckled, "let me come to refresh myself." He spoke irritably, and pushed past Prelice in a hurry. "Waiter! Waiter, a glass of champagne."

"I thought you were a teetotaler, uncle!" whispered Prelice.

Mr. Haken, betrayed by his chuckle, and wheeled suddenly, and spilt the wine he was about to sip. To his nephew's surprise he was trembling, and his stammering voice betrayed his agitation. "Who—who are you?"

Prelice whispered his name. "You needn't be alarmed," he added; "I won't tell Aunt Sophia that you are accepting her enemy's hospitality."

Haken drank off his wine in one deep gulp, and set down the glass, with his hands still shaking. "I would rather you did not tell her," he said in a low tone. "Sophia dislikes Mrs. Rover, and would be annoyed if she knew that I was here. I have come on business."

"What! Business at a ball? Invent a more credible story, uncle."

"It is true," insisted Haken, becoming more composed. "I have to see a political man from the Continent about a loan. He doesn't want it to be known that I am meeting him, so we thought that this would be the best place to ensure secrecy. Not a word of this, Prelice."

"Of course not," replied the young man, puzzled to know why Haken should take the trouble to explain; "but don't mention my name. I also wish to be unknown."

"What are you doing here?" asked Haken abruptly.

"I came to the ball, and also I have to see Ned Shepworth, who——"

"Shepworth," gasped Haken, backing nervously. "Oh yes! friend of our charming hostess; friend of mine also. Is he here?"

"No. He would not come to a ball when his promised wife is in prison."

"Of course not; very creditable of him, to be sure," muttered Haken, and took another glass of wine with a whispered apology. "I am teetotal as a rule, you know; but Society always tries my nerves, and I need sustenance. I wish the man I have to meet here had chosen my office in the city. But it wouldn't have done—it wouldn't have done. There would be trouble were it known that he was in London. What is the time, Prelice?"

"Don't mention my name or I'll mention yours," said Prelice impatiently, and drew out his watch. "It is eleven o'clock."

Haken nodded. "I must meet my man. Eleven-fifteen is the time. As to mentioning my name, what does that matter? I came here without my mask. Never thought of putting it on."

Prelice nodded in his turn. "I saw you when Rover received you."

"Then hold your tongue—hold your tongue. Not a word to Sophia, mind."

"Not a word," Prelice promised gravely; and Mr. Haken, drawing a long breath—it would seem to be of relief—at having extracted the promise, vanished into the many-hued crowd with his usual chuckle. While the millionaire gave vent to that chuckle there did not seem to be much chance of his concealing his identity.

Lord Prelice looked after him somewhat puzzled. He could quite understand why Haken did not want his wife to know of his presence in Alexander Mansions; but it was difficult to account for the old man's agitation and quite unnecessary explanations. As a rule, Haken was extremely reticent, and on such an important matter as a secret meeting with a Continental diplomatist, would be much more so. Yet he had gone out of his way to set himself right with his nephew, and by telling his private business, when a gay excuse of needing a night off, would have been sufficient to account for his presence. However, Prelice simply shrugged his shoulders, and did not deem the incident worth remembering. Why should not Simon Haken enjoy himself in this way if he liked, and turn Mrs. Rover's ballroom into an office, wherein to meet his foreign clients? All the same—and Prelice gave this a passing thought—it was strange that the chance meeting with one who knew him should so upset him. And it was still stranger that, if Mr. Haken wished to preserve his incognito, he should have arrived unmasked.

Having lost both his uncle and his charming blue domino, Prelice took a tour through the rooms in search of further adventures. He could only afford a few minutes, since he had to call upon Shepworth at eleven o'clock, and it was already that hour, as he had told Haken. Still, a few minutes more or less would not matter, and Prelice wished to see if he could espy Mrs. Dolly Rover, in order to renew his acquaintance with her and to compliment her on the success of her ball. And it undoubtedly was a success, for everyone seemed highly amused, and the laughter and small talk went on incessantly. Many people were dancing to the music of a gaily uniformed Hungarian Band, and many more were ensconced in flirtation corners, making the best of the hour which would elapse before everyone unmasked for supper.

Prelice therefore wandered leisurely throughout the two flats, exchanging a few chaffing words with the different women who addressed him, and looking for the tall form of his hostess. Alas! there were many tall women, who looked as imperial and graceful as Mrs. Rover, and Prelice felt like Ali Baba's robber when he examined Morgiana's chalk-marks on the various doors. He therefore began, by way of some diversion, to admire the costumes of the women, which showed themselves more or less plainly from under the flowing dominos of silk. In fact, the heat of the night and of the rooms was so great that many ladies loosened the strings and buttons of their dominos, and permitted their frocks to be plainly seen. They would have removed their masks also in some cases, so stifling was the perfumed air; but the rule of the ball stopped them from doing so. Still, as many revealed the gowns they were wearing, it was probable that some would pay for their flirtatious sins when the supper hour and recognition came.

The young man had an eye for colour, but knew very little about millinery, so if anyone later had asked him to describe the various dresses, he would have been puzzled. But one woman wore a dress which attracted him from its oddity. It was a flowing gown of white silk, and from hem to waist the skirt was adorned with triple lines, at intervals, of narrow red velvet. The spaces between the triple lines were equal, and the lines of red velvet themselves ran apparently entirely round the skirt. The effect was bizarre, and rather fascinating; but what made Prelice note the dress so exactly was the wonderful ubiquity of the lady who wore it. He went into the ballroom of the right-hand flat, and there she was dancing; he strolled into the left-hand ballroom, and found her flirting in a corner with another partner. Then he stumbled across her in the corridor, and later discovered her at the buffet sipping champagne. Her domino was green, as was her mask, and she seemed to be in several places at once. Prelice was amused at her activity, and at the way in which she seemed to permeate the entire place. She was certainly getting all the enjoyment she could out of the ball. He spoke to her once, but she made no reply, and disappeared before he could address her again. Rather annoyed that she would not respond, Prelice yawned, and discovering that it was half-past-eleven, decided to descend and look up Shepworth.

The stairs were crowded, not only with people leaving and arriving, but with flirting couples, who were cooling themselves in the purer air, which ascended from the main entrance of the mansions. These expostulated loudly, and sometimes silently—if irritated gestures went for anything—with those who pushed past them to go up or down. Prelice came in for his share of blame, as he cautiously steered his way to the second floor. Here there were but few people, as the guests kept to the third-floor stairs and to those leading to the fourth. A look at the left-hand door as he came down showed Prelice that it was Number Forty, so he pressed the button of the electric bell, and waited for the door to be opened. As he did so, and while he was leaning against the wall, still wearing his mask and domino, the ubiquitous lady in the green domino with the oddly trimmed frock descended the stairs alone. She cast a swift look at him as he passed, and it was not until she vanished below that Prelice became aware that the scent of the tuberose was again in his nostrils. He had half a mind to run after her, and—assuming the privilege of a masked ball—ask her if she was wearing such a flower. But, in his idle way, he did not think it was worth while, and remained where he was.

No one came to answer the bell, so Prelice judged that Shepworth's servants were out, perhaps fraternising with Mrs. Rover's domestics at the ball overhead. He rang again, however, believing that Shepworth must be within and awake by this time. As again the door did not open, Prelice raised his hand to the knocker. To his surprise, the door yielded a trifle, and then he discovered that it was slightly ajar, but so little so that he had believed it to be closed. For the moment there was no one on the landing, so he stepped into Shepworth's flat, without closing the door after him.

"I say, Ned. Ned, are you in?" cried the young man, pausing in the corridor, which was similar to that overhead in Mrs. Rover's flat. "I say, Ned! It is me. It is Prelice." And he slipped off his mask.

There was still no reply, and then Prelice smelt stronger than ever that strange odour, which had evoked the Easter Island vision. His thoughts again flew back to the heathen festival, and he walked along the corridor wondering why the scent should follow him here. On the left-hand side he peeped into a drawing-room, but it was empty. The door opposite was surely that of the dining-room. It was closed, but Prelice opened it and walked in to look for his friend. Shepworth was in the room sure enough, but Prelice uttered an irrepressible cry when his amazed eyes fell on the barrister.

In a deep saddle-back chair, placed between the fireplace and the near window, sat Shepworth, bolt upright, with his hands resting upon his knees, in the hieratic attitude of an Egyptian statue. His intensely calm face was pearly-white, his brown eyes were fixed in a glassy, unnatural stare, and he appeared as rigid and stiff and unbending as though hewn out of granite. There was no disorder about his clothing, the evening-dress he wore was as accurate and neat as though he had got ready to go to the ball overhead. Prelice stared at him, tongue-tied and motionless with astonishment. Then his eyes mechanically wandered round the room. They fell immediately upon another figure seated on the far side of the dining-table, with outstretched arms sprawling nervelessly across the cloth. On them rested a huge head covered with shaggy red hair.

Drawn, as by a loadstone, Prelice stole forward with staring eyes, and saw, with a sudden shudder, that the man at the table was stone-dead. He had been stabbed ruthlessly in the back, under the left shoulder-blade. Everything in the room was in absolute order. Only one man, dead, sat at the table, sprawling half across it, and the other man, insensible, was stiffly seated in the armchair. And the whole apartment was permeated with the scent which suggested Easter Island; suggested also that other murder at Lanwin Grange.

CHAPTER VII.

SHEPWORTH EXPLAINS.

An unsteady footstep roused Lord Prelice from his momentary stupor, and he wheeled automatically to see a little man, masked, and wearing a black silk domino, swaying to and fro at the open dining-room door. But the sight of the two apparently dead men, and the presence of their possible murderer, seemed to sober the new-comer in a single moment. Before Prelice could spring forward, he gasped and fled. Almost immediately his voice, tense with terror, was heard shouting the news of his discovery to the revellers on the stairs.

Prelice cursed under his moustache, and ran into the passage to close the outer door, which he now remembered he had foolishly left ajar. Possibly the little man, being intoxicated, had stumbled up the stairs on his way to the ball, and finding the door open, had so far mistaken his way as to stagger in. Prelice wondered if the stranger was Haken or Rover, both small of stature; but he recollected that he had never seen either drunk. Besides, drunk or sober, Rover or Haken would never mistake Shepworth's flat for the one overhead.

At the outer door Prelice swiftly changed his mind. He saw that the murder of the red-headed man was similar in all respects to that of Sir Oliver Lanwin. Then Miss Chent had been given time to recover, and so had been accused of the crime, although she protested that she had been in a state of catalepsy, induced by the scented smoke. Shepworth likewise was insensible, and, judging from the odour in the dining-room, from the same cause. It would be better, decided the young man rapidly, that Shepworth should be seen by a score of witnesses thus insensible, for then it could be proved that so helpless a man could not have struck the blow. Thus, when a crowd of startled people came pouring down the staircase, and into the flat on the second floor, Prelice threw open the door widely, and admitted them with a hurried explanation.

"There has been a terrible crime committed," he declared, leading the way to the dining-room. "I came here a few minutes ago to find Mr. Shepworth, the owner of the flat, insensible as you see, and this other man stone-dead. He has been stabbed."

"Stabbed!" Several voices echoed the word, and one woman gave a faint scream. The passage was crowded to the very door of the dining-room, and as many as could were looking over one another's shoulders to view the sinister scene. And like a ball from one person to another was tossed in various tones the ominous word "Murder!"

"Who stabbed the man?" asked a medium-sized masker in a blue domino, who had placed himself directly in front of the mob, blocking the doorway. He addressed Prelice, and his manner was offensively suspicious.

"I do not know," disclaimed that young gentleman quietly, for it seemed absurd indeed that he should be suspected. "I came here to see Mr. Shepworth only ten minutes ago."

"How did you enter?" The tone of the question was still offensive.

"The outer door was slightly ajar," explained the other suavely. "I pushed it open, as I had an appointment with my friend. I decline to defend myself further, as you seem to suspect me."

"Send for the police! Send for the police!" said many voices; and a rough male voice was heard recommending that Prelice—only the voice called him the murderer—should not be allowed to escape.

"What nonsense," cried the young man indignantly, raising his voice on hearing so direct an accusation. "I have nothing to do with the matter. I am Lord Prelice, if anyone here knows me."

The utterance of a title had a magical effect, and several people began to unmask; amongst these was the aggressive masker who had questioned

Prelice.

"You can explain to the police," said this man sharply.

"Certainly, Captain Jadby."

"You know me?"

"I saw you in Court to-day, and also in Geddy's Restaurant, Burns Street."

Jadby nodded, but did not relax his suspicious manner. "It is strange that you should be here," he said, marching into the room.

"Not at all," rejoined Prelice hotly. "I had an appointment to see Mr. Shepworth, and came only a few minutes ago."

Jadby took no notice of this speech, but lifted the shaggy red head of the dead man. Apparently he knew who he was, for after a single glance he dropped the heavy head again, and wheeled round with an amazed face. "Steve Agstone," he gasped, "the missing witness!"

Prelice also startled, backed against the wall with outstretched hands and open mouth. In a flash he saw how dangerous was the position of the barrister; and indeed many confused voices were muttering as to the guilt of Shepworth. Captain Jadby, letting his eyes fall on the dead man, made himself spokesman for all.

"Shepworth murdered him to win the case," he said, nodding. "I ask your pardon, Lord Prelice, for suspecting you."

"I would rather you continued to do so," cried Prelice angrily. "It is absurd to think that Shepworth killed this man. Look at him," he pointed to the rigid form in the armchair; "he is incapable of raising a hand."

"Miss Chent was also incapable," sneered the captain, "yet——"

"She is innocent," stormed Prelice fiercely; "she no more killed her uncle than did Shepworth this witness."

Everyone was listening eagerly with open eyes and ears to the altercation; and it is impossible to say how long it would have continued, but for the entry of the police. Two constables pushed their way through the crowd, and forthwith —when they had taken in the situation—began to clear the place. The crowd of pleasure-seekers, now unmasked for the most part, were driven outside. Some fled down the stairs, anxious to get away from the scene of the tragedy, while others returned to the Rovers' flat. But the fact of the murder ruined the ball. It broke up, like Macbeth's famous banquet, "with most admir'd disorder," and in ten minutes the rooms were deserted. Everyone ran away, as though from the plague, and Mr. Rover, looking like a frightened rabbit, came down to make inquiries.

"Is Shepworth dead?" he asked tremulously of a stalwart policeman whom he found guarding the closed door of Number Forty. "Everyone says that Shepworth is dead; and my wife has fainted."

"The doctor is with Mr. Shepworth now," said the constable gruffly. "I don't know what's the matter with him, and it ain't my duty to say anything, sir."

"Oh dear! Oh dear!" Rover wrung his small white hands. "How very, very dreadful all this is. Who is the other man—the dead man?" He handed the officer half-a-sovereign so as to gain a reply.

Dogberry unbent. "They do say, sir, as the corpse is Steve Agstone, who is the missing witness in the Lanwin murder case."

"How wicked—how very wicked. But if Mr. Shepworth is dead——"

"He ain't, sir," the constable slipped the gold into his pocket; "he's in a faint of sorts I believe. And they do say as he killed Steve Agstone, so as to save the young lady he's defending. Now I can't tell you more, sir, and I've said too much already. Just go home and keep quiet, sir. The police will look after this matter here."

Rover, still wringing his useless hands, and muttering to himself like the weak-brained little man he was, wearily climbed the stairs to his deserted ballrooms. As he ascended, two women and a man came down, white-faced and shaken. They tried to enter Number Forty, but the constable stretched forth a brawny arm to prevent entrance.

"But we must come in," said the man deferentially; "we are Mr. Shepworth's servants. I am his valet, this lady is the cook, and yonder is the housemaid. We have a right to enter."

"You can't until the doctor and the inspector have done with your master," said the constable stolidly. "And why aren't you in bed?"

The cook, a large, red-faced lady, gaily dressed, replied. "Mr. Shepworth allowed us to join Mrs. Rover's servants at the masked ball."

"Then none of you were in this flat when the murder was committed?" questioned the policeman, doing a little detective business on his own account.

"Oh, lor', no," cried the housemaid timidly; "we've been upstairs since nine o'clock helping Mrs. Rover's servants with the party. Do let us in, Mr. Policeman."

"Stay where you are until orders come," commanded the officer sternly; and the trio sat disconsolately on the stairs. With the instinct of self-preservation, they had thoroughly explained their absence from the scene of the crime, and now felt perfectly safe.

Meanwhile in the dining-room a young medical man, who had fortunately been present at the ball, was reviving Shepworth with brandy and ammonia. The windows had been thrown open, and the fresh air was filling the room so rapidly that scarcely a trace of the tuberose fragrance remained. Prelice, having laid aside his mask and domino, was standing near the door with his hands in his pockets, watching a man in uniform, who examined the dead along with the official doctor whom the police had called in. The first individual was Inspector Bruge, a keen-looking, sharp-eyed man, with a clean-shaven face and closely clipped grey hair, and an abrupt red-tape manner. Captain Jadby was not present, having departed with the rest of the too curious onlookers; but Lord Prelice remained, as he had been the first to discover the crime, and Bruge wished to hear his account of it. Already the Inspector's note-book was in his hand to note down the result of the official doctor's examination. There was a dead silence in the room, faintly broken by the distant roll of vehicular traffic, with the occasional hoot of a motor horn. The bell of a near church boomed out midnight so unexpectedly that Prelice jumped. He might well be excused for doing so, as his nerves were considerably shaken.

"Twelve o'clock," said Bruge crisply. "When did you discover the crime, my lord?"

"At half-past eleven," replied Prelice, shivering. "Good heavens, is it only half-an-hour since then? It seems like years."

"We were on the spot in ten minutes," said Bruge with official satisfaction, "and haven't been long in getting things ship-shape. Now that these ladies and gentlemen have gone, we can look into matters. Doctor," he glanced at the young man attending to Shepworth, "is your patient reviving?"

"A trifle," answered the other, rising; "help me to place him near the window —in a draught."

"It is a long faint," said the Inspector, helping to wheel the armchair to the open window.

"It is not a faint at all. The man is in a cataleptic state, induced by the administration of some drug."

"Induced by the odour of a burning herb, you mean," said Prelice, looking at the rigid face of Shepworth, which was as expressionless as that of the dead man at the table.

"What's that?" questioned the Inspector, turning his head.

Prelice waved his hand. "I'll explain later, and after I have seen my friend Dr. Horace."

"Horace! Horace!" The medical man who was examining the corpse looked up at this remark. "I know him slightly. A great traveller, isn't he?"

"Yes," answered Prelice quickly; "he travelled with me to a little known part of the world called Easter Island. Lucky that he did so, and that I was with him. Between us we may be able to solve the mystery of this cataleptic business."

"You know that it is catalepsy, induced by some odour?"

"Of course I do. I have seen a man in that state before." And Prelice pointed to the rigid form of Shepworth.

"Where?" asked Bruge, looking at him with keen eyes, somewhat puzzled.

"On Easter Island."

The Inspector would have asked further questions when the elder doctor rose from examining Agstone's body, and stretched himself. "Well, Thornton?" he asked curtly.

"The man is dead right enough!" said Thornton, with a shrug; "that stab under the left shoulder-blade reached the heart at one blow. I don't see the weapon with which it was committed—the crime I mean."

"We haven't searched the flat yet," rejoined Bruge brusquely; "and if you remember, Thornton, the weapon which killed Sir Oliver Lanwin was not found either."

"What has this case to do with Sir Oliver Lanwin's death?"

Bruge looked surprised. "Don't you read the papers, doctor? There is a murder case on at the New Bailey which resembles this in every particular. Sir Oliver Lanwin was stabbed seated at his desk, and under the left shoulder-blade. His niece, who is accused, says that she is innocent, and was in a cataleptic state, just as this Counsel of hers is. What we see here," mused Bruge, "will go a long way towards helping her to prove her innocence. Mr. Shepworth need not have got rid of Agstone in this way."

"He didn't," cried Prelice sharply; "I'll stake my existence that Mr. Shepworth is perfectly innocent."

"My lord, we know that the prosecution hoped to convict Miss Chent on Agstone's evidence. It was necessary that the defence should keep him out of the way. And here is the man, very forcibly removed, and in the rooms of the young gentleman who is not only helping to defend Miss Chent, but who is her affianced husband. It looks strange."

Prelice pointed to Shepworth, who now showed signs of reviving. "I say to you, as I said to those people who burst into the flat when the alarm was given, that Shepworth is incapable of lifting a hand."

"Ah! but we don't know how long he has been incapable," said Bruge cunningly. "When was Agstone murdered, doctor?"

Thornton, who was twisting a cigarette, answered promptly enough. "I should say, judging from the condition of the temperature of the body, some time between ten and eleven o'clock."

"And can you tell," asked the Inspector, turning to the other doctor, "how long Mr. Shepworth has been insensible?"

"No!" said the young physician promptly; "but he'll tell us himself soon. He is coming round."

Even as he spoke Shepworth opened his eyes, and stared vaguely at those in the room. His gaze wandered in a bewildered manner from the Inspector to Prelice, and from Prelice to the two doctors. Finally, he looked meditatively at the dead body, which was stretched right across the blue cloth of the dining-table, with its glassy eyes staring at the ceiling. A shudder shook the barrister's frame, and as though moved by wires, he sprang stiffly to his feet.

"Prelice! Prelice!" he cried, and his voice grew stronger as his strength came back, as did his colour and senses. "Look! Look! Isn't it the same as in the Grange library! Agstone is dead, and I have been in a trance."

"You know then?" asked Bruge swiftly, "that the dead man is Agstone?"

"Yes! I have seen him many times, at the Grange. But how did he come here? Who murdered him?" And his eyes questioned those present dumbly.

"That is what we wish to ask you," said the Inspector.

Shepworth passed his hand across his forehead, which was now moist with perspiration. "The police," he murmured, "and Agstone dead. Will you place me in the dock beside Mona?" he asked Bruge passionately.

Prelice sprang to his side, and caught him by the hand. "Ned, Ned!" he urged, "pull yourself together and tell us how Agstone came to be murdered in this room."

"I can't tell you," cried Shepworth, wrenching away his hand. "I can tell you no more than Mona could. She was in a trance, and saw nothing, only coming out of it to find the dead beside her. I was in a trance, and saw—— Ah!" he

51

broke off, and his wild eyes went roving round the room, "where is the woman?"

"What woman?" asked Bruge suddenly, and kept his eyes on Shepworth's face with a look of severe scrutiny.

"The woman who came in, masked and cloaked. She came in. Agstone admitted her. She waved the bronze cup before me, and then I—I—— Oh! what does it all mean?" he asked, breaking down, and with every reason, considering what he had undergone.

Prelice shook him gently by the shoulders. "I am beside you, Ned. I am looking after you. Only tell us everything you remember."

Shepworth stared straight before him, and then, as though a spring had been touched, he began to speak swiftly and coherently. "I was sitting reading in the drawing-room, when I heard three heavy blows struck on the wall of this room. As my servants were all upstairs, assisting at the ball, I wondered who was in my flat, and came out to inquire. The door of this room was closed, and I opened it to find a thick white smoke, smelling sweetly and sickly, curling from a bronze cup placed on the table. The fumes choked me, and I staggered instinctively to open the window. Before I could reach it, I fell."

"Senseless?" interpolated Thornton keenly.

"No!" Shepworth turned irritably. "How could I be senseless when I heard and saw everything?—up to a point, that is."

"What did you see?" questioned Bruge eagerly.

"I could move neither hand nor foot, nor could I call out," went on Shepworth slowly, "and I lay on the floor, half propped up against that chair. Then I saw," he shuddered, "a large hairy hand push aside the tablecloth, and shortly a man crawled from underneath. It was Agstone, for I recognised him without difficulty. He growled in a pleased manner, and lifted me into this chair. Then he went out, and remained absent for some time. When he returned a tall woman was with him, wearing a mask and a green domino. Taking the bronze cup, from which the white smoke still poured, she waved it under my nose. My senses left me, and I knew no more until I woke to find you all in my room. And Agstone is dead," ended the barrister, trembling. "Agstone is dead."

"And Agstone," said Bruge significantly, "is the chief witness for the prosecution."

CHAPTER VIII.

A PRIVATE EXPLANATION.

Shepworth made no reply to the insinuation contained in the remark of the Inspector. His brain was still dazed with the fumes of the white smoke, and after telling his story he sat indifferently in his armchair. Prelice watched him closely, recognising the mental confusion, then laid his hand on the poor fellow's arm. "You had better come and lie down," he said gently, and glanced at Thornton.

"Certainly, certainly!" answered that gentleman briskly, and in reply to the unspoken query of Prelice; "a few hours' sleep will cure Mr. Shepworth completely."

"Can I stay with my friend?" demanded Prelice, turning to Bruge.

The Inspector nodded absently, as he was evidently following some train of thought. "Will it be necessary to make a further examination of this?" he inquired, looking at the dead body and at Thornton.

"No, no—not at present. When it has been removed to the dead-house I will see to a further examination. I have seen the body before rigor mortis has set in, so that is all that is necessary. The man has been stabbed some time between ten and eleven, and he is as dead as a coffin nail." Thornton drew on his gloves. "Good-night!"

"Good-night," replied the Inspector. "Allow me to see you to the door." And he conducted both the medical men out of the room, leaving Prelice alone with his still dazed friend.

But Shepworth was not so dazed as he pretended to be, for the moment the door was closed he sprang to his feet. "Dorry, Dorry," he gasped, swaying, "the knife—look for the knife!" Then he dropped back again in the chair, too weak to stand.

"What do you mean?" demanded Prelice sharply, and much puzzled.

Shepworth clutched him. "I did not tell all," he stuttered hurriedly; "it would not have done to tell all. Listen, Dorry. Agstone came back again alone— alone, I tell you—before he brought the lady. I was still conscious, although unable to move in any way. He held the knife in his hand—the jade-handled paper-cutter with which Sir Oliver was murdered. I had it, as you know; it was concealed in my desk—in my study. Agstone must have found it. Agstone must have used it. No! Agstone is dead. I forgot. But someone must have used it to kill Agstone. Oh, my head, my head!" He grasped his hair, and rocked to and fro; then with an effort: "Look for the knife—under the table perhaps—under the——"

Before he could end the sentence Prelice, realising its importance, sprang forward, and lifted a corner of the tablecloth, which trailed on the ground. At the same instant Inspector Bruge appeared again, unexpectedly. His keen eyes immediately fixed themselves on Prelice.

"What are you doing, my lord?" he asked imperatively.

"Making a search," retorted the other bluffly. He did not know what else to say, and hoped that his ready and natural explanation would lull any newly aroused suspicions entertained by the officer.

It did to a certain extent. "You must allow us to do that, my lord. I think you had better take Mr. Shepworth to his bed. And we may as well cover this thing until it is taken away," added Bruge, gathering up the folds of the tablecloth to lay them over the stark-dead creature staring at the ceiling.

Shepworth moved at the same moment as Bruge; but Prelice, guessing that he wished to interfere, held him down with an iron grasp.

When the lifted cloth exposed the bare legs of the table, both the young men caught sight of an object lying underneath. Bruge, stepping back, espied it also, with his trained faculty of instant observation, and stooped to pick it up. The jade-handled paper-cutter lay just where the feet of the dead man had rested before the body had been shifted on to the table. The wonder was that it had not been discovered before; but then it had been concealed by the drooping cloth.

"The weapon with which the crime has been committed," murmured Bruge in a complacent tone; "after stabbing his victim, the assassin must have allowed the knife to fall under the table, or perhaps threw it there intentionally. A jade handle! H'm! It looks like a dagger too—an Eastern dagger. Where have I seen it—where?" And the Inspector fell into a brown study, turning and twisting the paper-cutter slowly.

Prelice pressed Shepworth's shoulder to keep him quiet, and cleared his throat to answer. "It is the knife used to kill Sir Oliver," he said, and felt Shepworth jerk his body in surprised remonstrance at this unnecessary frankness.

Bruge glanced up in amazement. "Why, so it is," he remarked wonderingly —"the very dagger. I remember now that I read the description given of this in the newspaper report of the inquest at Hythe. H'm! So that is how I fancied that I had seen it before." He balanced the knife on the palm of his hand. "A very good piece of description it must have been to so enable me to recognise this. But you," he glanced suspiciously at Prelice, "how did you know?"

The young man shrugged his square shoulders. "That is easily explained," he replied suavely. "I went to hear the case at the New Bailey to-day, as I thought that my friend here," he again pressed Shepworth's shoulder significantly, "was to speak in defence of Miss Chent. At the Court I heard the knife described. It is quite simple, you see."

"I wonder how it comes to be here?" mused Bruge, nodding acquiescence to this lucid explanation. "Odd, isn't it?"

"Not at all," rejoined Prelice easily; "the assassin of Sir Oliver Lanwin brought it here to kill Agstone."

"But Miss Chent is in prison," remonstrated the Inspector; "she could not have——"

"She never did in any case," interrupted Shepworth faintly, but rousing himself sufficiently to defend his promised wife. "She is innocent."

"It is natural that you should say so," remarked Bruge, with polite scepticism, then added significantly: "Did you expect Agstone?"

Shepworth's eyebrows went up wearily. "I? No! Why should I have expected a witness for the prosecution to call upon me? I have told you all that happened until I entirely lost my senses. The first I saw of Agstone was when he crawled from under that table. Then the smoke had rendered me, not unconscious, but unable to speak or move."

"Can this smoke you mention, do that?"

"I speak from experience, Mr. Inspector; and Miss Chent, if you remember, told the same story."

"Oh, I see that the two crimes are connected," said Bruge hastily. "The circumstances are the same as regards this mysterious smoke and its curious power. But you say," he added, turning to Prelice, "you say, my lord, that the assassin of Sir Oliver brought the knife to kill Agstone. Yet we see," he waved his hands towards the corpse, "that Agstone himself is a victim."

"Quite so; but he may have brought the knife for all that."

"Then you imply that Agstone murdered his master?"

"I imply nothing," retorted the young man restively; "but the knife could not have got here unless someone brought it, and as it was missing from the Lanwin Grange library, only the murderer who used it could have possessed it. Moreover," Prelice pressed Shepworth's shoulder to make him particularly note the next sentence, "moreover, Mr. Shepworth saw the knife in Agstone's hand."

Bruge wheeled swiftly towards the barrister. "You did not say that?"

"Not when the doctors and you were in the room," said Shepworth languidly. "I am only beginning to recover my senses, remember; but I told Lord Prelice that Agstone, after he left this room, returned and looked in, to see if I was insensible I suppose, before he brought in the lady. Then he had the knife in his hand."

"And what do you infer?" asked Bruge pointedly.

"There can only be one inference drawn," said Prelice, before Shepworth could speak; "Agstone must have had the knife in his pocket."

"Then Agstone must have murdered Sir Oliver," said Bruge triumphantly.

Shepworth shrugged his shoulders, and staggered to his feet. "I feel too dizzy to give an opinion," he said, leaning heavily on his friend. "We know that Agstone was devoted to Sir Oliver. Why should he have murdered him? Besides, he accuses Miss Chent."

"Naturally," cried the Inspector, who followed eagerly the scent of the red herring which Prelice had drawn across the trail. "If Agstone is guilty himself he naturally would throw the blame on another person; and if he was possessed of the knife he must be guilty. It was missed from the Grange library and reappears here."

"The masked lady might have brought it," suggested Shepworth.

Bruge, extremely pleased with his own theory, shook his head sapiently. "Mr. Shepworth saw the knife in Agstone's hand before he became insensible. You can swear to that?" he asked the barrister.

"Yes," said Shepworth truthfully; "I can swear to that."

"And you can swear that the masked woman killed Agstone?"

"No; I can't say that. When she waved the bronze cup before me I became entirely insensible."

The Inspector looked more knowing than ever. "Of course," said he in a complacent way, "she did not wish you to see her stabbing Agstone."

"But why should she have stabbed him?"

"We can't say until we know the lady. Did you recognise her?"

"No; she was masked and cloaked."

"A green domino, I think you said."

"And a green mask," supplemented Shepworth.

"She must have been at Mrs. Rover's ball," mused Bruge.

"Not necessarily," interpolated Prelice; "but as many people masked and cloaked were ascending and descending the stairs, she may have taken advantage of the ball to get into this flat unobserved."

"Quite so," assented the Inspector; "but who admitted her?"

"Agstone must have done that," said Shepworth.

"Probably; but who admitted Agstone?"

The barrister shook his head. "I can't say," he replied in a tired tone. "I heard a noise—three heavy blows struck in this room—as I told you, when seated in the drawing-room. I did not know that anyone was in the flat."

"What time did your servants go to assist at the ball?"

"Shortly before nine o'clock, when the dinner was over."

"You had dinner then?"

"Oh yes. I came from the Court worn out, and slept for a long time. I then had a light dinner."

"Agstone could not have been at the table then—under it I mean?"

"I think not," said the barrister slowly; "it is not a large table as you see. I would either have heard him, or I should have felt him with my feet."

"Your servants may have left the outer door ajar."

Shepworth nodded. "Perhaps. You can question them. But after dining I returned to the drawing-room before nine o'clock."

"And you did not re-enter this room until you came to see what the three heavy blows meant?"

"No; I did not."

"They must have been struck to make you enter the room."

"I think so, Mr. Inspector. Agstone wished to be smothered with the smoke. That was why the bronze cup was smoking on the table."

"Where is the bronze cup?" Bruge looked about him.

"I can't say. I last saw it when the lady waved it under my nose."

The Inspector meditated. "It's a queer case altogether," he mused, "and undoubtedly it is connected with the Lanwin murder," he mused again, and then looked up abruptly. "I believe that this second murder will exonerate Miss Chent," he said quietly.

"I hope so," rejoined Shepworth, walking towards the door heavily, and still leaning on Prelice's shoulder. "If she is condemned for murdering her uncle, I should certainly be arrested and tried for murdering Agstone. I had every reason to kill him, since on his evidence hangs the fate of Miss Chent."

"You may as well speak in the past tense, Mr. Shepworth, seeing that the man is dead. For my part, I believe that Agstone murdered his master, and was ready to throw the blame on Miss Chent so as to save his own skin. Only the assassin of Sir Oliver could have been possessed of the knife."

"Am I to consider myself arrested?" demanded the barrister.

"No," rejoined Bruge promptly, and held open the door; "but, of course, we must keep an eye on you," he added, smiling ambiguously.

Shepworth nodded languidly, and went out with his friend. "Come into my study, Prelice," he said almost in a whisper. "That knife——"

"Hush!" Prelice gripped the barrister's arm hard. He quite understood what Shepworth wished to do. "Not so loud."

But he need not have been so cautious, for the door of the dining-room had been closed by Bruge, who was now probably searching the clothes of the dead man for more evidence. The two young men went into the study, which was at the end of the passage, and there found that the desk had been forced open—that is, all the three drawers on each side, six in all—in a most dexterous manner. Agstone had apparently come provided with house-breaking tools, so as to gain possession of the dagger. "But how did he know that I had it?" asked Shepworth, perplexed.

"I daresay he was watching through the Grange window, and saw you take it from Miss Chent," suggested Prelice.

Shepworth nodded. "Let us put the room tidy," he said hurriedly, and closing the door; "I don't want the police to fuss about here."

The room really was untidy, for in searching for the knife Agstone had scattered the loose papers lying on the desk all over the carpet. The young man collected these, and placed them in order; then Shepworth closed the drawers of the desk carefully. In a few minutes—after replacing a chair that had been kicked over, and smoothing a rug that had been rucked up—the study looked quite in order. Nevertheless, Shepworth stared anxiously at the now innocent-looking desk. "I hope the police will not examine it," he said nervously.

"I don't think so, since you have explained so much, Ned. Their attentions will be confined to the dining-room wherein the murder took place. Will you go to bed?"

"No." Shepworth sat at his desk. "I don't want this examined. Let us sit here and have some strong coffee."

Prelice shook his head. "Don't," he advised; "better let us steal to your bedroom, and say nothing about having been here. If the police examine the desk you can pretend ignorance, and express surprise. On the other hand, if Bruge comes in and makes the discovery while we are here, he will naturally demand why we kept silence, and inquiries would lead to difficulties. Leave the thing to chance."

Shepworth agreed with this reasoning, since it was useless, and even dangerous, to create difficulties at the present juncture. The two walked silently to the bedroom, and here the barrister stripped, to put on his dressing-gown. Then, lying down outside the bed, he placed his hands behind his head, and stared at the ceiling, while Prelice lounged in an armchair close at hand.

"Why did you tell Bruge about the second entrance of Agstone with the dagger?" asked Shepworth suddenly.

"Because he had already seen the dagger," rejoined Prelice promptly. "It is as well to tell the truth when possible, and just as well that the Inspector should think Agstone—who cannot now contradict—brought the dagger. You heard what he said yourself about Agstone's possible guilt. Our frankness will probably save Miss Chent, as the murder of Sir Oliver will be attributed to Agstone because he possessed that paper-cutter."

Shepworth groaned. "But if Bruge knew that I took it from Mona?"

"Then there would be serious trouble. Let things remain as they are, Ned. We know that Miss Chent is innocent, and must save her."

"But we don't know that Agstone is guilty. He certainly is not, on the reasoning of Bruge."

"No; seeing that we know Agstone did not bring the dagger here. But the man is dead, and if he can be made to act as scapegoat for an innocent woman, so much the better."

The barrister sighed. "We are environed by difficulties," he murmured; then added significantly and unexpectedly: "Jadby called to see me this evening."

"What!" Prelice was startled. "I thought that you had quarrelled."

"So we had—so we did—and with fists too. But when I was reading in the drawing-room, and thinking of my poor girl shut up in prison, I heard a ring at the front door. The servants had gone to the ball, as you know, so I had to open the door myself. Captain Jadby was there, and after a stiff greeting he asked for an interview. I took him into the drawing-room, and——"

"One moment. Did you close the outer door?"

"Of course. Why do you ask that?"

"I fancied that you might have unconsciously left it open, and that Agstone might then have entered to conceal himself."

"No," said Shepworth decisively. "I am certain that I closed it. With Jadby I went to the drawing-room, and there he frankly expressed his regrets that we had quarrelled. He wished to make it up, and to join forces with me to save poor Mona."

"Because he loves her?"

"Quite so. He makes no secret of the fact that he is madly in love with Mona. Our hand-to-hand fight at Lanwin Grange rose solely from the fact that he would insist upon forcing his attentions on her. She appealed to me as her lover, so I tackled Jadby, and knocked him down. However, he seemed to be sorry that he had behaved like a bounder; so we shook hands, and then sat down to consider how we should act with regard to Mona's position."

"H'm!" Prelice looked sceptical. "From the glimpse I caught of Jadby I should not think he was the sort of man to forgive a punch in the eye, much less the loss of the girl he loves. He might have come here with the intention of trapping you; he might have admitted Agstone."

"No," replied Shepworth quickly. "I was with him all the time. I opened the outer door to admit him, and closed it when he departed. As he was under my eyes while in the flat, he had no chance of admitting Agstone secretly. I don't know how the man managed to enter and conceal himself under that table, but Jadby had nothing to do with it. Moreover," added the barrister decisively, "Jadby told me that he was as ignorant as everyone else of Agstone's whereabouts."

"Oh, a blighter like Jadby would say anything."

Shepworth protested. "I think we have judged Jadby wrongly."

"My dear Ned, you are altogether too good for this wicked world. I don't trust Jadby for one instant. He plays for his own hand."

"I know he does. He admits that he intends to claim the estate of Sir Oliver, and that he loves Mona. But he swears that he will take no steps until she is set free. Then she can marry me if she chooses."

Prelice laughed ironically. "And you believe him?"

"He seemed to be in earnest."

"About setting Miss Chent free? Oh yes; I am sure of that; but he intends to marry her, you may be sure. Jadby is very philanthropic. How does he propose to save Miss Chent?"

"By finding Agstone, and sending him out of the kingdom."

"And Agstone appears shortly after that proposal. H'm! H'm! H'm! I must have a personal interview with Captain Jadby, and ask him——"

"Ask him what?"

"If he has ever visited Easter Island."

"What on earth do you mean?" demanded Shepworth curiously.

But Lord Prelice refused to explain further.

CHAPTER IX.

DR. HORACE.

Next day everyone, from the man in the street to the lady in her drawing-room, was talking about the murder at Alexander Mansions. As a rule, those in Society talk very little about such horrors; but on this occasion people, more or less fashionable, felt that the crime had been committed, so to speak, on their very doorsteps. Mrs. Rover's ball had been broken up by the discovery of the crime, and many of the guests, crowding down to Shepworth's flat, had seen a murdered man for the first time in their frivolous lives. No wonder the tragedy made a sensation.

Moreover, the second crime in London was connected—no one knew exactly how—with the first crime at Lanwin Grange, Hythe. Sir Oliver had been murdered by his niece, who was now being tried for the offence. The victim had been a baronet, and the prisoner was a well-known figure in the social world. Now the missing witness, upon whose evidence was supposed to hinge the condemnation or acquittal of Miss Chent, had been violently done away with. And—hinted gossip—in spite of appearances, the barrister to whom the flat belonged must have killed the man, so that damaging evidence might be finally suppressed. Thus the two crimes had much to do with Society as a whole, and the newspaper placards informed the lower orders of "A Tragedy in High Life." Stump orators in Hyde Park chose the placards and the moment to talk of the decay of the upper classes, and of the need of a revolution to sweep away tyrants born in the social purple.

Finally, there was another thing which interested fashionable folk. Many guests at the masked ball had been robbed of valuable jewellery, and the police were entirely at a loss to trace the thieves. Undoubtedly, what Mr. Simon Haken had prophesied jokingly to his host had come cruelly true: swell mobsmen and light-fingered ladies had taken advantage of the use of masks at the ball to mingle with the legitimate guests, and appropriate gems and gold of great value. Bracelets, ear-rings, chains, brooches, and even rings—many of these had vanished, and scarcely a single woman had escaped the rapacity of the unknown thieves. This in itself was sufficient to make Mrs. Dolly Rover's entertainment notorious, and that a terrible murder should cap the climax of such roguery was almost too much for belief. Next day the journals sold like hot cakes, and the one topic of conversation with high and low had to do with this astounding criminality.

Lord Prelice returned to his rooms in Half-Moon Street just as the dawn broke over an astonished and indignant Mayfair, and threw himself on his bed to recuperate. Tough as he was with travel and adventure, he needed sleep very badly after the exciting events of the dark hours, and as he dropped off into slumber it struck him forcibly that the time of superabundant leisure had gone by for ever. Formerly an idler, who took comparatively little interest in life, and certainly none in the doings of other people, he found himself committed, through friendship, to a strenuous career. Ever since Lady Sophia's visit on the previous morning he had gradually become entangled in other lives, and until the crooked ways of these had been made straight he saw no chance of reverting to his happy-go-lucky existence. Prelice, having a high ideal of friendship, resolved to help Shepworth, and, through him, Miss Mona Chent, with all the brain power and physical power and social power at his command. And the opportunity of doing so was not unpleasing to an active-minded man, who had hitherto fritted away his intelligence in butterfly pursuits.

He woke at noon to receive a telegram, which his man brought in, with an apology for disturbing him.

It proved to be from Shepworth, and contained the amazing news that the barrister had been arrested for the murder. Considering that Inspector Bruge had assured Shepworth—and in Prelice's presence—that there was no chance of any suspicion being cast upon him in any way, the young man had to read the wire twice or thrice before he could fully grasp its sinister significance. It seemed absurd. Dozens of people, including Bruge and two medical men, had seen the insensible form of the accused man, and were content at the time that he could not raise a hand, much less execute a crime, which needed clear-headedness and strength. And it was the more ridiculous to arrest Shepworth, because the barrister had given a plain account of what had happened,—so far as he remembered—which was similar in most respects to what had taken place at Hythe. Of course, Prelice recollected the way in which he and Ned had concealed the true story of the knife; but it was impossible that Shepworth, now quite in possession of his wits, should have told an unnecessary truth. If he had, Prelice believed that he would be arrested also, as an accessory after the fact. The thought made him uncomfortable, until he brushed it away. Ned was not exactly an idiot, and on whatever plea he had been arrested, it certainly could not have to do with the story of the knife.

But it was necessary to learn what had taken place, and also to bail Ned out, so that they might work together to elucidate the mystery. This would be difficult considering the charge was one of murder; but Prelice indulged in a cold bath to freshen his physical powers, and after dressing rapidly, took a hansom back to Alexander Mansions. Here he was confronted at the door by the same burly police constable who had prevented Shepworth's servants from re-entering their master's flat some hours before. He treated Lord Prelice in the same way.

"You can't come in, my lord. Inspector's orders."

"I wish to see Mr. Shepworth," argued Prelice vexedly.

"It's against orders, my lord."

"Is he within?"

"Yes, my lord, but he isn't allowed to see anyone."

"Will you take a note in from me?"

"No, my lord. I can't do that."

"Can I see Inspector Bruge?"

"He is at the police station, my lord."

Prelice stamped with vexation at the obstacles placed in his way. He did his best to argue this official machine into something resembling reasonable humanity, but without success. Shepworth, he learned, was to be taken to prison later in the day, and the constable hinted that, since the charge was so serious, there would be no chance of the barrister being let out on bail. There was no other course open but to see Inspector Bruge, so Prelice drove to the Kensington Police Station, only to find that the man he wished to see had gone to Scotland Yard, presumably about the case.

Apparently there was nothing to be done at the moment in connection with this new trouble, so Prelice was half minded to repair to the New Bailey, and listen to the further progress of the charge against Miss Chent. Now that Agstone was dead, he did not think that she would be convicted. Also, the repetition of the circumstances of the Hythe crime in Alexander Mansions would assuredly strengthen her position, since the jury would now be compelled to believe her story of the stupefying smoke, which formerly had been regarded as absurd. And it was when the thought of the smoke entered his mind that Prelice recollected that Dr. Horace lived in the neighbourhood. He therefore walked to Rutland Square, and asked at Number Twenty for his former fellow-traveller. Chance stood the young man's friend, for the doctor was within, and saw him at once.

"This is an unexpected pleasure, Prelice," said the doctor, beaming. "I thought you were in the West Indies."

"I returned only a few days ago. Are you busy?"

"My friend, I am always busy." And Horace indicated a case of beetles and butterflies, with which he was dealing when his guest entered.

The room was a large one, with two broad windows looking out onto the quiet square, but all available space was taken up with records of the doctor's travels. The floor was carpeted with wild-beast skins, for Horace was a noted hunter; the walls were decorated with Polynesian war-clubs, with Zulu assegaies, with Redskin wampum belts and beaded moccasins. Also, there were Japanese gods, Chinese jars of grotesquely decorated porcelain, Hindoo swords, Persian tiles reft from mosques, and African canoe paddles rudely carved. As Horace never allowed any servant to meddle with his treasures the room was extremely untidy and dusty, and generally neglected, With the exception of a gigantic dining-table of mahogany and two chairs there was no civilised furniture, yet the place was so crammed with barbaric curiosities that Prelice could scarcely find a clear place to stand in. Finally, he stumbled through a narrow passage of Egyptian mummies and gigantic Maori idols to an uncomfortable cane chair near the window. Here he sat down, and looked at his host with some disgust.

"Why the dickens can't you live like a civilised being when you are in London?" he asked, lighting a cigar to dispel the frowsy smell of the room.

"I am perfectly comfortable," said Horace, clearing a place on the table to sit on. "This is my home; I live here."

"You camp here, I think. I never saw such a messy place in my life."

"Huh," grunted the doctor, filling a German pipe with strong tobacco. "You shouldn't come here in a Bond Street kit. Well, what is it? Are you longing to be on the trail again?"

"I am on a sort of trail certainly," admitted Prelice slowly, and inspecting the ash of his cigar. "A manhunt. Ah, your eyes light up at that, you bloodthirsty old pagan."

"A manhunt," repeated Horace meditatively, "and in London—slow business."

"Well, I don't know, Horace. It is one requiring a great deal of subtility. I have come for your assistance."

"Huh!" said the doctor again, and nodded. "I'm with you."

Prelice reflected for a few moments before beginning an explanation of his errand. He did not know how much to tell and how much to withhold. Horace saw his hesitation, and ascribed it to the right cause.

"I must know everything, Prelice," he said quickly, "else I do not assist. I have no notion of working in the dark, and failing through ignorance."

"You can read my thoughts as usual, I see," commented the visitor; "some more of that clairvoyant business, I expect. Well, I have a case to lay before you which will tax your occult powers to the utmost."

"Fire away," said Horace, and placing his hands on the table rocked to and fro, looking absurdly like a monkey. "The Missing Link" they called him in the Wilds, and certainly the name was deserved. Horace was a small man with a long body, short legs, and lengthy arms; very powerfully built, and very shaggy in appearance. Prelice looked at the doctor's large head covered with tangled red hair; at his beard and moustache of the same hue, untrimmed and untidy, concealing nearly all his flat face; and at his big horn-rimmed spectacles, which hid the brightest and keenest of blue eyes. He wore an old pair of flannel trousers, and a still older flannel shirt, the sleeves of which were turned up over two hairy wrists encircled with Matabele wire bracelets. To complete his barbaric looks his large ears, furry as those of a faun, were adorned with gold rings. A more quaint or a more extraordinary figure was not to be met with outside a Freak Museum. And Dr. Horace should have been exhibited in one, if only on account of the beautifully executed tattooing, which Prelice could see on his sunburnt arms, and on his chest, through the unbuttoned shirt.

No one would have taken this man-monkey to be a clever and learned scholar with a heart of gold and a fund of knowledge second to none. Prelice knew and esteemed him, and had fought with him—for the doctor was obstinate— and beside him in the Naked Lands at the Back-of-Beyond, when both held their lives in their hands. All the same, being fastidious, he sincerely wished that when the doctor returned to civilisation, he would leave behind him in the wilderness his uncouth manners and shabby dress and general appearance of being a prehistoric man of Lady Sophia's favourite Stone Age.

"Go on, go on," said Horace impatiently, "don't keep me waiting. I have lots to do, and can't waste time."

"You have lots to do in the way of dress, I think. Come and have a Turkish bath, and visit the nearest barber. Then I can take you to my tailor to be clothed properly, and——"

Horace interrupted characteristically by throwing his pipe at the young man. It was deftly fielded and returned. "Do you remember Easter Island?" asked Prelice when the doctor was again smoking; then in reply to a consenting grunt: "I see you do. And the Sacred Herb, eh?"

Horace scowled. "How do you come into the matter?" he growled.

"Into what matter?" queried the other.

"Oliver Lanwin's murder. It's in all the papers."

"Quite so; but why should my remark about the Sacred Herb make you think that I referred to Lanwin's murder?"

"Is there any need of an explanation?" asked Horace coolly. "If you didn't guess, as I did, that the Sacred Herb was used to make that smoke, why do you talk of the matter at all?"

"Then you think that the herb——"

"Course! Course!" growled Horace, beginning to rock again. "Lanwin haunted the South Seas. I knew him there. He must have got the herb from Easter Island, as it is the only place it grows in. When I read the girl's yarn of the smoke, I guessed straight off that Lanwin had been trying to induce a trance with the burning herb."

"Do you think that Miss Chent murdered him?"

"No! The library was filled with the smoke of the herb. Anyone not used to the fumes would go down like a shot, as she did."

"Then you believe Miss Chent's story?" asked Prelice eagerly.

Horace nodded. "She could not have made up such a clever yarn."

"Then why in Heaven's name," questioned the young man, rising, "did you not volunteer your evidence to save her?"

"Will it save her?"

"Assuredly! Everyone regards her story of being stupefied with the smoke as absurd. If you tell what we saw on Easter Island, in front of the statues———"

"Tell it yourself."

"I intend to. I am going to the Court now, and you," said Prelice with emphasis, "*you* are coming with me."

Horace knocked the ashes out of his pipe. "Why should I?" he demanded, with a stolid air.

"That's a long story," retorted Prelice restlessly.

"I can give you ten minutes. Don't talk through your hat."

Knowing his man, the visitor did not waste time, but bluntly detailed how he came to be drawn into the Lanwin murder case. But he naturally suppressed his feelings for the beautiful prisoner, and put down his interest, with some emphasis, to pure friendship for Shepworth. On reaching the end of the Hythe portion of the story, he paused to draw breath. "Is that all?" asked Horace grimly.

"The first part only," replied Prelice promptly, and narrated the events of the previous night from the time he went to Mrs. Rover's *bal masqué* to the time he left the Kensington Police Station to call upon his listener. During this latter part of the history Dr. Horace became restless, and wandered about his untidy room, stumbling over obstacles, and softly swearing, with a wonderful command of language. He appeared to be inattentive, but in reality had not lost a single word. When Prelice stopped he came to a halt before the young man. "I'll go with you to the Court," he declared. "The first thing to do is to save the girl. After that we can consider how to get Shepworth out of his difficulty."

"He is innocent, of course," observed Prelice, trying to read the rugged face of his new ally.

"Never said he wasn't," grumbled the doctor; then reflected for a few moments, raking his long beard with out-spread fingers. "See here," he burst out finally, "will you allow me to engineer this business?"

"I shall only be too glad. Are you going to use occult methods?"

"I don't need to. I have my own ideas, having read the newspapers."

"Then you think that Agstone murdered Lanwin?"

"No more than I think Shepworth murdered Agstone. On your own showing your barrister friend brought the knife to the flat. And it is on the false evidence of the knife, which you and Shepworth supplied, that Inspector Bruge seems to judge Agstone."

"Still——"

"Oh, don't talk poppy-cock," interrupted the little man impatiently.

"You are not polite, Horace."

"Was I ever polite?" demanded the other scornfully.

"No! To do you justice, you are always consistently rude!"

"Then why expect the impossible?" retorted Horace, and again stumbled about the crowded room, swearing softly. When again abreast of Prelice, who was sorely puzzled by this strange conduct, the doctor thrust out a large hairy paw. "Shake," said he brusquely.

Prelice did so promptly, and inquired: "Why?"

"Because you are giving me pleasure in allowing me to help you."

His friend looked at the odd creature perplexedly. "I don't understand what you mean," he declared, frowning.

"Never mind," returned Horace, with a chuckle; "when it is necessary for you to understand I'll straighten out things."

"Then you have a theory?"

"I have more than that; I have certain knowledge."

"Of what, in Heaven's name?"

"High cockalorum, snip snap snorum," was the jocular and enigmatic reply, "come to my bedroom, and we can chatter while I dress."

"Well," said Prelice as he sauntered after his friend, "I am glad that you are not going in that rigout. It isn't the fifth of November."

"Silly ass," snapped the traveller; "get a dressed-up doll to help you."

"All right. Come to a toy-shop and help me to choose one."

Dr. Horace began to laugh. "Why can't you talk sense?" he growled.

"I shall do so if you will set the example."

"Very good. I have some of the Sacred Herb here. Shall I take it to the New Bailey, and give judge and jury and counsel a practical illustration of how Miss Chent and Shepworth went into trances?"

"You can if you like. By the way, did you give any portion of that herb away, Horace?"

The doctor, who was plunging his hairy face in water, gurgled and grumbled, but made no reply. Prelice was nettled. "Why can't you be plain with me, confound you?"

"All right." Horace began to dry his face vigorously. "I don't believe that Miss Chent is guilty, or that Shepworth killed Agstone."

"I knew that before," said Prelice dryly; "you tell me nothing new."

"Oh," retorted Horace mockingly, "you want to hear something new, like an Athenian of St. Paul's period. Very good. Do you know why I take so deep an interest in this case?"

"No, I don't; unless it is to help me and Ned."

"I don't care a red cent about you and Ned. But I care a trifle about Agstone, poor devil."

Prelice sat up straight, and stared. "In Heaven's name, why?"

"Because," said Dr. Horace slowly, and looking at Prelice's puzzled face in the glass, "because Steve Agstone is my brother."

CHAPTER X.

THE VERDICT.

Here was a surprise indeed. Prelice knew that Dr. Horace had worked his way up from a humble position, and laid no claims to being of gentle blood. But he had never referred to the existence of a single relative, and the young man had always believed him to be alone in the world. Now it seemed that Agstone was his brother. And when Prelice recollected that Agstone was the same hirsute, red-haired, uncouth animal in appearance, it flashed across his mind that the brothers were twins. The extraordinary thing was that he had not noted the close resemblance before, since he had seen Agstone dead and Horace alive, within the last few hours. But the idea of connecting a common sailor with an eminent scientific man had never entered his mind.

In the cab, on the way to the New Bailey, Horace gruffly gave his companion a few facts to substantiate his statement, but Prelice observed that he said as little as he could.

"My full name is Horace Agstone," explained the doctor bluntly, "but as I got on in life and rose in the world I dropped the last and kept to the first. Steve is my elder brother by one year, and we are the sons of a Suffolk labourer. I had the brains of the family, and in one way and another managed to cultivate those same brains, with the result—no very great one—you see. Steve went to sea, and we did not meet for years and years. When he returned to England with old Lanwin he went down to Suffolk to look up the family. Our parents were dead and buried, but Steve learned my name and address from the vicar. He came to look me up, but as we did not hit it off very well, we considered it best to live our lives apart, as formerly. That's all."

Prelice threw his cigarette out of the cab, and stared at the horse in a meditative way. "Strange that you should be connected with this case also," he remarked dreamily.

The doctor grew red, and looked fierce. "What the devil do you mean by that? I have nothing to do with the case."

"Your brother——"

"I have nothing to do with my brother. He and I were born of the same mother, but beyond that we are—I mean we were, seeing he is dead—nothing to one another. If he chooses to kill people and be killed, that is his affair. No one can connect Steve Agstone with Dr. Horace, save the vicar of Burfield in Suffolk, unless you betray me. Not that I care, mark you, Prelice. I learned that fable of the old man and his ass very early in life, and never trouble about people and their opinions."

"I don't intend to betray you," said Prelice coldly, but flushing all over his freckled face; "you can be brother to Satan for all I care. Moreover, I have given confidence for confidence. If I know about your relation to Agstone, you know about the knife's evidence, which I and Shepworth suppressed."

"Right! Right! Don't get your hair off," said Horace, gripping his companion's knee in a painful manner. "You and I are chums of the Wild, old son, and those of that breed don't go back on one another." He released Prelice's knee, and leaned back, thoughtfully. "Of course, it was a shock for me to learn of Agstone's death."

"Didn't you see it in the morning papers?"

"No. I have more to do than to read riff-raff rubbish. You were the first to inform me. Well!" Horace leaned his arms on the splash-board calmly, "Steve's gone to see father and mother on the Astral Plane. I expect he will quarrel with them as usual. They never got on together."

Prelice suppressed a smile at this odd, unchristian way of viewing death, and nodded. "I quite understand why you don't believe Agstone to be guilty!" he remarked after a pause.

"Meaning that I'm a born fool," retorted Horace genially. "Make no mistake, old son. If Steve were guilty, I should not defend him in any way; but he was too devoted to old Lanwin to murder him. Besides——" The doctor suddenly checked himself. "But that's neither here nor there, my son."

"What isn't?" asked Prelice alertly.

"Never you mind; ask no questions and you'll be told no lies. Here we are at the door of the Temple of Falsehood. Get out."

Prelice alighted with his companion, sorely puzzled to know what this enigmatic remark meant. That Horace knew of something which had to do with the Lanwin case he was perfectly sure; that the something implicated the late Mr. Agstone he was also certain. But Prelice knew his friend sufficiently well to be satisfied that he would not explain, unless it appeared to him needful to do so. All that could be done was to trust blindly to the rugged old sinner, and perhaps he would be able to lead those concerned in the case out of the labyrinth of crime. He certainly appeared to hold a clue.

Dr. Horace, more brusque and domineering than ever, pushed his way into the crowded Court, eliciting comments the reverse of complimentary. Of these, with characteristic cynicism, he took no notice, but secured good places for himself and Prelice. In a few minutes he scribbled a note, and sent it to Cudworth, K.C. The Counsel read it with a puzzled air, glanced at the writer across the crowded Court, and whispered to the usher. Shortly Dr. Horace was requested to go to the lawyer's table, and was soon in deep conversation with the big barrister. While this was taking place Prelice stared at Miss Chent, who looked weary and sad as she sat in the dock. The strain of her perilous position was beginning to tell upon her, which was scarcely to be wondered at. Again her roving eyes caught sight of Prelice, and again she blushed, this time drawing a corresponding signal from him. Apparently the natures of these two were sympathetic.

The case was rapidly drawing to a close, as the witnesses for the prosecution had been examined, and now those for the defence were giving evidence. From a solicitor at his elbow the young man learned that Cudworth had succeeded in proving the destruction of the will in Mona Chent's favour. This had been done by the production of half burnt and minutely torn scraps of paper rescued from the grate in the library. These, pieced together, had revealed the mention of the prisoner's name, and of the ten thousand a year, and of the love and affection felt by the testator for his niece. As the will could not be found, and it was certain that Sir Oliver had framed no new testament, the presumption was that the burnt document was the will in question, and despite all efforts the other side could not prove otherwise. This was assuredly a great point in the prisoner's favour, as had she murdered her uncle she would certainly not have destroyed a deed which made her wealthy.

It was with great surprise that Prelice saw Shepworth placed in the witness-box to give evidence, since he had left him practically imprisoned in his own flat. Possibly Inspector Bruge had received instructions from Scotland Yard, on detailing what had happened in Alexander Mansions, to afford the judge and jury the opportunity of seeing how similar the murders of Agstone and his master were to one another. Shepworth was perfectly cheerful and composed, much more so than he had been on the previous day, so apparently he had no fear that his arrest would lead to his conviction. Indeed, he was so clearly innocent that Prelice expected he would be set free after the inquest proceedings on Agstone's body had taken place. Meanwhile he caught his friend's eye, and smiled, after which he smiled again encouragingly at Mona.

Shepworth's evidence was to the effect that Miss Chent loved her uncle, and would never have harmed him in any way. Sir Oliver, in the course of an occult conversation, had referred to a certain herb—he did not give it any name—which when burned produced trances. Apparently, when prisoner entered the library to make up her quarrel with Sir Oliver, the baronet had been testing the herb, and the fumes had reduced Miss Chent to an unconscious state. Then Shepworth went on to detail his own experience, and narrated the same story as he had told to Prelice, to the two doctors, and to Inspector Bruge. Finally, he mentioned that Agstone had re-entered the dining-room, before returning with the masked lady, holding a knife. As Shepworth, naturally, was not asked if the knife was concealed in his desk, there was no need for him to commit perjury, which he would have been unwilling to do, even to save the girl he loved.

While the barrister was giving his evidence Lord Prelice was called to Cudworth's side, and introduced by Dr. Horace. He learned that the Counsel wished him to appear as a witness and substantiate Shepworth's story, which the young man was perfectly willing to do. It thus happened that when Shepworth retired Cudworth examined Prelice, and heard from him how Shepworth had been found unconscious, and how many people, including Captain Jadby, had seen him in this helpless state. This evidence induced the recall of Jadby, and he reluctantly swore that the barrister was indeed unable to strike the murderous blow which had slain the old sailor.

Both Shepworth and Prelice had given evidence as to the finding of the knife under the table by Inspector Bruge, and that officer himself next appeared to say how he had picked it up. Mrs. Blexey, Madame Marie Eppingrave, and two of the Grange servants were then called to depose that the paper-cutter with the jade handle, found in the flat by Bruge; and produced in Court, was the same that had lain on Sir Oliver's writing-table in the library, wherein the crime had been committed. Thus the jury, and indeed everyone else, believed that Agstone had murdered his master, and then had brought the knife up to Alexander Mansions, presumably to kill Shepworth; but, of course, the question as to who had killed Agstone was not touched upon.

The final witness was Dr. Horace, and he dealt entirely with the questions of the perfumed smoke alluded to by the prisoner and by Shepworth. Producing a grotesque brown root and several stems covered with purple leaves, more or less withered, the doctor deposed that it was a certain plant growing in Easter Island, and nowhere else, so far as he knew. The natives gave it no name, but termed it "The Sacred Herb," and it was used by their priests to induce trances, in which the spirit was supposed to leave the body, and appear before the gods incarnate—so to speak—in the gigantic statues of the island.

Belmain (for the prosecution): "Did you give any portion of this herb to Sir Oliver Lanwin?"

Witness (emphatically): "No! I was acquainted with Sir Oliver in the South Seas, but I never met him in England. We did not get on well together, and were better apart."

Belmain: "Then how did Sir Oliver become possessed of this herb, which, by your own showing, is to be found only in Easter Island?"

Witness: "I cannot say how Sir Oliver got the herb. Of course, he was sailing the South Seas for years, and probably went to Easter Island. If he did, he certainly would have secured a portion of the herb from the native priests, seeing that he took so profound an interest in occult matters."

Belmain: "Then you think that Sir Oliver was experimenting with the herb when prisoner entered the library?"

Witness: "I think it extremely likely, considering the presence of the white smoke, and the tuberose perfume, which is exactly the kind of scent given off by the herb when burnt. The fumes of the herb would choke prisoner in the way she stated, and reduce her to unconsciousness."

Belmain (significantly): "To complete unconsciousness?"

Witness: "I think so, seeing that she was not accustomed to the smoke of the herb. A slight smoke would place anyone in a cataleptic state merely, but a dense smoke would take away all consciousness. It did so apparently in the case of Miss Chent, and although Mr. Shepworth was simply cataleptic at first, the waving of the bronze cup under his nose plunged him into the deeper state."

Belmain: "How did Agstone become possessed of the herb to burn in Alexander Mansions?"

Witness: "I really cannot tell you. Perhaps he went to Easter Island with his master, and got some leaves of the herb; or it might be that, when taking the knife away from the library, he also secured the leaves which were lying on Sir Oliver's desk."

Belmain (quickly): "How do you know the leaves were there?"

Witness (coolly): "I am only surmising. If Lanwin was experimenting with the herb, he must have got out his packet of leaves and roots. I expect, not being used to the herb, he was reduced either to catalepsy or to unconsciousness, and while thus helpless was murdered."

Belmain: "By Steve Agstone?"

Witness: "I am not prepared to say." (Very dryly.)

"A very improper question," rebuked the judge; and Belmain sat down feeling that he had not scored off this rugged witness.

Before Dr. Horace left the witness-box the judge, prompted by the foreman of the jury, requested him to burn some leaves of the herb at once. "But do not reduce us to a state of catalepsy," said the judge, with a smile; "we have to finish our business, you know."

A china plate was brought, and on this Horace gravely laid two or three leaves of the Sacred Herb. On applying a match, a thick curl of pungent white smoke arose, like a summer cloud, and the odour of tuberoses was perceptibly indicated in the heavy atmosphere of the Court. Prelice, who was standing near the witness-box, and so smelt the perfume very strongly, suddenly felt sick, and swiftly pushed his way into the fresh air. He was inclined to faint, being susceptible to odours, and but that a good Samaritan addicted to alcohol had produced a flask of brandy, he would have become unconscious. When quite restored, he thought how very powerful the herb was, when even so slight a breath of the smoke could muddle his senses. No wonder that Miss Chent and Sir Oliver and Shepworth had become unconscious when the full power of the burning purple leaves was poured through the rooms.

Prelice did not feel inclined to re-enter the Court, and sat outside in the vestibule, smoking a cigarette. Here he was joined by Captain Jadby, which rather surprised the young man, as he thought that the sailor's love for Mona Chent would have kept him in the Court. Also, Prelice was surprised when Jadby approached him in quite a friendly way, and with an apology.

"I hope you have forgiven me for my rudeness last night, Lord Prelice," was his ingratiating remark.

"I never gave it another thought," retorted Prelice brusquely. "Pray do not apologise again. You did so last night."

"Thank you," said Jadby, smiling all over his smooth, feline face. "I am glad that you take it in such a spirit. By the way, I never knew that you were acquainted with Dr. Horace."

Prelice stared at this impertinent remark. "Very probably," he said stiffly, "but then you know nothing about me."

"I know that you went to Easter Island, Lord Prelice. I heard of your visit when I went there myself."

"Oh," said Prelice alertly, "then you visited the Island also."

"I have just said so," rejoined Jadby coolly, "but I did not bring away any of the herb, if that is what you mean."

"It is *not* what I mean," said the other, wondering why Jadby should say such a thing. "I don't accuse you of murdering Sir Oliver, even though you inherit the property."

He was thus pointed and rude to get rid of the smiling man before him, as he felt the same antipathy to Jadby as he would have done to a cat, the one animal which Prelice could not endure. But the sailor was not at all annoyed, or if he was, did not show it. Rather did he smile in a very satisfied way. "Yes, I do inherit the property," he remarked, "and there is a good reason why I should."

"Really," observed Prelice, considering what the reason might be, but unwilling to ask.

"Yes, really," retorted the captain, still smiling; "of course, I am sorry for Miss Chent, but when she marries me all will be well."

"You forget, sir. She marries Mr. Shepworth."

"They are engaged," replied Jadby, with a shrug, "but I do not think that they will ever be married. Mrs. Rover——"

Prelice interrupted imperiously. "What do you mean by mentioning Mrs. Rover's name in this connection?" he demanded, flushing.

"Oh," said Jadby, with his hateful smile, "I understood that you and Mr. Shepworth were intimate friends. Good-day!" And before Prelice could stop him, Captain Jadby had vanished amidst the crowd, leaving, like the wasp he was, a sting behind him.

Prelice frowned. He recollected Shepworth's blush, Lady Sophia's remarks, and now considered Captain Jadby's hint. It would seem that his friend was either in love with Mrs. Dolly Rover or was entangled in some way. If that was the case, he could not possibly love Mona, and if he did not—— Prelice's face grew crimson, and his eyes brightened. Then he shook himself free of the thought. Jadby was implying that Shepworth was behaving dishonourably, and Prelice could not bring himself to believe that such was the case. He had known Ned too long to doubt him. All the same, he felt that an explanation would clear the air, and concluded to ask Shepworth for one as delicately as possible. Upon that explanation would depend his future movements.

Lord Prelice walked up and down the vestibule, musing on Mona, on her perilous position, on Shepworth's possible entanglement with Mrs. Rover, late Miss Constance Newton, and on the enigmatic hints of Dr. Horace dealing with the mysterious cases, in which friendship had involved him. Thus thinking, he lost all note of time, and it was only when a Court official came to turn on the electrics that he became aware of the passing of time. Glancing at his watch, he found that it was several hours since he had left the Court, and he determined to enter again, and hear the speeches of the Counsel for the Defence and Prosecution. But just as he turned in the direction of the Court he heard a cheer, and an excited throng of people poured out. In two minutes Prelice was in possession of the news, and learned that Mona Chent had been acquitted. She was free.

CHAPTER XI.

When London was made acquainted with the verdict, the majority of people were satisfied that justice had been done. Miss Chent's behaviour while in the dock, the open sympathy of the Grange servants, the occurrence of the second murder, so similar in all respects to the first, and the evidence of Horace with regard to the anæsthetic properties of the Sacred Herb of Easter Island, went far to enlist the public in favour of the accused girl. Perhaps, also, her youth and brilliant beauty had something to do with the loudly expressed pleasure of those who read in the newspapers that she had been set free.

Of course, there were the usual malcontents, who agreed with no one, and wrote to the journals stating that the verdict was wrong. A communication to *The Daily Telegraph* insisted that Miss Client must have lied, declaring that she fell senseless while unfastening the window for fresh air. If it had been the case Captain Jadby would have found her lying near the window, whereas she was discovered in the armchair near the fire, some distance away. But a supporter of the late prisoner replied to this by pointing out that the murderer of Sir Oliver undoubtedly had picked up the girl while she was insensible, and placed her in the chair. The first correspondent retorted that Sir Oliver was dead, and his murderer conspicuous by his absence, when Miss Chent entered the library, and so could not have shifted her from the floor on to the chair. To this the defending writer wrote that there was no proof of Sir Oliver being dead when Miss Chent entered, as it was apparent that the fumes of the herb had drugged him into insensibility, and therefore the murderer must have entered later to kill the baronet, and remove his niece from the place where she fell, by her own showing, to the chair in which she was discovered by Captain Jadby. And so the war of letter-writing went on; and although Mona was free from the danger of hanging, her character was still stained, in the opinion of some people, with the blood of her uncle.

Prelice was furious when he read this correspondence, but, on the face of it, did not see how he could defend Mona, since he had no evidence to bring forward in her favour. On the testimony of the knife it was generally considered that Agstone had murdered his master, and then had come to Alexander Mansions to kill the barrister. But, of course, both Shepworth and his friend, knowing the true story of how the knife came into Agstone's possession, were by no means certain that the old sailor was guilty. The mystery of Sir Oliver's death was no longer one to the public—as everyone had been misled by the suppression of the evidence dealing with the knife— but it continued to be one to those who had suppressed that same evidence. But of one thing Lord Prelice was certain—namely, that Mona's character would have to be completely cleared by the discovery of the real criminal.

With this idea in his mind, he went next day to Alexander Mansions, and learned—somewhat to his surprise—that Shepworth was within. Inspector Bruge informed him of this at a chance meeting on the stairs, and affably told the constable guarding the door of Number Forty that Lord Prelice was to be admitted to see the prisoner. "Not that he is a prisoner," said Bruge, nodding; "we are merely detaining Mr. Shepworth until the inquest is held on the body of Agstone."

"When does the inquest take place?" asked Prelice, lingering to ask necessary questions.

"To-morrow, at three o'clock in the afternoon, at the Greyhound Hotel, Kensington. Beyond the fact that the jury will bring in a verdict of wilful murder against some person, or persons, unknown, I don't think that we—the police that is, my lord—can give any evidence to indicate the assassin of Agstone."

"Then why accuse Mr. Shepworth?"

"I don't accuse him."

"If you don't, why arrest him?"

"It is best to be on the safe side," said Bruge dryly; "and notwithstanding what Mr. Shepworth may have written to you, my lord, the arrest has not taken place. He is merely detained, pending the inquest."

"And under suspicion?" flashed out Prelice loyally.

The Inspector shrugged his square shoulders. "If you like to put it in that way," he said indifferently.

"But it is absurd to suspect Mr. Shepworth," cried Prelice excitedly; "many people saw him insensible, in the same way that Miss Chent was insensible. If she is guiltless—and a competent jury have acquitted her—Mr. Shepworth also must be innocent. The evidence of Dr. Horace——"

"Quite so, my lord," interrupted Bruge, with rather a bored air; "but all that will be discussed at the inquest. We need not enter into it now, considering we have insufficient premises to go upon."

"If anyone murdered Agstone——"

"Which they certainly did, since no man can stab himself in the back."

"It must have been the lady seen by Mr. Shepworth," finished Prelice.

"Hum! That might have been a hallucination."

"And the moon may be made of cream cheese," retorted Prelice heatedly.

"It may be," assented Bruge gravely; "I know no reason to the contrary, my lord. But this talk leads to nothing, and I am very busy. Go in and see your friend. You will find Dr. Horace with him."

"Dr. Horace?" echoed the young man, staring.

Inspector Bruge nodded. "So you may guess that, when thus permitted to see his friends, Mr. Shepworth is not a legitimate prisoner. By the way," added Bruge formally as he took his leave, "I am delighted that Miss Chent has been acquitted."

"Of course. She is innocent."

"Entirely innocent in my opinion, and very beautiful also. Mr. Shepworth is a lucky man, my lord. Good-day."

The Inspector descended the stairs, leaving Prelice somewhat puzzled. The young man could not quite determine whether Bruge believed Shepworth to be innocent or guilty. At one time he said one thing; again, he hinted at another. However, it was useless to ponder over the enigma; so Prelice entered the flat, after a word or two with the uniformed Cerberus who guarded the door, and was conducted by a somewhat pale parlour-maid to the library. Here he found Dr. Horace, looking more uncivilised than ever, in deep conversation with Ned. The latter sprang up when his friend entered. Shepworth had lost some of his ruddy colour, and his eyes had dark circles under them. Otherwise he appeared to be quite composed, and not at all like a man accused of a serious crime. And in spite of Bruge's protestations, Prelice believed that the Inspector did so accuse him, mentally at all events.

"You are just in time, Prelice," cried Shepworth, grasping the new-comer's hand warmly; "in addition to the mysteries of these murders we have another to solve in the person of our friend here."

"There's no mystery about me," said Horace gruffly. "I merely advise you to leave matters as they stand."

Prelice looked as astonished as Shepworth. "But I say," he cried, "you wanted to take a hand in the game yourself, Horace."

"I *have* taken a hand," retorted the doctor coolly, "and I have won. My aim was to save Miss Chent from being unjustly convicted; for whomsoever murdered Lanwin, I am convinced that she is innocent. As she is now free, and the prevailing opinion seems to be that Agstone is guilty, why stir up muddy water and waken sleeping dogs?"

"You forget," said Shepworth rather tartly, "that I have to be cleared myself.

Bruge says that I am innocent, but the fact that he has practically arrested me proves that he thinks the contrary."

Horace, who was smoking his ungainly German pipe, shook his shaggy head vigorously. "When the inquest takes place, you will be discharged without a stain on your character. That being the case, my advice to you is a speedy marriage with Miss Chent, who is also free. Don't bother your head further about these two murders."

When Horace mentioned marriage with Mona so pointedly Prelice darted a side glance at his chum, bearing in mind the hints of Captain Jadby and Lady Sophia. As he expected, Shepworth coloured and looked confused. "At present I am not rich enough to marry Mona," he said in a halting way; "and by the burning of the will she loses the property."

Horace chuckled silently. "Which goes to Captain Jadby?"

"Yes. The earlier will comes into force now that the latter one has been destroyed."

"In that case," observed Horace, complacently puffing at his pipe, "I should advise her to marry Captain Jadby."

Shepworth, still looking uneasy, went to stare out of the window, and it was Prelice who replied. "I'm hanged if she'll do that."

"Why not?" inquired the doctor, with a keen glance. "Jadby has the money by Shepworth's showing; he isn't bad-looking, and he loves her devotedly. Also, it was Sir Oliver's wish."

"Jadby's a cattish ruffian," cried Prelice warmly, and with a sudden access of colour; "we don't know where he comes from or——"

"From the South Seas, my old son."

"Or who he is," continued Prelice impetuously. "It would be a shame that so delightful a girl should marry a shady buccaneer. Ned, you are engaged to Miss Chent—why don't you speak?"

"There is nothing to say," replied the barrister somewhat coldly. "If Miss Chent will take me, a pauper as I am, I shall only be too charmed to make her my wife."

Prelice raised his eyebrows. A conviction was forcing itself upon him that Ned had no real love for the girl. But if that was the case, why had he become engaged to her; why had he so vigorously defended her of late? Then there was Mrs. Dolly Rover; but Prelice knew nothing about that mysterious lady, as he had not seen her since returning to London. He had half a mind then and there to demand an explanation from Ned; but the presence of Dr. Horace restrained him, and with an afterthought of wisdom, he determined to interview Mrs. Rover herself before coming to an understanding with the barrister.

As it was therefore unnecessary to pursue the subject, and as already Horace was asking him mutely why he should take such an interest in an engaged young lady, Prelice changed the subject by an attack on the doctor himself. "I can't understand why you should wish to abandon the search into these cases when you were so keen yesterday to run the show on your own."

Horace quite understood the slang of the concluding remark. "I merely quoted a proverb about letting sleeping dogs lie," he said coolly.

"Why? Are you afraid for a certain person?" questioned Prelice, meaning Agstone and the listener's relationship with Agstone.

"Oh no," retorted the doctor, quite aware of what Prelice was referring to. "The person you hint at is dead, and everyone believes him guilty of the first murder. It doesn't matter who killed him, as Shepworth here is sure to be acquitted. I don't care a damn one way or the other, as you will respect my confidence."

"What confidence?" asked the barrister suddenly.

"One that I made to Prelice here," said the doctor dryly; then heaving up his squat figure from the armchair, he waddled towards the door. There he paused, and addressed himself to Prelice: "If you go on prying into this matter," he said, with uplifted finger, "you will be very, very sorry, my son."

"What do you mean?"

"Gammon and spinach," said Horace, again enigmatic, and hurled himself out of the room, still smoking his unwieldy pipe. The two young men stared at one another.

"Is he mad?" asked Shepworth.

"Mad like Hamlet, south-sou'west," rejoined the other in a vexed tone; "unless he is in league with that Jadby bounder, whom he knew in the South Seas, I don't know what he means by backing out."

"But surely you don't suspect Jadby?" asked Ned, startled.

"Why not? He was at Mrs. Rover's ball."

"Nonsense. She doesn't know him!"

"Remember the jewel robberies," said Prelice dryly; "a great number of people unknown to host or hostess were at that ball."

"But Jadby!" Shepworth bit his fingers perplexedly. "You can't suspect him? He came and saw me, and then went away. It was a woman whom Agstone brought in. She must have killed Agstone."

Prelice shrugged his shoulders, and sauntered about the room.

"Perhaps!" he remarked carelessly, sauntering about the room. "I certainly have no reason to suspect Jadby, save that he was at the ball."

"How do you know?"

"He was one of the crowd that rushed in to see you insensible, and he wore a domino and mask, as did the rest of them."

"Then how did you spot him?"

"He unmasked."

"That shows his innocence," declared Shepworth quickly, "for if he had come to the ball to slip down and murder Agstone, he would not have revealed himself."

"Hum! Hum! Perhaps not." Prelice threw himself into a chair. "However, I shall keep an eye on Jadby."

"Then you are still searching into the case?"

"Into both cases," corrected the other, lighting a cigar; "I want to learn who killed Lanwin, and who murdered Agstone."

"Out of friendship for me," cried Shepworth, grasping his chum's hand. "You are a brick, Dorry."

Prelice returned the grasp, but blushed a trifle. He knew that love for Mona prompted the desire to search, as much as friendship for the man before him. If he could only understand Shepworth's attitude towards the girl and towards Mrs. Rover! Again it was on the tip of his tongue to ask a leading question, but he suppressed the desire, and kept to his earlier resolution to see the lady in the flat overhead.

"By the way," said Prelice carelessly, "have you seen Miss Chent?"

"No," answered Shepworth rather ruefully. "I wish I could have seen her, but Bruge hurried me away from the Court to keep me as a kind of state prisoner here. However, Mona wrote me a short note thanking me for all I had done, and said that she was going down to Lanwin Grange."

"But if that belongs to Jadby——"

"The will isn't proved yet," interrupted the barrister quickly, "and until it is, Mr. Martaban thinks Mona should stop at the Grange."

"Mr. Martaban?"

"The late Sir Oliver's lawyer—a kind, clever old chap. He has taken Mona down to the Grange; and Mrs. Blexey, who is devoted to her, will look after the poor girl until I am free to visit her."

"You'll go down, of course," said Prelice nervously.

"Oh yes; as soon as the inquest is over and Bruge sets me free. I do not see how I can be arrested. But meanwhile, Dorry, you could do me a great favour?"

Prelice raised his eyes. "What is that?"

"Go down at once to Hythe and see Mona."

"But I don't know her," said Prelice, taken aback, although his face grew hot and his heart bounded at the idea of meeting this adorable girl, with whom he now knew himself to be in love.

"I'll give you a card of introduction. Tell her that I'm all right and will be down as soon as I can."

"All right," assented Prelice, feeling a guilty joy in thus yielding to a delightful temptation. "But the case?"

"That can look after itself until the inquest is over. Then, when I have seen Mona, and her future is settled by Martaban—her living and income and all that I mean—we can look into matters. I am as keen as you are to get at the truth of these two murders, Dorry. We can dispense with Horace."

"I wish I knew exactly why he backed out," muttered Prelice thoughtfully; "it is so unlike Horace to jib."

"Perhaps he has something to do with the matter himself, seeing that he possessed the Sacred Herb," said Shepworth jocularly.

"Nonsense. Horace would kill one man and a dozen men in fair fight, but he's not the chap to stick anyone in the back. By the way, tell me one thing, Ned. This lady, who came in with Agstone, and waved the cup under your nose to make you insensible—she wore a green mask, you said?"

"Yes; and a green domino also."

Prelice nodded. "Did you catch a glimpse of her frock by any chance, or did your senses fail you?"

"They did not fail me too quickly. I *did* see her frock. It was a white dress with thin lines of red running horizontally across it."

"Many lines?" asked Prelice breathlessly.

"It seemed to be ruled like a page of music," said Shepworth. "Why, what is the matter?"

"Matter!" echoed Prelice, who had risen and was dancing round the room like a school-boy. "What you say gives me a clue. I saw that dress at the ball. The lady who wore it was scented with tuberoses——"

"With tuberoses?"

"Or with the Sacred Herb. I must find out who she is."

"How can you?"

"I don't know. I can't say. But if we can find her we may learn if she killed Agstone, and why she did it. That discovery will lead to learning who murdered Lanwin. It is the beginning of the end. Give up the case indeed!" cried Prelice exultantly—"why, it's the only thing that renders life in London bearable."

"But do you think that this lady is guilty?" asked Shepworth doubtfully.

"Of course I do. Otherwise, why should she be scented with the perfume of the Sacred Herb, which has to do with both crimes?"

Shepworth shook his head, unable to answer this question.

CHAPTER XII.

MRS. DOLLY ROVER.

Shortly after the reference to the unknown lady, Lord Prelice took a hasty leave. There was nothing more to be said, as matters up to date had been threshed out thoroughly between them. Until the inquest had been held on the body of Agstone, and Shepworth's immediate future was decided, no move could be made towards elucidating the mysteries. Moreover, Prelice was mortally afraid lest Shepworth should alter his mind about making him ambassador to Miss Chent at Hythe. Strong-willed as the young man was, when he chose to exercise that same will he could not deny himself the pleasure of being in Mona's company, if only for ten minutes. Besides, he very much wished to learn if she truly loved Ned, for by this time he felt sure that Ned had no very deep affection for her.

In his hurry to catch a train to Hythe, Prelice quite forgot his determination to see Mrs. Rover, and learn how matters stood between her and the barrister. But the powers that direct the actions of men, and the lives that are made by such actions, brought about a meeting with the lady almost immediately. After shaking hands with the pseudo-prisoner, Prelice left the flat, to find Mrs. Rover arguing vehemently with the constable posted at the outer door. She wished to enter and see Shepworth; the constable, pursuant to strict orders, was trying to point out that his duty lay in stopping her, a point which Mrs.

Rover obstinately refused to see.

"I wish to enter," she kept repeating. "It is necessary that I should see Mr. Shepworth, and——"

"Will I do instead?" said Prelice, suddenly appearing at the open door.

"Dorry!" cried Mrs. Rover, giving him the pet name of his youth. "What are you doing here?"

"I am talking to you," said the young man, shaking hands, "but just now I have been chatting with Ned."

"Then why can't I chat with him also?" demanded the lady.

Prelice shrugged his shoulders. "Ned is allowed to see no one, unless Inspector Bruge gives permission."

"What rubbish! Let me go in!" And Mrs. Rover, in a flaming temper, tried to push past the policeman.

"You can't, ma'am," he said firmly and respectfully; adding to the pale parlour-maid, who still lingered, out of sheer curiosity: "Close that door straight away."

"I'll report you," cried Mrs. Rover, when she saw the door practically banged in her angry face.

"All right, ma'am. But dooty is dooty."

"Constance! Constance!" whispered Prelice, touching her arm. "Don't make an exhibition of yourself before the servants. The man is only doing his duty. Come upstairs, and we can have a chat."

"What about?" demanded Mrs. Rover swiftly; and Prelice saw, or thought he saw, a glint of fear in her eyes.

"Well," he answered, smiling, "I have not had an opportunity of talking to you since I returned to town, so it is natural that I should wish for a short conversation."

Mrs. Rover, who apparently was an extremely obstinate woman, paused irresolutely, looking at the stolid policeman with a battle light in her eyes. But the constable met her gaze firmly, so finding that feminine persistence could do nothing in the face of an official barrier, she turned away biting her lip. "Come upstairs, Dorry," she said, beginning to ascend; "I can do nothing with that fool."

Prelice smiled at this Parthian arrow, and slipped a florin into the constable's hand to pacify him for the parting insult. Then he ran up after the lady, and reached her on the next landing. "You ought to be pleased, Constance," he said slyly; "you've had the last word."

"I should like to have had the last half-dozen," she retorted, putting a Yale latch-key into the lock.

"I think that you have even achieved that," replied Prelice dryly. "It is extraordinary that women never will learn that the law is stronger than sheer temper."

"I am not in a temper," snapped Mrs. Rover, sweeping into her flat. "I never was calmer in my life—never, never, never."

"I am quite content to believe that," said her companion acidly; for as Constance Newton, Mrs. Rover had not been noted for imperturbability. It was all the better, in Prelice's opinion, that her temperament should be thus fiery, as he would discover from her rash tongue much that a more cautious and composed woman would withhold. Moreover, Constance and her visitor had been friends for many a long year—witness her calling him Dorry—and she was accustomed to speak frankly to him about her troubles. Had Prelice been in England when the stockbroker was courting the lady, it is doubtful if Constance would ever have become Mrs. Rover. And Prelice strongly suspected that Mr. Rover found Ned Shepworth an inconvenient third in his married state.

"You are looking very well, Constance," said Prelice when the two were seated in the drawing-room, which was more gorgeous than artistic.

"I'm not well then. I'm nearly worried to death."

"So sorry. Tell me all about it."

"I'll do nothing of the sort."

"I beg your pardon. Let us chat about the weather."

"Do you think that I have time to waste in discussing barometers?" She rose, impetuously.

"Don't know, I'm sure," replied Prelice, keeping his temper admirably.

"Well then, I haven't."

"Would it do any good if I gave you a thorough shaking?"

"Yes, it would. If Dolly shook me I should respect him; but he lets me lead him the life of a dog, and doesn't even bark, much less bite."

"I see, you prefer a bull-dog to a poodle."

"Ned isn't a——" Mrs. Rover stopped in the centre of the room, grew red, and could have bitten out her tongue for so incautious a speech. "What rubbish you talk!" she said, trying to smile carelessly.

Prelice looked at her gravely. "I hope you are talking rubbish too."

"I wish I were dead and buried!" whispered Mrs. Rover, and once more sat down to burst into violent tears.

Expert in the handling of the sex, Prelice knew better than to offer a single word of consolation. He lay back in his chair, quietly watching the progress of the storm. Mrs. Rover was going through the usual programme of upset woman. She had raged, now she wept, and would shortly be offering an apology for her conduct on the plea of nerves.

Constance had certainly grown into a handsome woman. When Prelice had left England seven years before she was merely a school-girl, very gawky and very awkward. Now she appeared tall, majestic, and beautiful after the voluptuous style of Juno, Queen of Olympus. Her hair and eyes were dark, her features delicate and regular, and her figure was finely formed, even if a trifle inclined to stoutness, as it assuredly was. Prelice had somewhere seen an old print of Catherine II. of Russia, and it struck him that Mrs. Rover greatly resembled the Empress, although she was undeniably a more lovely woman. It was unfortunate that her face should have been marred by a sullen expression, hinting at a superlatively bad temper. But many people— unobservant as most people are—never noted this defect. They only saw before their ravished eyes a handsome, well-bred, graceful woman, perfectly dressed, and quite able to hold her own in the most exacting society. Yes, Constance had improved greatly. Prelice admitted that, but he wished to find out if she possessed the same beauty of character as of person. From what he had heard and what he had seen, he had grave doubts on this point.

"Pray excuse me," said Mrs. Rover, offering the expected social apology in a faint voice. "I'm rather upset; my nerves are out of order. The season has been trying, and then that horrid ball bowled me over, with its robberies and murders; not to speak of Dolly, who is—who is—— Oh, I don't know what he is."

"Do you think it is good taste to discuss your husband with me?" asked Prelice rather tartly.

"You are the only true friend I have in the world, Dorry."

"Then you have made no acquaintances since I left England seven years ago, Constance?"

"Oh, acquaintances?" she echoed contemptuously, rolling her damp handkerchief into a ball. "I have hundreds of these. But a friend—oh, Dorry, there isn't a single person I'd trust with a shoe-lace."

"He or she would not thank you if you did," replied Prelice, smiling; "a shoe-lace is not good security for anything."

"That's just it," wailed Mrs. Rover, dabbing her red eyes with the handkerchief; "people like one for what they can get out of one. But there isn't a soul to help me—poor me."

"Won't Ned?" asked her companion very deliberately.

Mrs. Rover darted a keen glance at him, and rose to alter the position of her hat in front of the mirror over the fireplace. Prelice knew quite well that she was watching him in the mirror, and carefully smoothed all expression out of his good-humoured face. "Ned!" repeated Mrs. Rover, patting her back hair; "oh yes, Ned, of course. Do you think they will hang him?" she demanded, wheeling round, rather white, and breathing hard.

"Good heavens, no. What put that into your head?"

"He isn't allowed to see me. The arrest——"

"Ned hasn't been arrested. The fact that he was seen insensible by heaps of people proves his innocence. Bruge is simply detaining him as a necessary witness, although I admit that Bruge is taking a somewhat high hand in the matter. Don't bother your head about Ned, Constance. He'll soon be free to marry that girl."

"Mona Chent!" Mrs. Rover clenched her hands, and breathed still harder, while Prelice anxiously watched the effect of his deliberate introduction of the name. "Oh yes." She went off into a meaningless trill of laughter. "She's free, isn't she? Lucky girl, for I quite believe that she killed her uncle."

"Why do you believe that?" demanded Prelice.

"Everyone says so."

"Everyone does *not* say so. The majority of people think that the verdict is a just one. I do myself."

"Do you know her?"

"No. What has that to do with it?"

"You won't like her when you do know her," said Mrs. Rover spitefully. "She's a horrid girl; I never liked her."

"That's a pity; you won't be able to visit Ned's wife."

"She isn't his wife yet," breathed Mrs. Rover, trying to keep her temper in check; "perhaps she never will be."

"Oh," Prelice spoke with calculated daring and cruelty, "do you then think that Mr. Rover will die?"

"You coward—you——" She broke off. "What do you mean by that?"

"I would rather you explained, Constance."

"I have nothing to explain. Did you come here to insult me?"

"Of course," replied Prelice, rising; "and now that I have done so, I may as well take my leave."

She seized him by the lapels of his coat before he could reach the door. "Don't go, don't go," she panted; "I do so want a friend. I'll tell you all; you shall know everything."

"If it is against your husband, I sha'n't listen."

"You shall! Sit down, and hear what I have to say."

Prelice was a strong young man, but for the moment her feminine strength prevailed, and he found himself forced into his former seat.

"I wouldn't say what I'm going to say to everyone," panted Mrs. Rover, who was very strongly moved, "but, even though we have been apart for so many years, I still regard you as my best friend. You and I were boy and girl together, Dorry—you remember——"

"Ned also," interposed Prelice pointedly.

"Yes! Yes. Of course. I always loved Ned."

"Constance, what are you saying?"

She rose, and beat her hands together. "The truth—the truth! I liked you, Dorry, I always liked you, but I loved Ned, and I shall love him until I die!" She looked like a tragedy queen.

Prelice grew impatient, being a very matter-of-fact young man. "Don't be melodramatic, Constance. Sit down, and explain quietly."

With that wonderful adaptability of women, at which man never ceases to marvel, Mrs. Rover sat down, and composed herself with a violent effort. When next she spoke it was in so cold and icy a tone that Prelice, had his eyes been closed, could have sworn that another person had joined in the dialogue. "You know that my father, the General, was not rich, and that my mother was extravagant. I was the only child, and my parents wished me to make a wealthy marriage, so that their affairs might be put right. That is, my mother wished it, for my father, dear old man, desired me to consult my own heart. I did, and it told me to marry Ned. We were half engaged. My father was willing in spite of his difficulties, but my mother would not consent. Ned was poor, you know; he had only five hundred a year of his own, and has not yet made a success at the Bar. Then Dolly Rover came along." She stopped, and bit her lip, while her hands moved restlessly, as though boxing her husband's ears.

"What about Mr. Rover?" asked Prelice soothingly.

Then the natural woman came out, and she rose in a rage. "I hate Dolly like poison," she cried, pacing up and down the room, twisting her hands together; "he's a horrid, sneaky little cur, who——"

"Don't abuse your husband, Constance," interrupted Prelice impatiently; "it does no good. You married him of your own free will."

"I did nothing of the sort. I married him to save my father from going through the Bankruptcy Court. It would have broken his heart, dear old father, and he would have died. Dolly knew that I hated him, and that I loved Ned. But he demanded his price, like the mean dog that he is. My mother was on his side too, and I could not bear to see my father suffer. I parted with Ned, and married Dolly. That is, I sold myself, on condition that father's debts were paid. I kept to my part of the bargain——"

"And didn't your husband keep to his?"

"No," Mrs. Rover stamped violently; "he paid a portion of the debts; enough to avert bankruptcy merely. But he left father the worry, and of that worry father died. My mother has married again—a rich man—so she is happy. And here am I tied to Dolly—ugh! the name—while my heart is breaking for Ned."

"It is a hard case," said Prelice, sorry for the miserable woman; "still, your self-respect, Constance."

"That is right—preach, preach, preach. So like a man," she mocked. "I have kept my self-respect as you term it. I am a good wife to Dolly, although I detest him. I have never said a word against him to anyone, and I wouldn't to you, but that I must speak or suffocate. I can trust you, Dorry, and you understand how I feel, and what I feel. I love Ned. I want to marry Ned, and here I'm tied to—to——"

Prelice interrupted. "It is hard on you, Constance, I admit," he said, "but you must make the best of it. You say that you lead your husband the life of a dog."

"Of a pet dog, of a poodle. He's so meek and mild and sneaky that I can't respect him. He merely sniggers when I grow angry, and chuckles how he got the best of me over the marriage by not paying all father's debts. Oh, what is the use of talking! I love Ned, and Ned loves me."

Prelice jumped up. "I can't believe that," he declared, growing angry, "for Ned is engaged to Miss Chent. If he loves you, why is he——"

"Don't ask questions," interrupted Mrs. Rover angrily; "or if you must ask them, go to Ned; or better still, to Mona Chent herself."

"What can I ask Miss Chent?" demanded Prelice sharply.

"It's very warm weather," mocked Mrs. Rover, "and I think there will be a thunder-storm."

The young man looked at her, and saw her mouth set obstinately. He knew as well as if she had spoken that there was nothing more to be got out of her for the time being. But what she had said made him all the more determined to see Miss Chent, and learn the truth about the engagement to Shepworth. Meanwhile he took the wind out of Mrs. Rover's sails by falling in with her humour. "It will be a good thing if it does thunder and rain," he remarked, glancing out of the window; "it will clear the air."

Mrs. Rover looked as though she would have struck him, but being unable to parry his thrust, threw herself sulkily on the sofa. Prelice took up hat and gloves to depart, but halted at the door with premeditated craft. A sudden thought had struck him. "Constance," he said in a natural tone, "I am in love."

"Indeed," she said indifferently.

"Yes; with a lady who was at your ball."

The remark made her rouse herself, and she sat up with a look of curiosity. "Who is she?"

"I want you to tell me that. I could not see her face, and very little of her figure, owing to the domino, but she seemed to be so charming when we talked together"—this was a lie to gain information—"that I quite lost my heart."

"It's easy lost," said Mrs. Rover, curling her lip. "The woman may be as ugly as sin under her mask. How was she dressed?"

"In a green mask and domino," Mrs. Rover stiffened, "and with a white dress streaked with lines of red velvet. Why do you laugh?" he asked, for Mrs. Rover was trying to suppress her mirth.

"Why?" she cried, shaking with merriment, "because *I* wore that dress and mask and domino."

"You?" Prelice looked horrified.

"Yes. Why do you look at me like that?"

"You?" Prelice backed to the door in silent horror. He could not trust himself to speak, and finally disappeared, leaving Mrs. Rover petrified with amazement, perhaps with dread.

CHAPTER XIII.

LANWIN GRANGE.

In the exercise of his profession, a legitimate detective would have waited to question Mrs. Rover. Since she had said so much he would have forced her to say all, in order to get at the truth as speedily as possible; but Lord Prelice was new to the business, and his emotions were not entirely under control. On leaving Alexander Mansions he felt that he was in possession of a most dangerous and perilous secret, the publication of which would cause even a greater sensation than that produced by the crimes themselves. The shock of learning that Mrs. Rover was the woman who had been brought by Agstone into Number Forty was very great, and quite confused Prelice's usually strong brain. He did not dare to call again on Shepworth, lest he should say too much.

It will be seen that Prelice, being an untrained detective, jumped somewhat hastily to a conclusion. Mrs. Rover had admitted that she wore the dress, the mask, and the domino which Shepworth had seen on the unknown lady. But Constance did not know that Ned had so described her appearance, and, if she had, would probably not have admitted that she had assumed such a costume at her *bal masque*. But the mere fact that, even in ignorance of Shepworth's description, she had, as the saying goes, given herself away, should have proved to Lord Prelice that she could not be guilty. Had Mrs. Rover entered Number Forty in Agstone's company, and had she struck the blow, she assuredly would not have incriminated herself so unthinkingly. Rather would she have denied that the frock mentioned by Prelice belonged to her.

After the first shock, and while Prelice was in the train going to Hythe, he began to revise his earlier opinion on the above-mentioned grounds. His common-sense came to his aid, and told him that, if guilty, Mrs. Rover would not have confessed even to a half-truth. Certainly, had she not done so, her maid, knowing what dress her mistress wore at the ball, might have blurted out the secret; but then, so far as the world knew, no inquiry would have been made about the wearer of that especial frock.

Of course, assuming that in a thoughtless moment Mrs. Rover had foolishly confessed the truth, Prelice could find a motive for her behaviour in committing the crime. It might be that Agstone wished to kill Ned, and that Mrs. Rover, to save the life of the man she loved, had struck down the sailor unawares. Having committed the deed, she could easily slip back to her own flat, and mingle with the masked crowd.

But then again, as Prelice further argued, while the train drew near to the coast, Mrs. Rover must have known that in murdering Agstone she was not only securing the freedom of Mona Chent, whom she hated, but also was placing her lover in a dangerous position. Agstone was a necessary witness for the prosecution, whom Shepworth of all men did not wish to see placed in the box, so the supposition would be, were the man found dead in Number Forty, that Shepworth had killed him to save Mona Chent. As a matter of fact, this is exactly what had taken place, and in saving Ned from the sailor's knife Mrs. Rover, always presuming that she was guilty, had simply condemned her lover to a death on the scaffold. But that Prelice had been clever enough to admit the crowd of guests, so that all might see the barrister's helpless position, it is certain that the man would have been arrested, and probably sentenced to death, since it would have been extraordinarily difficult for him to clear his character in the face of circumstances. Therefore on these assumptions, for that they were and no more, Prelice after much reflection decided that Mrs. Rover was innocent.

Finally, the young man recollected that a woman dressed as described, by Ned, and in the costume which Mrs. Rover confessed to wearing, had passed down the stairs while he was waiting for entrance to Number Forty and immediately before the discovery of the crime. She could scarcely have been Mrs. Rover, for as that lady could have easily proved an *alibi* by returning to her guests and casually unmasking at the right moment, it would have been useless for her to leave the mansions. Of course, the lady—whether Mrs. Rover or a stranger—certainly might have followed Prelice down to the door, knowing that he would be certain to discover the tragedy, and might merely have descended to return to the ballroom overhead when the young man entered Shepworth's flat. But then, again, the person in question could not have known that Prelice, masked and unknown, was going to enter Number Forty, so there would be no reason to track him there. And to conclude, the murderess—if a woman was guilty—must have known that Shepworth, being in a cataleptic state, must have seen and remembered her very peculiar frock.

On the whole, Prelice arrived at certain conclusions, by no means inimical to Mrs. Rover, by the time he alighted at Hythe Station. He believed that Constance was innocent for four reasons. Firstly, if guilty, she would not have confessed to wearing the dress, since such a confession would necessarily lead to her detection. Secondly, by killing Agstone she would not only have placed Shepworth in a dangerous position, but by getting rid of an inconvenient witness would have enabled Mona to escape possible condemnation. Thirdly, she would not have followed an unknown man—as Prelice was by reason of his mask and domino—down the stairs with the intention of seeing what took place. Fourthly, and lastly, she would not have sought safety in an incriminating flight—as the similarly dressed woman on the stairs apparently had—when she would have been much safer in her own ballroom and amongst her own guests. Only by such a course could she have provided an *alibi*.

No! Mrs. Rover, in spite of her startling admission, was innocent, and the sole conclusion that Prelice could arrive at, was the existence of a double— outwardly at all events. He remembered the extraordinary ubiquity of the green domino in the red-streaked white dress, and decided, very naturally, that there was another woman in the field. But what woman possessed a motive sufficiently strong to urge her to murder Agstone? As Prelice felt quite worn out with arguing in Mrs. Rover's defence, he decided to leave the answering of this new question to the portentous moment, when further evidence might reveal the identity of the unknown lady. Meanwhile, on arriving at Hythe, he rested himself at a quiet hotel, and soothed his troubled brain with an hour's necessary sleep. Later on, after an invigorating bath and an excellent dinner, he started to walk towards Lanwin Grange.

It was summer, and romance was in the air—at least Prelice scented its presence by some sixth sense. He was going to see the girl he loved—the girl with whom he had not, as yet, exchanged a single word. Therefore, although past the peacock age, he was particularly attentive to his appearance when assuming his evening clothes. As he strolled inland along the leafy lanes, through the July warmth of the twilight, this somewhat premature wooer looked as comely and well groomed a swain as any damsel, not demanding an Apollo, could desire. And it was a great proof of Prelice's infatuation that, in looking forward to meeting Mona, he almost forgot that he was merely the emissary of the man to whom the girl was engaged. The whole position was extraordinarily queer. He adored this girl, without being personally acquainted with her; she was affianced to his best friend; and yet he could not be certain if that same best friend really loved the girl herself. Even a Palais Royal farce could offer no more fantastic complication than this. Prelice felt that, after running round the wild world in search of the unusual, he had returned to find Romance sitting on his doorstep.

The way to the family seat of the Lanwins twisted inland and uphill through deep lanes and umbrageous woods. On emerging high up from the belt of trees Prelice found himself on a wide, unshaded road, snaking over bare Downs. For some distance he toiled upward; then the road mounted a rise to slip down into a cup-shaped hollow brimmed with cultivated woods. In the midst of these he saw an old grey house, seemingly prevented from falling to pieces by the ivy which covered its mouldering walls. From the lips of the hollow stretched the rolling grassy Downs, dotted with nibbling sheep, grey in the shadows of the coming night. But it was not yet night, for the sky was filled with a luminous light, all-pervading, yet emanating from no certain point. A breathless peace brooded over the vast, treeless uplands, and an even deeper peace seemed to enwrap the ancient mansion. It appeared to be the veritable palace of the Sleeping Beauty, set amidst enchanted woods. And Prelice thrilled with the idea that Beauty herself, awake and unkissed, awaited some prince in the seclusion of her faery castle.

Following the road, which here grew somewhat narrower, Lord Prelice descended into the hollow, passed under the shade of overhanging trees, and came out into a kind of artificial glade, smooth with carefully tended lawns and brilliant with flowers. The Grange itself was somewhat sunken in the ground, entirely level with the lawns, and looked like part of the woods themselves, so clothed was it with darkly green ivy. There appeared a weather-worn escutcheon over the great doorway, and lights gleamed from oriel windows in the east wing. But to the left Prelice saw the three tall French windows opening on to a wide terrace which had been referred to at the trial. These windows appeared quite out of keeping with the Tudor architecture of the mansion, but the visitor eyed them with great interest. It was through one of those windows that Agstone and Jadby had looked, to see the tragedy of Sir Oliver's death. And had that not taken place Prelice might never have been brought into contact with the most charming girl in the world. His heart beat loudly as he rang the bell.

Afterwards Lord Prelice never could explain clearly how he had first come into the presence of his goddess. In a bewildered manner he waited in the antique hall, after delivering his card to a pompous footman, and in a bewildered manner was led into a long, low, wide drawing-room with oriels at the farther end, brilliant with family crests in stained glass. So far as he could recollect, he did not look at the cumbersome Georgian furniture, or at the aggressively modern grand piano, which seemed to be out of place, or at the portraits of cavaliers and their ladies decking the mellow-hued walls, or even at the painted ceiling, or the carpet tinted with rainbow colours, subdued by time to grateful sobriety: he had no eyes save for a tall slim girl arrayed in a white dress, with a somewhat pale, worn face, who welcomed him in the sweetest of voices and with the most grateful of smiles. "I am glad to see Ned's best friend," she said, and her voice sounded like faery music in the new-comer's ravished ears, "and to thank him."

"To thank me!" muttered Prelice, staring at the lovely face in the mellow lamplight.

"I saw you in that terrible Court," she said swiftly, "and the way in which you looked at me gave me comfort. Other people—my friends, they call themselves—stared as though I were a wild animal, but you, Lord Prelice ——" She threw out her hands with an eloquent gesture full of grace. "Ned wrote and told me that you were his friend."

"I am here to be yours also," stuttered Prelice, suppressing a wild desire to kneel and worship.

"We are friends already. It does not need words to confirm a friendship offered and accepted mutely and with gratitude."

Prelice felt more bewildered than ever. Here was a girl so entirely unconventional that she defied the usages of Society, which prescribed the etiquette for a primary meeting between bachelor and maid. It was marvellously sweet to be thus greeted; but Prelice must have revealed his delighted surprise too clearly, for Miss Chent laughed. "I am afraid that my proffer of unasked-for friendship surprises you," she said, smilingly; "but, you see, my poor uncle instructed me somewhat in psychology, and I look at the inner, rather than the outer."

"You said yourself, Miss Chent, that the friendship was asked for in Court," said Prelice earnestly; "and it was. As Ned's best friend, I claim to be yours also. I bring a message from Ned."

"You shall deliver it presently," said Mona, turning to a stout, white-haired gentleman with a genial face who was standing near the window silently. "Just now you must allow me to introduce Mr. Martaban, another loyal friend. Also," she waved her hand towards a spindle-legged Versailles table as the two men shook hands, "you must have some coffee."

Prelice accepted gratefully, as he would have taken poison from the hands of this delightful girl, so long as she served it, as she did the coffee, with her own white hands. Martaban took a cup also, and resumed the seat from which he had arisen when Prelice entered. Miss Chent pointed out a chair to her visitor, and herself reclined on a Louis Treize sofa. Then the three began to talk on immediate and earthly matters, and Prelice was forced to descend from transcendental heights. In that room, at that hour, and in the presence of such an angel, it seemed desperately hard to abandon romance for reality. But there was no help for it.

"Ned's message?" questioned Mona anxiously.

"He is all right, and will be down as soon as he can get away," replied the emissary, delivering the exact words of his friend.

"Then you don't think that he is in danger of being accused of this second crime?"

"No, no!" interposed Martaban in a genial but authoritative voice. "I have told you before, and I tell you again, that, under the circumstances, no one can accuse Mr. Shepworth. And that," added the solicitor, bowing towards the young man, "is due, my lord, to your wise action in admitting the crowd to see Mr. Shepworth insensible."

Prelice nodded his thanks. "Ned is perfectly safe," he said quietly.

Mona clasped her hands with a thankful gesture. "I am so glad—I am so thankful," she whispered softly; "he has been a dear, good friend in standing by me, when I so sadly needed help."

"Oh!" Prelice was rather indignant. "Seeing that he is something more than a friend to you, Miss Chent, he could scarcely fail to lay himself and his life at your feet. It is only what an English gentleman would do to any lady he respected, much less loved."

Mona coloured, and turned aside her face, rather embarrassed by the impetuous outbreak of her lover's friend. "Both English gentlemen and English ladies held aloof when I was in danger," she said simply, "so you can understand how much I prize the friendship both of Ned, and of Mr. Martaban here, seeing that they never believed that I was guilty."

"No one could believe that," cried Prelice, still impetuous, and throwing his usual discretion to the winds; "the moment I set eyes on your face I knew that you were innocent."

Miss Chent coloured again, and rather retreated from the confidential attitude she had assumed. Prelice was going ahead too fast, and her womanly nature, in spite of occult training, was taking alarm. "I must say that, seeing you did not know me, the belief was somewhat rash," she rejoined coldly; "however, I thank you."

"And you will allow me to help you?" asked Prelice eagerly, but timidly.

"Help Miss Chent," said the lawyer, looking keenly at the young man's glowing face. "In what way?"

Prelice laid down his cup, crossed his legs, and delivered himself of his opinion. It was just as well that both Mona and Martaban should learn of his determination to enter into their lives. "Everyone is delighted, with few exceptions," he said somewhat incoherently to the girl, "that you have been acquitted. But some insist that you must be guilty. Forgive me for inflicting pain," he added rapidly, "but it is necessary, so that you may entirely understand me. You are safe from the law, Miss Chent, but, with some idiots, your character is not yet clear. Also Ned, in spite of the absurdity of the thing, may be accused of making away with Steve Agstone in your interests. In order to set everything right it is necessary for us to make certain who killed your uncle, and who killed the sailor."

"But Agstone killed Sir Oliver," said Martaban quickly; "the evidence of the paper-cutter, which——"

"Quite so, quite so," interrupted Lord Prelice hurriedly, and skating quickly over this thin ice, "but we can't prove Agstone's guilt, beyond all doubt, without further evidence. For Miss Chent's sake, the truth—whatever it may be—must be made public."

"And what do you think is the truth?" demanded Martaban, puzzled.

Prelice, bearing Mrs. Rover in mind, shuffled again. "I am not prepared to give an opinion off-hand," he replied politely. "But what I wish you and Miss Chent to understand is, that Ned Shepworth has accepted my services towards hunting down the author, or authors, of this double crime. I wish Miss Chent, if she will, to accept them also."

"Willingly and with gratitude," said Mona, extending her slim hand.

Prelice contrived to press it in a friendly way, and not kiss it, as he felt strongly inclined to do, but the effort was great. "Then we can go ahead," he said easily; "and as I am now admitted to the inner circle as it were, I should like to know exactly how matters stand. About you, Miss Chent, for instance. Do you remain here?"

The girl flushed, and glanced, rather embarrassed, at her lawyer. "Yes!" replied the latter. "Captain Jadby, who undoubtedly inherits, now that the second will has been destroyed, has made no move towards assuming possession of his property. Moreover, there are certain legal formalities to be gone through before he can become the legitimate master of the Grange. Until everything is straight, I suggest that Miss Chent remains in her home."

"It is not my home, but Captain Jadby's," answered the girl, colouring painfully. "I would much rather go away. But," she added piteously, yet with a proud effort of self-restraint, "I have nowhere to go to. Uncle Oliver has disinherited me, and my parents died insolvent. If I leave the Grange I go into the world penniless and alone."

Prelice winced at the picture she drew. "There is always Ned," he remarked lamely.

Miss Ghent shot a swift glance at his distressed face, and answered coldly in his own words. "Yes, there is always Ned."

The young man felt more puzzled than ever. Her voice did not sound like that of a girl in love, and as he had gathered from Constance, the man Mona was engaged to, had not given her his heart. But if this was the case—and it was beginning to appear obvious—why had the two agreed to marry? Prelice did not know what to say, so Miss Chent, seeing his embarrassment, explained in a somewhat embarrassed fashion herself.

"Ned is poor," she remarked with deliberate self-control; "he has his way to make in the world. It would never do for me to burden him with a pauper wife."

"Two are stronger than one, Miss Chent. There is strength in unity."

"Not in this case," she retorted; and quietly dismissed the subject.

"Will you come to my house, my dear?" said Martaban, who seemed to be devoted to his luckless client, "my wife will be glad to have you."

"So will Aunt Sophia," interposed Prelice quickly, and struck with a brilliant idea. "You know my aunt, Miss Chent? Lady Sophia Haken. She is a friend of yours."

"Save yourself, Mr. Martaban, and Ned, I have had no friend since I was put on my trial for murder," said Mona in a level voice. "I decline to trouble any person until my innocence is proved."

"It has been proved at the trial," said Prelice; and Mr. Martaban echoed the speech.

"Legally, but not socially," she rejoined, rising. "I accept your services, Lord Prelice. Learn who killed my uncle, and who stabbed poor Agstone, and earn," she faltered—"and earn my—my gratitude."

Prelice looked disappointed. Yet what else could the girl say?

CHAPTER XIV.

MRS. BLEXEY'S OPINION.

Despite the threatening clouds on the horizon, which hinted at coming trouble, the days passed very quietly at the Grange. As an elderly male chaperon, Mr. Martaban remained to look after his client, and the very respectable Mrs. Blexey was also useful in this necessary capacity. Prelice, unable to tear himself away from the too dangerous society of Mona—and dangerous it was considering his feelings and her engagement to Ned—lingered at the Hythe Hotel. Shepworth, strange to say, did not put in an appearance.

"It's odd," remarked Prelice, when strolling over the lawns on the third day of his arrival, "it's odd that Ned doesn't come down."

He put the observation in the form of a query, and so Mona, who strolled beside him, was forced to reply. But she did so unwillingly, and as briefly as was possible. "Very odd," she said indifferently.

Lord Prelice cast a puzzled side glance at her beautiful face, which looked ethereal and rosy under a red sunshade. Even as yet he could not understand what were her feelings towards his friend. And as he was more in love than ever, the situation was perplexing from its very vagueness. In sheer desperation, he tried to make her talk of Ned (which she did very rarely), by continuing the topic. "Ned," said the young man, eyeing the trees, the lawns, the sky, and the house, with a fine affectation of indifference, "Ned has been acquitted at the inquest, and the jury gave a verdict of wilful murder against some person, or persons, unknown, in the orthodox style. Agstone has been buried, and here am I waiting for an interview with Ned to settle some course of action towards elucidating these criminal problems. Yet he has not come down, and has not even replied to my letter."

Miss Chent shifted her sunshade from one shoulder to the other. "I expect he'll come down when he is ready," said she calmly.

"Oh Jerusalem! Excuse the swear-word, Miss Chent; but if I were Ned I should have come here ages ago."

"You did, Lord Prelice. But if you are so anxious to interview Ned—and I quite admit the necessity—why not go up to London?"

Her companion wriggled uneasily, and searched his brains for an excuse to remain in his uncomfortable paradise. "Well, you see—er—that is, my dear young lady, I am—to put it plainly—er—my aunt, you know Lady Sophia, is coming to Folkstone."

"She arrived there last night, Lord Prelice."

"Eh—what—you don't—er—you don't say so?"

Mona laughed, and the young man was glad to hear her laugh. She gave way rarely to merriment during the undecided present. "Why did you write about me to Lady Sophia?" asked the girl gently.

"I?" Prelice was quite prepared to lie, but decided not to when he saw the expression of her face.

"Well, you see—that is, you understand—that an aunt is an aunt."

"I never thought that she was an uncle."

"Course not. But there, you see, my aunt expected me to write, and I have written."

"You needn't have made me the subject-matter of your letter."

"Who said that I did?" asked Prelice, growing scarlet.

"Lady Sophia herself. I received a note from her this morning, and, considering my position, a very kind note. It seems that you wrote asking her to stand by me, and she has come to Folkstone to do so."

"Loud cheers!" cried Prelice shamelessly. "I always thought that Aunt Sophia was a brick. She never believed you were guilty, you know," he went on confusedly; "said all manner of nice things about you to me whenever we met. Now she'll take you under her wing, and make things hot for any Society fool that dares to say a word against you."

"Why do you do this for me, Lord Prelice?" asked Mona in rather a faltering tone, and averting her too-speaking face.

"I am—that is—well—Ned's friend, you know."

"Oh," Mona's voice became steady, and she turned to look at him squarely, "so you enlist your aunt on my behalf for Ned's sake."

Was there ever such a perplexing girl! A moment ago and she seemed pleased at being championed by Lady Sophia, now her looks and her voice were cold. Prelice, in sheer desperation, blurted out the truth in a blundering manner. "A little bit for my own sake also."

"I am glad of that."

"Are you?" This time it was the young man's voice which became unsteady, for he did not know whether he was on his head or his heels. "That's all right." A sentiment of honour towards the absent Shepworth, who would not look after his own interests, made him end thus lamely.

Mona laughed again, and was as enigmatic as the Sphinx. "It is extremely good of you, Lord Prelice," she went on in a guarded manner. "Lady Sophia can help me greatly to recover my position in Society."

"You have never lost it," blurted out Prelice crossly.

"I did lose it, and I have lost it," she answered sadly, "and I shall never recover it entirely until the murderer of my uncle is discovered. Lady Sophia, who really likes me——"

"Loves you! Loves you!"

"No, no! She likes me; let us say that she has an affection for me. That is a greatly-to-be-appreciated state of mind for one woman to be in towards another. That's rather a German sentence, isn't it?"

"I don't know what you mean," muttered Prelice, beginning to find out that, after all his experiences in the four quarters of the globe, he was but a neophyte where women were concerned.

"I mean that Lady Sophia's liking or affection for me will do a great deal to rehabilitate me, but that the punishment of Uncle Oliver's assassin will do more."

"And your marriage with Ned will do most of all."

Mona mocked him. "Marriage covers a multitude of sins, doesn't it?"

Prelice clutched his head, but his hair was too closely cropped for him to grip. "I'm to be best man," he said feebly, and found a delight in torturing himself.

"Oh! Has Ned selected you for that post?"

"He did; when we were at Eton."

"I see. Then he was engaged when at Eton. How precocious!"

The young man groaned, and glanced at her despairingly, quite unable to understand her moods. Lately she had been sad, now her eyes were dancing with merriment. "I am glad you are happy," he said in a surly tone, for this mystery of her engagement tortured him.

"I am," she assented swiftly, "and for three reasons."

"May I hear them?"

"Certainly. In the first place, you and Ned will find out who killed my uncle and poor old Steve, so as to clear my character. In the second place, Lady Sophia is coming over to-day, and thus begins the necessary whitewashing for me to re-enter the world. And in the third place," she ended seriously, "throughout all this trouble I have had a firm conviction that God would help me. He *has* helped me by saving my life from a legal death, and He will help me to clear my character. Some day—perhaps in the near future—there won't be a single stain on my name. Now don't speak," she held up her hand; "you are about to say that there is not a stain now. But there is. To remove it, I trust in God first, and in you second."

"What about Ned?" asked Prelice restlessly.

"Oh, in Ned also," she rejoined, and looked at him quietly. As he made no observation—and he could not out of sheer perplexity—she turned on her Louis Quinze heel. "I am going in to get ready for the visit of Lady Sophia," she said abruptly.

Prelice watched the red sunshade vanish into the house, then dug his stick into the turf, and swore volubly. He had a considerable command of language in this respect, but rarely exercised his vocabulary. On this occasion he did, since ordinary words failed to soothe him. And even as it was, swearing did little good, so Prelice started to walk violently and aimlessly, only desirous of restoring his temper to its usual state of cynical calm by abnormal exercise.

He could not make Mona—as he called her mentally—out in any way whatsoever. She was certainly engaged to Ned, and yet she spoke of him quite unemotionally, as she would have done of—well, not of an acquaintance perhaps, but of a friend. She could not possibly love him, and if she did not, should certainly not be engaged to him. Ned had no money and no position, so she assuredly could not be seeking to better herself by the marriage. Certainly gratitude might induce her to become his wife, since he had stood by her; but then—and here Prelice swore again—she had been engaged to him some time before the death of Sir Oliver, and when no gratitude could possibly have entered into her acceptance. And if she was merely grateful, Ned would not marry her on that account, especially since, on the authority of Mrs. Rover, he loved another woman. For the third time Prelice swore over the problem, and determined to throw all delicacy to the winds, so far as Shepworth was concerned. The moment Ned arrived at the Grange he would ask him plainly what he meant, and what she meant, and what the whole infernal complication meant. It was quite impossible that a young aristocrat with a large income, and a healthy frame, and a loving heart, should sit on thorns any longer.

"Blankety—blankety—blank," raged Prelice, and looked up on hearing an exclamation of horror at his elbow.

His aimless walk had led him to the kitchen garden, and to a bed of pot-herbs, which Mrs. Blexey was laboriously picking. Being stout, and like Hamlet scant of breath, the housekeeper wheezed like a creaky wheel as she stooped to gather some sage and thyme. But she retained enough breath to cry out with horror, when hearing this handsome young gentleman swearing—as she afterwards described it—like the late Mr. Blexey, who had been a skipper of renown in the way of bad language.

"I beg your pardon," said Prelice, showing his white teeth in a smile which won Mrs. Blexey's heart. "I'm a little put out. Didn't know any lady was within earshot."

"Bless you, my lord, I'm not a lady, and never laid claim to be one, so swearing, though not proper, don't worrit me over-much. It calls back old times, sir."

"Really. Did you swear yourself?"

"Me!" Mrs. Blexey looked indignant. "Why, I belong to the United Inhabitants of the Celestial Regions."

"What?"

"It's my religion," said Mrs. Blexey simply; "what you might call my sect, my lord. There's very few of us, but we all go to heaven."

"There's nothing like being certain of your destination," said Prelice dryly, and was about to move on, when the housekeeper stopped him.

"Your pardin, my lord, but I've been trying to catch your eyes ever since you came here, but never managed it till now. In a kitchen garden too," ended Mrs. Blexey mournfully, "which don't seem to be the place for a lord of high degree to speak in."

"It suited him to swear in it, however," murmured Prelice frivolously; then added in louder tones: "What do you wish to speak to me about?"

"Not about him that is gone," remarked Mrs. Blexey, referring to her lost spouse, "though his language—begging your lordship's pardin—was as like yours as bean-pods. And because of such talk, he'll never come back—never. Them as has him, will keep him."

"Indeed. Are they—whomsoever they may be—fond of him?"

"I don't think so, my lord. You see, he's—well, he's dead, my lord."

Prelice put up his hand to twirl his moustache and hide a smile. "Then you think that——"

"I'm sorry for Blexey," interrupted the housekeeper firmly; "but he didn't belong to the United Inhabitants of the Celestial Regions, so he——" She pointed stealthily downward.

"Let us hope it is not so bad as that," said Prelice, choking with suppressed laughter. "You wish to speak to me," he repeated politely.

"To catch your lordship's eyes as it were."

"That has been accomplished. What next?"

Mrs. Blexey groaned, and made an effort. "It's about Miss Mona."

The young man's merriment died away, and he looked keenly at the red-faced, shapeless old woman. "What's that?" he demanded in the imperious tone which formerly he had used towards recalcitrant soldiers.

Mrs. Blexey, being timid, dropped with a thud on to the sage and thyme, and placed a podgy hand on her ample breast, gasping like a fish out of water. "The heart, my lord—mother's side—it ain't strong. If your lordship would speak less like a gun going off——"

"Certainly," interrupted Prelice in his most silky tones. "What have you to tell me about Miss Mona?"

"It ain't about her exactly, my lord. But there's the will, you know, and that Madame Eppingrave, as she called herself, though I don't believe it is her name for all her airs and graces, and she nearly as old as me, and as stout too, for all her tight lacing."

Prelice, leaning against the mellow brick wall where the nectarines grew, stared at the fat woman, who was still prostrate amidst the herbs. "If you knew of such things, Mrs. Blexey, why didn't you explain in Court?"

"Because I don't believe in Courts or in them as is in Courts," said Mrs. Blexey, fanning herself with a pink sun-bonnet. "They got me to give what they called evidence, and say things against my dear, pretty Miss Mona. I nursed her, sir. I was born in the Grange, and have served the Lanwins all my life. When Mrs. Chent went away with her husband, I followed; and when she and him died, I came back here with Miss Mona, as Sir Oliver wished, to be the housekeeper."

Prelice nodded sympathetically. "I know that you are devoted to Miss Mona," he said, approving of this devotion.

"You are too, my lord, ain't you?" asked the old woman pointedly.

The young man grew as red as the brick wall against which he was leaning; but Mrs. Blexey, seeing this sign of anger, went on hastily. "I don't mean boldness, my lord; indeed, I don't. But Miss Mona does need a friend sadly, my lord, and she tells me that you are one."

"I am," said Prelice firmly, and flushing again, "and I am glad that she spoke thus of me. But about this Madame Marie Eppingrave?"

"I never liked her, my lord. An oily flatterer she was, with a gimblet eye and a buttery tongue. She was always trying to get the better of Sir Oliver, and gave him that nasty thing that made the smoke."

Prelice naturally looked startled. "Why, Sir Oliver brought the herb from Easter Island himself—at least I fancy he did."

"I don't, my lord; and what's more, he didn't. I went into the library to ask master what he'd have for dinner, and Madame Eppingrave—if that is her name, the old bag-o'-rags—was showing master a lot of dry stems and purple leaves, and talking about trances and suchlike rubbish. That was just a week before Sir Oliver's death."

"What do you make of that, Mrs. Blexey?" asked Prelice thoughtfully.

"I don't make anything of it, sir. But it was strange that the nasty smoky weeds she gave master should bring about his death."

"Madame Marie had no reason to wish Sir Oliver dead?"

"Oh no, my lord. Why, she lost a good friend in him, and often must have desired him to be alive and kicking. All the same, sir, she gave him them withered leaves, and through them master came by his end."

Prelice nodded absently. He required time to think over the matter, and turned away to be alone. Then a thought struck him, and he returned to the housekeeper. "What about the will?" he demanded.

"It wasn't burnt."

"You must be mistaken The Court——"

"Much them lawyers knew about it," cried Mrs. Blexey, struggling to her feet. "I never said it to them, because they said as it would help Miss Mona to get out of their nasty clutches if the will was proved to be burnt. So I said what I was told, for Miss Mona's sake. But Sir Oliver was writing out another will ——"

"How do you know?" asked Prelice sharply, and much disturbed.

"I saw him writing it," said Mrs. Blexey firmly. "It was never signed, to my knowledge. But you can take my word for it, my lord, that the unsigned will was burnt, and that Miss Mona is entitled by the other to the property."

CHAPTER XV.

JADBY PLAYS A CARD.

Mrs. Blexey's communications certainly afforded Lord Prelice ample food for reflection. What she had said about Madame Marie—as the young man mentally termed her—implied that the fortune-teller was somehow implicated in the tragedy of Sir Oliver's death. Yet he had been a good friend to the lady, and by his death she lost a valuable client. It was impossible to think that she had killed the baronet herself, or had been a consenting party to his death. But undoubtedly, according to Mrs. Blexey's firm asseveration, she had given Lanwin the roots and leaves of the Sacred Herb, and from using these in the prescribed way to induce a trance, Sir Oliver had been rendered helpless. Had he not been chained hand and foot by the fumes of the herb he could not have been killed, as, in spite of his lost leg, he was no despicable antagonist. The herb, therefore, was the main factor in the tragedy, and Madame Marie had placed the same in the man's hands.

Of course, it was just possible that someone—name unknown—had found Sir Oliver helpless, and so had taken the opportunity to kill him. Madame Marie may have discovered the guilty person, and, to recompense her for the loss of a wealthy friend, had been bribed by the same person to silence. This pointed to the guilt of Captain Jadby, who might have been anxious to get rid of the baronet so as to enter into his heritage. But the assertion of the housekeeper about the new, unsigned will went far to show that the sailor was innocent. Captain Jadby assuredly would have destroyed the will which gave the property to Mona, and not an unsigned document, which mattered nothing to him.

Much puzzled by the new aspect of the case, Prelice sought out Mr. Martaban, and related what he had heard in the kitchen garden. The solicitor at first scoffed at the idea of the unsigned will being destroyed, but later cautiously ventured the remark that there might be something in it.

"Though, mind you," he remarked thoughtfully, "Mrs. Blexey does not prove her case, as we say in legal circles. She states that Sir Oliver made a new will in his own handwriting, but she cannot prove that this was the particular will which was burnt."

"But Sir Oliver's handwriting would be recognised," urged Prelice.

"It was," replied Martaban tersely; "the will leaving the property to Miss Chent was in my late client's handwriting also. He always preferred to write out his own testaments."

"To draw them up you mean."

"Not in this especial instance, my lord. The will leaving all to Captain Jadby, and made in the South Seas years ago, is a personal document, since I have seen it. The unsigned will also was personal, as so far as I know Sir Oliver did not employ any lawyer to draw it. But I drew out the document by which Miss Chent inherited, and Sir Oliver copied it himself, and had it signed by Mrs. Blexey and Agstone. So you see that we can't actually say which will was burnt, as there is not sufficient remaining of the document. From some of the scraps found, which alluded to Miss Chent as 'my dear niece,' it would seem that the will in her favour must have been destroyed, since Sir Oliver when angered would not have spoken kindly of her in the document alluded to by Mrs. Blexey."

Prelice nodded absently. "I presume that the new will would also have been signed by Mrs. Blexey and Agstone as witnesses?"

"I think so, since Sir Oliver trusted both, but according to the housekeeper the will was not witnessed. For all we know, it may not even have been signed."

"Mrs. Blexey says that it wasn't."

"I think she is right," said Martaban thoughtfully, "since the testator has to sign in the presence of the witnesses, and Mrs. Blexey would probably have been one."

"What about Captain Jadby?"

"He was absent on many occasions, and had he signed as a witness he would not have benefited."

"Madame Marie Eppingrave?"

"Humph!" Martaban considered. "She and Agstone might have signed certainly, but in that case she would have come forward to state to whom the new will left the property. It could not have been Jadby, since the old will held good, if the second was destroyed."

"Madame Marie may have been bribed by Jadby to hold her tongue about the third will, so that the first could stand."

"Which points to the fact that the second must have been destroyed. Yet Mrs.

Blexey says that it was not."

"I agree," admitted Prelice; "but, as you say, she does not prove her case."

Martaban nodded. "The sole way in which the case can be proved is by the production of the second will."

"Or of the third," remarked Prelice quietly. "The assassin of Sir Oliver burnt one will—we know not which—and holds the other. He will produce it when he is ready."

"And so lay himself open to arrest," ended Martaban neatly. He paused, and went on deliberately: "I advise a waiting game."

"A waiting game?"

Martaban nodded. "Let the other side move first."

"Do you mean Captain Jadby?" asked Prelice abruptly.

"And this unknown assassin, who holds one of the last two wills. Jadby, we know, retains the first, which gives the property to him. He will probably come down to insist upon his rights. I shall refuse to let him have the Grange or the income until the other wills are proved to be destroyed, or at least until he proves that the burnt will is the one giving the property to Miss Chent."

"That was proved at the trial."

"Quite so; but Mrs. Blexey's story requires that the case should be reopened."

"Not for the trial of Miss Chent!" cried Prelice in alarm.

Martaban laughed heartily. "You can make yourself easy on that score, my lord. No one can be tried twice for the same offence. Well?"

"I agree with you that it is best to wait and see what Jadby does, and then we can checkmate him, as you suggest. Meanwhile I shall go to London, and call on Madame Marie in New Bond Street. She may know of something likely to elucidate the mystery of the Lanwin Grange crime."

"If she does," said Martaban, with a chuckle, "she certainly will not speak out. A clever woman, Madame Marie."

"I can deal with clever women," said Prelice, rather conceitedly.

"Deal with Miss Chent then," finished the lawyer, and the conversation ended for the time being.

It was all very well for Martaban to suggest dealing with Mona, but that young lady was much too feminine for Prelice to tackle. He could make nothing of her. Sometimes she was kindness itself to him, and then she would hold him at arm's length with freezing politeness. Even as yet he could not determine her relations to Ned, otherwise than that an official engagement existed. She gave him no chance of learning the exact truth. When he praised Ned she would assent cordially to the most enthusiastic eulogiums, and yet when he hinted—and being in love, he could not help hinting—that Ned did not behave as a lover should, she entirely agreed. In desperation, he would have spoken to her about Constance Rover, but a feeling of loyalty to his absent friend prevented his doing this. Once or twice Prelice determined to leave for London, and wash his hands of all these mysteries, of which Miss Chent was not the least. But he was so deeply in love that, awkward as the position was, he could not tear himself away. Yet, like a true gentleman, Prelice never revealed by word or deed, or even look, that he was at Mona's feet.

It was with a feeling of relief that Prelice came one day to the Grange, and found Lady Sophia officially established as Mona's friend. All day long the young man had been walking off his feelings on the Downs, trying by violent exercise to calm his agitated nerves. He tore along at top speed for miles, cursing himself for a fool in submitting to be lured by a will-o'-the-wisp, since, seeing how matters stood between Mona and Ned, he could not hope to make the girl Lady Prelice. But however far he went, the loadstone of the Grange, magnetised by Miss Chent's mere presence, always drew him back to her dainty feet, there to sigh hopelessly for the moon. On this occasion he arrived back to afternoon tea, and was greeted effusively in the drawing-room by his aunt.

"Though I can't say that you look well, Prelice," said Lady Sophia, putting up her lorgnette. "What have you been doing with yourself? Late hours and indigestible suppers, no doubt."

"Ask Miss Chent," replied Prelice, somewhat sulkily; "she knows what a rake I am."

Mona, who was presiding over a well-provided tea-table, glanced at the dark circles under the young man's eyes, at his lack of colour, and noted his cross looks. The survey, for some reason, appeared to give her a large amount of satisfaction. "I don't know Lord Prelice's character," she observed demurely.

"He's a dormouse—always asleep," said Lady Sophia, sipping her tea.

"So Ned told me, and his nickname also. But he's a very energetic dormouse, surely, in exploring the world as he has done."

"Humph! It would be much better if he stayed at home and married."

Prelice could not stand this observation in Mona's presence. "That is entirely a personal matter, Aunt Sophia," he snapped.

"Not at all," answered the lady coolly; "as you are the head of the house, its members should have some say in your marriage. Unless you marry a nice girl, I sha'n't call on her."

"Have some more tea, Lord Prelice," said Mona, sorry to see how very annoyed he was, yet secretly pleased, Heaven knows for what reason.

"Thank you." He passed his cup. "I am glad to see you, Aunt Sophia, and surprised," he ended with emphasis.

Lady Sophia put up her lorgnette again. "One is always surprised to find virtue in unexpected places," she remarked coolly. "I plagiarise that from Molière, my dear. Yes, I *am* virtuous coming over into these wilds on a hot day, and I want the reward of my virtue."

"What reward do you want?" asked Prelice gruffly.

"The right to look after this dear girl." Lady Sophia patted Mona's arm. "I propose that she shall come abroad with me for a few months. Then next year we can return, and I can present her again at Court. I never believed the rubbish that people talked, my sweetest Mona, so you can safely trust yourself under my wing."

"I shall be delighted," said Mona, giving the elder lady's arm a little affectionate squeeze. "But don't you think I ought to remain here until the truth is found out?"

"You silly child, the truth has positively been shouted from the housetops. Everyone knows that you are innocent—not," added Lady Sophia in her usual inconsequent fashion, "that I should blame you if you were guilty. I never liked Sir Oliver."

"He was very kind to me," said Mona impetuously; "he meant well."

"That condemns him. People one doesn't like always mean well. However, he's dead, so we'll say no more about him. But you'll come to Germany with me, my dear. I'm going to some Bad—I can't tell you the name exactly—it's too long, and sounds too much like swearing. But it's a new Bad that has to do with the new disease."

"And have you got the new disease, Aunt Sophia?"

"I never was healthier in my life, my dear boy; but there's a cave near this Bad, with bones and skulls of the Stone Age. I want to see what like the poor, dear things were, in those happy times."

"They won't look pretty as merely bones," said Prelice dryly.

"Perhaps not. Only dogs like bones. But I daresay there will be some dear little axes, with which they cut off the heads of animals that lived before the flood. And beads too, perhaps. Fancy, beads. It brings the poor, dear things so near to us to think they wore beads."

While Lady Sophia rattled on thus, talking about everyone and everything to set Mona at her ease, the girl herself was listening. "I hear a fly," she said, starting to her feet expectantly.

"Where?" asked Lady Sophia, looking up at the ceiling. "What sharp ears you must have, child."

"Hark!" Miss Chent walked to the drawing-room door, opened it, and passed through. A moment later, they heard her voice raised in joyful welcome, and Prelice tried hard to suppress his jealousy. He did not need Lady Sophia to tell him that it was that "Shepworth man." All the same, he contrived to be fairly amiable, when Ned entered with greetings.

"How do you do, Lady Sophia? Dorry, I am glad to see you. What a hot day it has been! Thank you, Mona, I shall be glad to have a cup of tea."

Prelice stared, as Ned sat down in a comfortable chair near Miss Chent, for he could not understand Shepworth, who had so lately escaped peril, chatting in this silly fashion. The barrister did not look well either, as his face was pale and his eyes sunken. "I expected you down here before," growled Prelice after a pause.

"I could not get down," rattled on Ned, stirring his tea. "Another lump of sugar, please, Mona. There was much to do. But now that Agstone has been buried, and my character cleared, I have come down to circumvent our friend Captain Jadby."

Mona started nervously. "Oh, Ned, is there anything wrong?"

"Not at present, but Jadby will try and put things wrong. He will be here in a quarter of an hour."

"Here!" Mona rose in dismay. "Are you sure?"

Shepworth nodded, and cast a hasty glance at Prelice. "He came to me yesterday, and said that he was coming down to see you for a certain purpose. As Prelice is here, and I know very well what Jadby wants to say, I thought it best to come down too. By watching at the station I found what train he was going by, and nipped in also. At Hythe I secured the only fly, and so have got ahead of him." Shepworth glanced at his watch. "He'll soon be here; and then ——" He paused.

"And then?" queried Lady Sophia, astonished. "Bless me, Mr. Shepworth, what then? How mysterious you are. You surprise me."

"Captain Jadby will surprise you more," rejoined Shepworth dryly. "And so I am glad that you are here, Dorry."

"Why?" demanded that young gentleman, who was as astonished as his aunt.

Shepworth merely nodded mysteriously, and whispered to Mona, who nodded in reply with very bright eyes, and with another glance at the puzzled Prelice. He could not understand, even in the presence of the engaged couple, if they really were in love. Shepworth was certainly attentive, and Mona was extremely amiable. But there was something wanting in their behaviour. They had not kissed, for one thing, as engaged lovers surely would do. But perhaps that sign of future marriage had taken place in the hall. Lady Sophia, also puzzled, would have asked questions which her more diffident nephew was afraid to put, but that the footman brought in a card.

"Captain Jadby," said Mona, reading the same. "Ned, must I see him?"

"It will be as well," rejoined Shepworth significantly, "and in the presence of Martaban."

"He has gone out for a walk, and won't be back for some time," explained the girl nervously, "but I feel safe with you and Lord Prelice."

"Why with me?" Prelice asked, when the footman departed to usher in the South Sea sailor.

"You are always so kind," she observed in a low voice, and cast down her eyes, blushing scarlet, much to Prelice's amazement. He really did not know what to make of all this.

But Mona's sudden colour ebbed from her cheeks when Captain Jadby entered, for she appeared to be rather afraid of the buccaneer. Jadby, halting, and bowing on the threshold, did look rather lawless in spite of his civilised flannel garb. He had arrayed himself in white, and wore a scarlet cummerbund and a scarlet tie. These touches of too vivid colour, added to his smooth, dark face with fiery black eyes and curly black hair, and general hint at foreign blood, bespoke him the buccaneer from the fringes of the Empire. His manners also left something to be desired, for after bowing to Lady Sophia and Miss Chent, and greeting Prelice with a sullen nod, he turned towards Shepworth. Then his eyes flashed, and his mouth grew hard.

"You have stolen a march on me," he declared, coming forward.

"As you see," replied Shepworth very coolly; "after what you told me yesterday it was necessary."

"I wonder that you are not afraid to come," said Jadby, sneering viciously.

"Why should Mr. Shepworth be afraid?" demanded Mona, catching at Lady Sophia's hand to keep up her courage.

"Ask him," snarled the captain, posing picturesquely.

"Why should you be afraid?" Mona reiterated, turning to her lover.

"Captain Jadby can explain," replied Shepworth suavely.

"And may I suggest," said Prelice politely, "that in explaining, Captain Jadby might remember that there are two ladies present."

The buccaneer shrugged his shoulders, and pointedly turned his back on Prelice, a rudeness which that young gentleman noted carefully, intending to rebuke Jadby later for the same. "You are, I understand, Miss Chent, engaged to Mr. Shepworth," he said to Mona insolently.

She glanced at Shepworth, but kept her temper. "Everyone knows that news! It is common property."

"And I love you," he went on steadily.

"Rather a public place to speak like that to me, Captain Jadby."

"I am true to you, and he," pointing to Shepworth, "is false. He loves another woman."

"And I forbid you to mention that woman's name," cried Shepworth meaningly.

"Then you admit it!" cried the sailor triumphantly.

"He does," said Mona unexpectedly, "because I know it."

"What?" Jadby recoiled in dismay. His thunderbolt had fallen and failed.

"My engagement," pursued Miss Chent, "is merely official."

CHAPTER XVI.

DR. HORACE INTERVENES.

In the dead silence which followed Mona's enigmatic announcement a pin could have been heard to drop. Prelice's head was whirling. Here, at last, was the explanation, and he would now know the true relationship between the girl he loved and Ned, who apparently cared nothing for her. Shepworth stood quietly beside Miss Chent with a perfectly calm face, but his eyes were fixed threateningly on Captain Jadby, who appeared to be much amazed at the calm way in which Mona received his news. Lady Sophia glanced from one man to the other, and, having a shrewd idea of what was coming, made up her mind to depart, so as to spare herself a scene, and Shepworth an awkward explanation.

"Most interesting," she said, rising and shaking out her skirts, "but I have so much to do that I really cannot wait. Mona, child, you must come and see me at Folkstone, the Piccadilly Hotel, you know, though why Piccadilly by the seaside I really don't know."

"Will you not wait and hear what I have to say?" asked Jadby, who seemed desirous of having as many listeners as possible, so as to cast shame upon Shepworth.

"No, my good man," rejoined Lady Sophia, with all the polished insolence of a grand dame; "other people's affairs do not interest me. You had better go back to the South Seas, where I am sure you will be much more at home. Prelice, help me on with my dust-cloak." She pointed to a grey silk mantle, which her dutiful nephew duly adjusted on her shoulders. "Now, Mona, child, don't forget. Good-bye, Mr. Shepworth. Prelice, you had better come with me," she ended, sailing towards the door.

The young man hesitated, and looked at Mona doubtfully. She interpreted his look promptly. "Lord Prelice will stay, at my request."

"My dear," Lady Sophia at the door sunk her voice, "so very awkward, if you really know what that creature"—so she designed Jadby—"is going to say."

"It has to be said sooner or later," whispered Mona, "and I want Lord Prelice to hear."

"Oh!" A new thought seemed to strike Lady Sophia. She glanced from her hostess to her nephew, and then pursed up her lips, guessing in a flash what was coming. "You had better come with me, Prelice," she repeated, raising her voice, and at the sound of it Mona shrank away.

But Prelice looked dogged, and declined to come. "I must stop and support Miss Chent," he said.

"Mr. Shepworth can do that," cried Captain Jadby insolently.

"He can," said the barrister, taking a step forward, "and he can support the cause of"—with emphasis—"any lady."

The advocate of the Stone Age, standing at the open door, raised her lorgnette, and surveyed the group. "Most interesting," she said, with cool impertinence; "quite a comedy. Let us hope that it will not merge into a tragedy." And, biting her lip, she departed, with a glare at her obstinate nephew.

Guessing that Lady Sophia was offended, and pretty certain of the reason, Mona did not dare to follow.

The motor car of Lady Sophia was heard whirring down the avenue in the hot sunshine, and only when the sound died away did Miss Chent return to the three men. "What more have you to say, Captain Jadby?" she asked politely.

"It seems to me that there is little need of an explanation," he answered, with another shrug, and compressing his lips.

"None at all that I can see," rejoined Shepworth in a cool voice. "I think Captain Jadby had better go."

"Not until I receive Mona's answer from her own lips," he snarled, and looked a very ugly customer in his impotent wrath.

"Miss Chent to you," said the girl equably.

"Mona! Mona!" vociferated the captain, "I have a double right to call you by your christian name."

"I did not even know that you had a single right," she retorted.

"I have; Sir Oliver wished us to marry."

"Quite so, and for that reason I became engaged to Mr. Shepworth."

Prelice gave a gasp, and turned to his friend. Ned nodded. "It is true, Dorry," said the barrister. "When I was stopping here, during the lifetime of Sir Oliver, this man," he indicated Captain Jadby with contempt, "pestered Miss Chent with his attentions. Sir Oliver was on his side—why, I can't say—but ——"

"I can tell you now," interrupted Jadby hoarsely; "I am Sir Oliver's son, and Mona is my cousin."

There was a second silence. "I don't believe it," said Prelice decidedly, and his opinion was echoed by Miss Chent and Shepworth.

Jadby threw back his handsome head scornfully. "It matters little what you believe," he said violently, "since what I say is the truth, and no denial can make it anything else. My mother was the daughter of a great chief of Tahiti."

"Oh!" broke in Prelice impulsively, "then you are a half-caste?"

"Yes," admitted the captain, his nostrils working and his native origin becoming more and more apparent as he lost his temper. "My father was married to my mother in native fashion, but that, I learn, does not entitle me to inherit my father's title and property, which it should do. However, my father made a will in my favour before leaving the South Seas. He never had much love for me, and therefore I dreaded lest he should change his mind and leave his property to someone else. I came to England to look after my interests, and then learned that a new will had been made leaving the money to Mona. My father, to give him his due, was ashamed of himself, and proposed that the affairs should be settled by marriage, so that both Mona and I should benefit. I loved her, and agreed to the arrangement, but she scorned me, and so——"

"And so her uncle died," ended Prelice, looking sharply at the captain.

Jadby whirled round furiously, and stamped. "My father's death has nothing whatever to do with my engagement to Mona."

"I never was engaged to you," she interposed swiftly; "it was because you persecuted me that I asked Ned to stand between us. I have known Ned for years, and he is a loyal gentleman."

"Very loyal," sneered Jadby, with quivering lips, "to love one woman and become engaged to another."

Shepworth would have spoken, but Mona prevented him. "There is no need for you to excuse yourself, Ned," she said coldly, and addressed herself to the fuming captain. "When I asked Mr. Shepworth to pretend to be engaged to me, so that your worrying might be stopped, he told me that he loved another woman——"

"A woman who is——"

Shepworth threw up his hand. "If you dare to say a word," he cried menacingly, "I shall break your neck."

"There is no need," said Mona again, while Prelice, keenly observant, held his peace. "I can explain to Captain Jadby, and then he can go."

"I have heard enough," said the sailor hoarsely, and glared. "To fool your uncle—my father," he added with emphasis, "and to fool me, you pretended to engage yourself to this man."

"You have stated the position accurately," said Mona with great calmness. "Mr. Shepworth and I have paid you out. We have played a comedy by which you, for your insolence, have been deceived."

"Mona!" The man took a step forward imploringly.

Miss Chent receded. "I am not afraid of you now," she declared in a clear voice, "although you did your best to frighten me. And I do not allow anyone to call me Mona save those I love. You may be my cousin for all I know, but I don't like you, and I shall have nothing to do with you. My fictitious engagement with Mr. Shepworth is at an end," she concluded, slipping off a ring and passing it to Ned, who put it in his pocket; "and you, I understand, have the property, since the will in my favour has been destroyed. There is no more to be said."

"There is this to be said," shouted Jadby, the veins on his forehead swelling dangerously, "that this house is mine, and you shall leave it."

Mona faced him coolly. "Mr. Martaban looks after my interests," she declared, quite composed; "as soon as he tells me to leave I shall do so, but until then I am mistress here, and I order you to go."

Jadby would have disobeyed, as he was furious at the failure of his two thunderbolts. He had hoped to overwhelm Mona by stating that he was her cousin, and he had hoped to separate her from Shepworth by telling of the latter's infatuation for Mrs. Dolly Rover. Having failed, he looked like a fool, and would have tried to recover his ground by insisting upon remaining, but that Prelice rose to his feet and Shepworth took a step forward. Jadby was no coward, for the drop of white blood in him came from a brave old stock; but the odds were too great. Moreover, he really and truly loved his cousin, and his soul was torn within him at the thought of losing her. With a sudden revulsion of feeling, the tears sprang to his dark eyes, although he was by no means a tearful individual. Putting out his hands blindly, he groped his way to the door. Mona's generous heart smote her when she saw the man brought thus low, and she sprang forward to lay her hand on his arm. "Do not go in anger, Felix," she pleaded, using his christian name, as Sir Oliver had often done; "if you are my cousin—and I believe that you have spoken the truth—let us part in peace. Shake hands."

Jadby dashed the tears from his eyes and her hand from his arm. Her appeal brought back the original devil to his semi-civilised heart fiercer than ever. "Will you be my wife?" he demanded savagely.

"No. I cannot."

"Do you love anyone else?"

Mona drew herself up, quivering. "You have no right to ask that."

"Perhaps not," raged the captain, with contempt, "because you love a man who is in love with a married woman, and——"

Shepworth ran forward, his face white and his eyes bright. "Silence!" he exclaimed, and took Jadby by the shoulders.

"I shall not be silent," shrieked the half-caste, becoming feminine and abusive in his towering passion. "You and your Mrs. Rover, who——"

What else he would have said neither Mona nor Prelice knew, for the barrister, becoming suddenly silent, after the manner of the angered white man, ran Jadby swiftly out of the room. The semi-Polynesian kicked and shrieked and swore, and even tried to bite. But Shepworth, with set teeth and grim eyes, forced him along the hall, and out of the front door. The next moment Jadby was lying on his back some distance away, with Shepworth blocking the door of the house he claimed.

"You devil!" yelled the half-caste, and he leaped up, to slip his hand behind him. The barrister flung himself down, while three shots rang out from the captain's derringer, then sprang to his feet on hearing no more. Apparently only three chambers had been loaded, for Shepworth, filled with wrath at this treachery, dared the worst, and ran blindly down the steps. Jadby flung away the still smoking weapon with an oath, and sped down the avenue, as though the fiend himself was after him. For some little distance Shepworth followed, until he lost him on the wide Downs, and then returned to the Grange, to meet Prelice coming down the avenue at top speed.

"Are you hurt, Ned?" shouted his friend.

"One of the bullets ripped my arm, but it's nothing to speak of," was Shepworth's reply. "Where's Mona?"

"She ran upstairs to see Mrs. Blexey. I'll send up and let her know that you are all right. I say, Ned, you have made a dangerous enemy."

"Oh, damn the danger," growled Shepworth, who was furious—"the low, mean, sulking hound. He insulted me before on account of Constance, and that was why we fought. He hadn't a revolver then, and I gave him a black eye, the brute."

"And are you really in love with Constance?" asked Prelice doubtfully.

"Yes," said Ned gruffly, and not seemingly inclined to talk about the matter just then. "I'll tell you all about it some day. Meanwhile let us reassure Mona, and get my arm bathed. It's only a scratch."

"But one moment, Ned," said Prelice, holding him back from entering the house. "You are not actually engaged to Mona—I mean Miss Chent?"

"No. I only agreed so as to save her from Jadby's insolence and Sir Oliver's persecution."

"Then Miss Chent is heart-whole?"

"Entirely, so far as I know," replied Shepworth dryly; and then wheeling to face his friend: "Why do you ask these questions?"

"I'll tell you all about it some day," said Prelice, echoing the former speech of the barrister. "Halloa, here's Mona—that is, Miss Chent herself." It was indeed Mona who appeared at the top of the steps, with Mrs. Blexey and two footmen behind her. She looked pale, and hurried forward. "Are you hurt, Ned?" she asked anxiously. "I heard the shots."

"It's only a flea-bite," said Ned quickly; "don't bother about it. I'll go to my room and bathe it."

"Let me do that, sir," said Mrs. Blexey; and Shepworth, nodding a faint assent, for he had lost some blood, went into the house, and up the wide oaken stairs. Prelice lingered behind with Mona.

"I am so glad," he said meaningly.

"That Ned has been shot? How cruel of you."

"No, no, no! You must be aware that I am glad, because——"

"I haven't time to listen now," said Mona, her face crimson and her eyes very bright. "I have to send a telegram."

"To whom?" demanded Prelice as she disappeared through the hall.

"To Dr. Horace," came back the reply; and then the young man in addition to his other puzzled thoughts had this new one concerning his former fellow-traveller.

"I wonder what she wants with Horace?" he asked himself.

The answer came at dinner, when Mona was in the safe presence of Ned, and Prelice could make no demonstration of the feelings he had for her—feelings which she had guessed long since existed. Shepworth's wound, which was worse than he admitted, had been bound up, and he was in very good spirits. Mona, startled by the events of the afternoon, looked pale, and was rather restless. But Prelice said nothing. In the first place, he could not in the presence of a third party, even though that party was his school-chum; and in the second, he was too happy to speak much. All he could do, and did do, was to fill his eyes and heart with the pale beauty of Mona Chent. After all, the gods had been very good to him by removing an apparently impassable barrier.

It was Shepworth who asked why Mona had sent the wire to Dr. Horace, and Prelice listened with great interest to her reply.

"After the case," explained the girl, more to Martaban than to the young men, "Dr. Horace sent and congratulated me on the verdict. Also he wrote a note saying that if Jadby proved dangerous—those were his words—that I was to wire to him, and he would draw Jadby's teeth—his own words again, Mr. Martaban."

"Do you know Dr. Horace?" asked the solicitor, looking puzzled.

"No. I never set eyes on him until he stepped into the witness-box to give evidence about the herb. But when I heard the shots I knew then that Captain Jadby was becoming dangerous, so I sent off a telegram to Dr. Horace. Just before dinner a reply came."

"And the reply?" asked Shepworth, also puzzled.

"Dr. Horace will be here by ten o'clock to-night."

Prelice stared. "It must be something very important to bring Horace down so promptly. Have you any idea of what he means?"

"No," replied Mona quietly; "all I know I have told you; but if this Dr. Horace can stop Felix from shooting people, it will be as wise to have him down."

"Felix," muttered Prelice discontentedly. Mona shot a smiling glance at him, not ill pleased to see how openly jealous he was, even though he had no official right to be so. "He is my cousin, you know," she said sweetly.

"I don't believe it," said Shepworth sharply.

"I do, and if you will look at Uncle Oliver's portrait up there," she turned to point at the wall, "you will see that there is a likeness between him and Felix, only Felix is darker," finished Mona.

Prelice did not argue, but sat restlessly in his seat. When Mona left the three men over their wine they had a long discussion concerning the present aspect of things, and formed a committee of three to decide what was best to be done. Lord Prelice insisted upon going up to London for an interview with Madame Marie, while Shepworth was equally certain that the trail of Jadby ought to be followed. As to Mr. Martaban, he openly bewailed the loss of the will, which would have placed Mona in possession of the Lanwin property.

As the dinner was late, the three men lingered for a considerable time talking of what was best to be done, and the stable clock struck ten before they were aware of the passing of time. At once Prelice jumped up and walked into the drawing-room. There, to his surprise, he found Dr. Horace, more shaggy and uncouth than ever, sitting comfortably beside Mona Chent. The two looked like Titania and Bottom the Weaver.

"How on earth did you come here?" asked Prelice, amazed.

"Walked," retorted Horace gruffly. "I caught an earlier train, and so got here before the time mentioned in my wire. Good-evening, Shepworth; so you've been killed. Eh?"

"Oh, I'm alive yet," laughed the barrister; and then Dr. Horace was introduced to Mr. Martaban, to whom he immediately addressed himself.

"I'm glad that you are here," he said in his usual growling tones. "I mean you, sir, the land-shark. I've some business for you."

"Is this the time to talk business?" said Martaban somewhat annoyed, as after a good dinner he did not feel able to give advice.

"Judge for yourself," said Horace, fishing a blue envelope, foolscap size, out of the breast-pocket of his shabby coat. "Look at that."

Martaban did so, and so did Prelice and Shepworth, peering over the shoulder of his dress-coat. Martaban uttered a cry of amazement.

"Why, it's the missing will!" he almost shouted.

CHAPTER XVII.

THE OLD, OLD STORY.

On hearing Martaban's surprised cry, everyone stood still and silent out of sheer amazement. The unexpected had happened with a vengeance; and Dr. Horace, quite delighted with the sensation that he had produced, rubbed his hairy hands with a grim chuckle.

"Quite dramatic, isn't it!" said Horace.

Martaban drew a long breath, and clutched the document, as though he feared that it would vanish into thin air, like Macbeth's witches. "I am surprised," he confessed, staring at the doctor. "How did you become possessed of this, sir?" And in asking that very pertinent question he anticipated the speech of the others.

Horace did not answer immediately. Without requesting permission, he produced his immense German pipe, already stuffed as full as it would hold with strong tobacco, and lighted it calmly. Prelice looked annoyed at this breach of good manners, and would have stepped forward to remind Horace that he was not in his native wilds, but that Mona, guessing his intention, made a little gesture to stop him. Seeing what Dr. Horace had done, she was prepared to forgive him everything. Besides, the great traveller was such an eccentric person that no one could be angry when he behaved like a bear. It seemed natural that he should. Meanwhile the lawyer, becoming impatient, repeated his query.

"How did I become possessed of it?" said Horace, lying back luxuriously and puffing out white clouds of smoke. "Well, I might say that I murdered Lanwin, mightn't I?"

"Yes, you might," remarked Mona, smiling, "but you will not."

"No," sighed Horace, with an odd expression on his large face; "it would be an anti-climax."

"Oh, hang your dramatic instincts," said Prelice crossly. "Why can't you answer the question?"

"I am about to, if you will hold your tongue and sit down. You always did have too much chin-music, Prelice. Well," he looked round with a grin, like a somewhat malicious monkey, "if you must know, I got that will from Agstone."

Mona dropped back into the seat whence she had arisen, and her example was followed by the three men. Horace's calm announcement took their several breaths away, and their individual legs could support them no longer. "It seems to me," cried Prelice, much annoyed, "that you are presuming on our credulity."

"No; I am telling you the truth."

"But did you know Agstone?" demanded Shepworth, staring.

"Oh yes. He was my brother."

"What! What! What!" quacked Martaban like an excited duck.

"Go slow, old son of a gun," said the doctor, smoking calmly. "I told Lord Prelice yonder of my relationship, and there is no need for me to explain the same to you, beyond stating the fact that Steve Agstone was my brother. He knew of my address in London, and came to see me on the day after the murder."

"Why didn't you give him in charge?" asked the lawyer.

Horace surveyed the red face turned towards him in an aggravatingly calm way. "For two reasons," he grunted—"firstly, Agstone was my brother, and dog doesn't eat dog; secondly, I had no reason to believe that he had anything to do with the death."

"But the knife which he brought to Mr. Shepworth's flat——"

"Oh yes!" Horace glanced at the two young men and chuckled; "but you see there was no mention of the knife when Steve came to see me. Still, I must admit that he feared lest he should be accused of the crime."

"Oh!" cried Mona, sitting bolt upright, "then he did not accuse me again?"

"Not to me," answered the doctor promptly; "in fact, Steve seemed to be rather friendly inclined towards you."

"No! No! No!" cried Mona earnestly. "He never liked me; he was jealous because my uncle loved me."

"Well," Horace looked at his pipe rather than at the speaker, "I should not say that if I were you. In my opinion Steve was not so very devoted to Lanwin as was made out——”

“But I thought——”

“Never mind what you thought,” said Horace rudely, and rose to walk up and down the room. “I am here to tell you facts. When I have explained as much as is possible for me to explain, I'm going.”

“Won't you stop here for the night?” asked Mona, surprised.

“No,” retorted Horace abruptly; “I won't. Now listen, as my time is valuable, and I can't remain here chattering nonsense, and——”

“And behaving rudely,” finished Prelice, with sarcasm.

“Oh, you're there, my son, with your monkey-brand manners. There, there!” he went on teasingly, as Prelice jumped up, flushing, “don't get out your little gun. There's a lady present.”

“I wish you would remember that.”

“Oh, so I do. There's a lady present who wishes to hear how I became possessed of a document which gives her ten thousand a year. Very good, don't interrupt, or——” Horace broke off with a gruff laugh. “What bad manners you civilised people have.”

Prelice looked despairingly at Shepworth. It seemed impossible to bring this uncouth person to the point. But Mona was laughing at the bearlike antics of the traveller, although Mr. Martaban's indignant face showed how his feelings were outraged. “This,” cried the lawyer, “is quite intolerable.”

“Cock-a-doodle-doo,” crowed Horace derisively; then unexpectedly whirled a chair round between his stumpy legs, and sat down, leaning his arms over the back, to address his audience as it were from an imaginary pulpit. “Listen,” said Horace gravely, and the smiles gave place to watchfulness on every face. “My brother came to see me on the day after the murder. I had already read of Lanwin's death in the papers, and asked Steve how his master came by his end. Steve swore that he did not know, but stated that he quite expected to be accused. He then lugged that blue envelope which Mr. Martaban is holding out of his pocket, and passed it along to me. Before I could open the envelope he was out of the house, and I never heard of him again until Prelice yonder brought me the report of his death in Shepworth's flat. When alone I opened the envelope, and found the will.”

“Why didn't you bring it forward at once?” fumed the lawyer.

“Because I thought that its production might implicate Steve, and I didn't wish to have Steve hanged for a crime which he did not commit.”

"Are you sure that he did not?" asked Shepworth, meaningly.

"One is sure of nothing in this old ramshackle world," said Horace philosophically; "but what I want you all to understand is that Steve told me nothing. Why he should bring me the will I can't say, and he did not wait to tell me how he became possessed of it. I should have brought it forward at the trial, but that the papers hinted at the burning of this will being a point in Miss Chent's favour. I therefore waited until Miss Chent was acquitted, and resolved only to use the will when Jadby—whom I don't like—tried to secure this property. Miss Chent sent me the wire to-night, saying that Jadby was making himself disagreeable, so I came down with the will. *You* have it, Mr. Land-shark," he added, looking at Martaban, "so that is a present for you, Miss Chent." He pulled out a small white paper packet from his breast-pocket, and flung it dexterously across the room. "You will find that useful should Captain Jadby prove to be troublesome, as he will now that he has lost the money. That is all my mission here." He jumped away from his chair unexpectedly, and trotted to the door, where he turned to survey the company. "Good-night."

"Stop, stop!" cried Mona, running to the door, through which he had so promptly vanished; and the others following, echoed her urgent cry. But by the time they reached the hall the door was wide open, and Horace had disappeared as completely as though the earth had swallowed him up. Beyond was the darkness, which veiled him. "Is he mad?" asked Mona, turning an amazed face to the three men.

"Mad or not, he has done you a service," said Martaban, looking down at the will, which he still held. "This is undoubtedly your uncle's last testament, which was *not* burnt. It is signed by Sir Oliver in the presence of Stephen Agstone and Emma Blexey. What a facer this will be for our South Sea friend," ended the lawyer, actually becoming slangy in his delight.

"Ought we to follow Horace?" Shepworth asked.

"No," replied Prelice, who was frowning at Horace's manners; "even if we caught up with him, he would say nothing. We must wait to see if he will again intervene in the case."

"He seems to have washed his hands of it," said Ned, sauntering back to the drawing-room.

"He did so before, yet when Miss Chent wired he came down. I wonder——" Prelice paused, and bit his fingers.

"You wonder what?"

"If Horace killed Sir Oliver and Agstone."

Shepworth stared. "That's a rotten bad shot, Dorry. Why should he?"

"Oh, I can assign no reason, but——"

"My dear old chap, it is absurd. I know you are thinking of the will being brought here by Horace; but why should not his story be a true one, since Agstone is his brother?"

"Well," Prelice threw out his hands with a despairing gesture, "I can't understand the whole business; it passes my powers of comprehension."

Before Ned could reply Mona summoned both the young men. Along with Martaban, she had been opening the parcel which Horace had thrown across the room, and was now exclaiming at its contents. "Ned, Lord Prelice, here is the Sacred Herb."

They hurried over to have a look, and there sure enough was the yellowish stalk of the herb from Easter Island, bearing seven or more purple leaves. In addition, there was a written paper, which Mona read aloud.

"Use the enclosed when Jadby comes to close quarters and makes himself unpleasant," she read in a bewildered manner; "also, it will be as well for you to use your power over Lord Prelice to prevent his searching further in this case. If he meddles with what does not concern him, it means sorrow, and perhaps a public scandal."

There was a dead silence. "Now what does that mean?" asked Mona.

No one knew; no one dared to suggest an explanation. Prelice was the first to speak. "I advise you, Miss Chent, to obey Horace, and keep this herb constantly in your pocket. He is not the man to give a warning without some grave reason. He has saved you once from Jadby, and this herb, as he plainly says, intimates that it will save you again."

"But why should——"

"Oh!" Prelice shrugged his shoulders. "I can explain nothing. And with your leave I shall go back to Hythe, Ned."

"I remain here for the night," replied the barrister.

"All right, I shall see you in the morning." And Prelice sauntered to the door, after bowing to Miss Chent. He did not dare to take her hand, for fear he should never let go of it again. But she hurried after him, and spoke anxiously in the hall as he put on his light summer overcoat. This hasty departure annoyed her, as she showed plainly.

"Why will you not remain and talk over this strange matter?" she asked.

"No, no!" answered the young man, averting his eyes and quickly opening the door himself, since no footman was at hand: "But if you will permit me, I shall come here at five in the morning."

"At five? Why at five?"

"Then is the breaking of a new day," whispered Prelice in a somewhat tremulous voice. "And in the gardens—in the light of the dawn—you can then say—-you can then say——" He repeated the phrase, raised his eyes to meet hers, and left with a hurried good-night.

Mona stood where she was, amazed and confused. "What did he mean?" she asked herself; and immediately her heart explained. A light broke over her lovely face, and she whispered to herself: "At five—in the gardens—in the light of the dawn."

Meanwhile Prelice rushed downward to Hythe through the darkness of the night. There was no moon, but the purple sky scintillated gloriously with stars. A warm wind, laden with the fragrance of wild flowers, was blowing with strange murmurings over the bare spaces of the Downs, and the young man's spirits thrilled to the beauty and peace of the night. He should have thought of the case; of Horace's queer warning, repeated for the third time; and of the behaviour of Captain Jadby, now converted from a secret foe into an open enemy. But he considered nothing of these pressing matters, which had to do with the everyday world. Rather did he think of Mona and her starry beauty; rather did he recall with joy the great truth, which he could scarcely realise, that he was free to woo her, without being disloyal to his bosom friend. Mona was not engaged to Ned; her heart was free to receive a loving occupant; and Prelice, striding through the leafy lanes, swore inly that he would be that occupant. Lady Sophia would be hostile; he knew that from the way in which she had taken leave of the girl. But what did that matter, so long as Mona received him at dawn, in the enchanted gardens of the secluded Grange?

All that night Prelice slept soundly. As a lover, the tumult of his heart should have kept him wide awake, but the transcendental heights to which his thoughts raised him so drew him away from earthly matters that he lost consciousness of physical surroundings. Lying on his bed, the sound of the breaking waves on the rugged beach below the hotel lulled him to sleep. And then his spirit soared to a higher world, spiritual and pure, in which there was no pain or sorrow or weary misunderstandings. When he awoke, with the rosy lights of sunrise streaming through the curtainless window, his spirit told him little of what it had seen in the superphysical world. But Prelice was conscious that somewhere in the vast spaces of the unknown he had met with Mona, and had talked with her for endless periods of time. True, according to the clock, he had slept but a few hours; but, living in eternity, as a true lover should, he took no count of earthly time—man's measure of the eternal. He had lived for thousands of years during the dark hours, kneeling at the feet of Mona, crowned Queen of Dreams, of Kisses. And now he was to see her again in the flesh, gracious and lovely, and—as he knew she would be—truly kind.

The spirit of the man having bathed in the fountain of sleep, rose therefrom pure and undefiled. It seemed meet to Prelice—although he was not usually so imaginative—that he should wear a suit of pure white as symbolic of the coming interview. And as he passed uphill clothed in spotless flannels, with the purity of the dawn stealing into his soul, he felt as though he had been reborn into a fairer and more perfect world. Passing swiftly over the grassy uplands, his eager feet bore him down into the hollow, through the ancient woods, and on to the bird-haunted lawn. And there, in the cold, searching, chaste light of the dawn hours, he beheld his lady standing amidst the dewy grass, waiting for his coming. And she also was clothed in white.

As Prelice came across the lawns, his eyes far off met those of Mona, which shone like twin stars in the rosy flushing of her face. According to precedent, he should have raised his hat; he should have greeted her with a hand-shake; he should have explained his desire for this unconventional meeting. But he did none of these things; neither did she desire that he should do them. Without a words without a pause, he came to her swiftly, and clasped her in his arms. Their lips met in one long kiss, and the awakened birds sang joyfully in the rustling trees. So might Adam have greeted Eve in Paradise, when God presented him with the helpmate who was to be the mother of all mankind.

"And you knew—you knew all the time?" murmured Mona on his breast.

"No, I did not know, more shame to me. I really thought that you were engaged to Ned."

"I don't mean that. But surely you knew—you guessed that I loved you, and you only?"

"No. How could I when——"

"I showed my love in a hundred ways," she said, with a playful laugh. "Oh, Lord Prelice, how very little you know of women."

"I know more than is good for me," he murmured, smiling.

"What?"

"That is, Lord Prelice does," he protested, hedging; "but George is an innocent boy, who knows nothing."

"Who is George?"

"I am." And he kissed her again, victoriously.

Mona laughed happily. "I am afraid that George is not so innocent as he makes himself out to be."

"Teach him to be good, my darling."

"A hard task you set me—George," she lingered lovingly over the name; "and oh, what you must think of me, who take so much for granted."

"I think that you are an angel," he cried fervently.

"Dear, I loved you from the moment I first saw you in that cruel Court."

"And I loved you," she whispered. "I thought that it was merely friendship, until we met again, and then—then, I knew!" She gave a delighted little crow of laughter, which stirred the young man's heart to its depths. Impulsively he dropped on his knees, and kissed her hands alternately, scarcely able to speak.

"I am not worthy of you," he muttered.

"Dear." She stooped, and raised him to her breast. "Let me find out your imperfections by myself."

"I have many," he said humbly.

"And I love you for them. I marry a man in the world of men, and not an archangel; in the same way as you take a faulty woman, and not a spirit of light. But we are spirits, although clothed in coats of skin," she ended gently, "and when the hour strikes we shall know each other."

"Do we not know each other now?"

"No. That is, Mona Chent knows George Prelice."

The young man jumped gaily to his feet. "Enough for the day is the delight therefore," he cried. "I am quite content to know Mona Chent until she becomes Mona Prelice. When will you marry me?"

"So like a man," laughed the girl; "you wish to settle an important future in five minutes. We must wait."

"Wait? Oh no, no! Why should we?"

"Because," Mona laid a gentle hand on his shoulder, "your wife must be like Cæsar's, above suspicion."

"You wish me, then, to go on looking into the case?"

"I do, unless you accept the warning of Dr. Horace."

Prelice threw his panama over the hedge "I accept no warning, since you make me strong to dare it. I shall go on with the case—to-morrow."

"Why to-morrow?"

"Oh, Mona, let me enjoy Paradise for twenty-four hours."

"No. You must act, and at once, lest we lose our Paradise altogether. I don't understand what Dr. Horace means, but in spite of his hints I wish you to look into matters in order to find out who murdered poor Uncle Oliver, and in order to clear my name. You must go up to London to-day and begin your search. It is a sacrifice I ask of you, no doubt, but then love—true love—means sacrifice."

"Very good," said Prelice sedately; "I shall go up by the midday train and interview Madame Marie Eppingrave."

"Why her particularly?"

"She gave the herb to your uncle. Mrs. Blexey mistrusts her. Now," he closed her mouth with a kiss, "not a word more. The gates of Paradise will close in a few hours. Until then——"

"Yes, yes! Until then?"

"Let us play at being Adam and Eve in a garden."

And they did.

CHAPTER XVIII.

THE POWER OF THE HERB.

It had been Prelice's intention to ask Ned about his love for Constance Rover before leaving the Grange, but on second thought he resolved to wait until he learned more concerning the murders before putting Shepworth in the witness-box. Nevertheless, he was somewhat upset to think that his best friend was entangling himself with a married woman. Prelice was no prude, and had not been a Sir Galahad himself; all the same, he did not think that Ned was acting rightly. Of course, the case was a hard one, since the two truly loved one another. Constance had been sacrificed on the family altar, and to a man who took advantage of her sacrifice to play the tyrant as much as he dared. The poor woman was very unhappy, and it was to be presumed that the man who loved her was unhappy also. It said a great deal for Shepworth and Mrs. Rover that they had not long ago defied conventionality and eloped. Since they had not gone this length, Prelice argued that they were trying to bear their several burdens as honourably as possible. But how long would such endurance last?

According to Shepworth himself, Mona knew of his love for Constance, since he had explained the same when the pretended engagement was made to save the girl from Jadby's wooing and Sir Oliver's persecution. But Prelice, in the first flush of his love, shrank from questioning her about so distasteful a subject; and on her side, Mona was loyally silent, until Ned chose to speak. Thus it came about that, although Prelice met his friend at breakfast, he made no remark about this very private business, and Shepworth did not volunteer an explanation. Rather did the conversation turn on the unexpected appearance of the lost will; and Martaban explained his future actions. These included an immediate journey to London with Mrs. Blexey, who had to make an affidavit as to the authenticity of the document.

Under these circumstances, as Shepworth could scarcely remain at the Grange when both Martaban and the housekeeper were absent, he arranged to go to London with them by the ten o'clock train. Prelice would fain have lingered in those delicious gardens with Mona, but as he knew her views, he kept to his determination. However, when the trio drove away to Hythe, Prelice had a golden hour or so all to himself, and very wisely made the most of it. It was with great regret that he took his way to the station at Hythe and to the train which was to bear him miles away from his goddess. But the memory of the last kiss which she gave him cheered his somewhat despondent mood all the way to Charing Cross. And on stepping on to the platform of the metropolitan station Prelice shook off his dreams, and addressed himself to the task in hand.

As the day was fine, and Prelice, as usual, felt the need of exercise to tame his exuberant spirits—which had quite recovered during the journey—he walked to New Bond Street, and somewhere about three o'clock found himself reading a brass plate inscribed "Madame Marie Eppingrave." And afterwards he entered a narrow and dark passage, to mount a steep flight of stairs, and finally came to the second floor of the building, where the fortune-teller received clients.

A dark-complexioned lad of fourteen, dressed in white robes, with a blue scarf round his waist, received the new-comer, and informed him that Madame Marie was engaged for ten minutes or so. Prelice therefore sat down, and glanced over some papers lying on a round table. These mostly dealt with occult matters up to date, and he speedily grew tired of reading much which he could not understand. The room was small and commonplace, and even ugly in its adornments. The table aforesaid, a few cane chairs, and an old horse-hair sofa completed the furnishings, and two dingy uncurtained windows overlooked Bond Street. There was nothing of the mystical about this very ordinary apartment, and Prelice concluded that Madame Marie certainly did not spend her earnings on magical frippery in order to impress those who called upon her. After a glance round he spoke to the lad, who was seated cross-legged at the door, and asked him if he was a Hindoo.

"No," answered the boy in very good English, and with a flash of snow-white teeth; "I come from the South Seas."

"Indeed," answered Prelice in his turn, and somewhat astonished. "Has your mistress been in the South Seas?"

"Yes, sir. She brought me from Tahiti, but I want to go back again."

Prelice reflected. Tahiti was the home of Captain Jadby, and the former haunt of Sir Oliver Lanwin. He wondered if Madame Marie had met the baronet there. But the lad was not likely to know that, so he asked him another question. "Does your mistress know Captain Felix Jadby?"

The effect on the boy was somewhat strange. He leaped to his feet, and muttered some words in his native tongue, which apparently were not complimentary to the captain, judging from the savage expression of his face. "Madame does know him," he said at length, "and he comes to see her here very often. I don't like him. He kicked me. I would kill him if I were in Tahiti, but here——" The boy shrugged his shoulders, to show that the English law was much too particular.

"Madame loves the captain, and wants to marry him," went on the boy, apparently so carried away by his hate that he said more than was wise, considering his dependent position, "but he loves another, and——" Here the sound of the inner door opening made the lad aware of his folly in speaking secrets to a stranger. He cringed, and caught Prelice's hand. "You will say nothing to her?" he implored.

"No, no," Prelice assured him, and slipped half-a-crown into his hand; "but later you must tell me more. I also dislike Captain Jadby."

"I'll tell you what I can to harm him," said the boy viciously. "He kicked me and struck me—me, the son of a chief. But don't tell her," he added, pointing with a trembling hand to the inner door; "oh, my soul, don't tell her, for she can send the spirits to torment me."

The young man promised again, thinking that the lad in a way was somewhat like Caliban in his fear of spirits, and looked upon Madame Marie as a sort of female Prospero, who could have him pinched black and blue. But he had little time to think about this new ally, who might be of assistance in undermining Jadby's schemes; for a lady, fashionably dressed, and holding a handkerchief to her face, emerged from the inner room. The lad showed her out, and Prelice waited for his reception. A silver bell sounded within, and the boy returned to point meaningly at the door, laying his finger on his lips in token of silence. Prelice nodded reassuringly, and stepped into the shrine.

If the approach to this holy of holies was commonplace, the shrine itself certainly was not. Prelice beheld a room of no great size furnished very oddly —that is to say, it was not furnished in the ordinary acceptation of the word. The ceiling was painted a dull red, and a plain carpet of the same hue was spread over the floor. Two windows looking on to Bond Street were filled in with painted glass, representing various mystical signs, and the four walls were hung with lustreless black stuff, which made the place look like a chapel during a funeral service. But the odd thing was that the red carpet was strewn with perfectly white cushions, and there was neither table nor chair. Tall pillars of black marble stood in the four corners, each bearing a glass ball on its summit, and between the windows was placed a bronze tripod, in which smoked a perfumed fire. What with the dim religious light, the black walls, the red carpet, and the snowy cushions of silk, Prelice felt somewhat dizzy. All this theatrical parade was evidently designed to produce a confusing effect, and unseat as much as possible the reason and judgment of Madame's dupes. Annoyed that he should give way so easily, the young man pulled his wits together, and looked at the priestess who had conceived this artful *mise en scène*.

Madame Marie, clothed in a long white silk robe, made perfectly plain, knelt —Japanese fashion—on a cushion in front of the tripod, and with her back to the painted windows. She was a stout, heavy-looking woman, of apparently no great height, with a colourless face, very large and smooth, and with masses of snowy, silvery hair, which tumbled down her back in waves of white. What her figure might be Prelice could not judge because of the robe, but he noted that her hands were slender and beautiful, and also ringless. Indeed, she did not wear a single ornament of any description, and kneeling perfectly motionless, with closed eyes, looked like an idol carved out of alabaster. It was cleverly done, and Prelice, the sceptical, could quite understand how the majority of people yielded to the carefully prepared spells of this managing woman. But it was when Madame Marie opened her eyes that Prelice became aware of the true secret of her power over weaker minds.

These were large and blue and clear, looking from under white eyebrows in a penetrating way, fathomless as the sea, and as mysterious. Prelice met this mystical gaze calmly, but felt his skin prickling, and his will power growing weak. Aware that the seeress was trying to hypnotise him, as she doubtless hypnotised her other clients, the young man concentrated his will to meet and baffle hers. For some time they stared at one another, Prelice looking down from his height, and Madame Marie gazing upward from her cushion. Then the woman closed her eyes again with a somewhat annoyed expression.

"You are not a weak man," she said in a deep melodious voice, like the sound of a mellow bell.

"No," answered Prelice calmly; "I am not!" And he sat down cross-legged on a cushion directly in front of the sibyl.

"Then why do you come to me?" she asked, looking at him steadily; "only weak persons wish to know the future. The man who is strong and self-willed and sceptical, as you are, need learn nothing of the future, which lies in his own hands."

"In the hands of God rather," corrected Prelice. "Do you know who I am?"

"You are Lord Prelice."

"How do you know?"

"I might say by magic, but you would not believe that. I always suit myself to the nature of those I meet, therefore I shall give a commonplace explanation. I saw you in Court, when you gave evidence during the trial of Miss Chent for murder."

Prelice nodded. "I might have guessed that. Do you know why I have come?"

Madame Marie folded her hands calmly before her, and replied equally calmly. "You have come to solve the secret of the murders."

"That is a very clever guess, and I rather think that you can solve the secret, Madame."

"Why should you think so?" she asked with absolute calmness.

"You gave the Sacred Herb to Sir Oliver."

"I did. The Sacred Herb of Easter Island—but I need not explain to you, since you heard what Dr. Horace said in Court. The herb induces trances, and Sir Oliver wished to go into a trance by its aid. I therefore gave him a few twigs."

"Why did Sir Oliver wish to go into a trance?"

"He desired to explore the Astral Plane, if you understand that——"

"I quite understand; I have studied Theosophy. Well?"

"There is nothing more to be said," rejoined Madame Marie, with a little shrug, which hinted at French blood. "He went into a trance, and while his spirit was absent from his body he was murdered."

"Who by?"

"I can't tell you. Even with my powers, and they are great, I am not permitted to know who killed Sir Oliver Lanwin. It was his Karma, and he had to bear it, since he reaped only as he sowed. The Karma of his murderer has nothing to do with me, therefore my sight is veiled, and I cannot read the truth; and if I could," added the woman with emphasis, "you must be aware, if you have studied the occult, that I would not be permitted to tell without permission from those who rule."

"The Lords of Karma?" asked Prelice, wondering if she was talking in earnest, or merely wriggling out of an awkward position.

Madame Marie bowed solemnly. "I see you understand somewhat; but may I ask you to be more open with me regarding the purpose of your visit. You can hardly have come to accuse me of these crimes?"

"No," said Prelice, studying her face carefully; "I think that you are innocent. Let us leave the murders alone for the moment; I want you to help me"—he paused to add effect to his next words—"with Captain Felix Jadby."

The woman's hands moved restlessly, and she began to lose her calmness when the name was pronounced. "I know nothing about Captain Jadby beyond the fact that I met him at Lanwin Grange; but he is not guilty of Sir Oliver's death, if that is what you mean."

"Oh dear me, that is not what I mean at all," rejoined Prelice in his most airy manner, and resolving to be very plain; "but the fact is that Captain Jadby is my rival."

Madame Marie rose as though moved by a spring, and he then saw that she was little, but tremendously dignified. "Your rival!" she repeated, and her marble-white face became crimson with angry blood. At length he had managed to break through her calculated calm. "I understood that Miss Chent was engaged to Mr. Shepworth?"

"Oh, the whole world knows that," replied Prelice, still airy in his manner, "but that was merely an official engagement to prevent Jadby from worrying Miss Chent. Sir Oliver was in favour of the engagement with Jadby, for reasons——"

"I know those reasons—I know that Felix," she let slip the name, forgetting that she had disclaimed intimacy—"that Felix is his son."

"His illegitimate son," said Prelice with emphasis.

"Yes, by the daughter of a chief to whom he was married in native fashion, Lord Prelice. Of course, Captain Jadby," she had the name stiffly by this time, remembering her slip, "came home to look after his interests, and wished to marry another woman; forgetting," cried Madame Marie, beginning to pace the room, "that he was engaged to marry another woman—myself, Lord Prelice—myself."

Remembering what the native boy had said, Prelice expressed no surprise, but rapidly resolved to work on her jealousy. "I congratulate Captain Jadby more than I do you," he remarked gravely.

"Oh, I know that he is not a good man," she cried, now quite the woman, and kicking several cushions out of the way; "but I loved him, I have always loved him, and he owes much to me. He promised, when we met in the South Seas, that he would make me his wife. Not that I am young or beautiful, but because he found in me—so he said—a good comrade. I gave him the money to come home and see his father, and to secure his inheritance if possible. But he saw that girl, and loved her. Oh, how I hate that girl who stole his heart."

"You need not," said Prelice very dryly. "Miss Chent dislikes Jadby immensely, and pretended to be engaged to Shepworth so as to escape his clutches, otherwise Sir Oliver might have worried her into consenting to a marriage which she hated; but Jadby came down the other evening to Lanwin Grange, and knows now that the engagement was a false one. What he does not know," ended Prelice emphatically, "is that Miss Chent is now engaged to me."

"To you!" Madame Marie stopped in sheer surprise, then went on pacing the room, talking half to herself. "But why should I be astonished? I saw her look at you in Court; I noted how you glanced in her direction. I told Jadby that you loved her, and that she loved you."

"Oh, you couldn't be certain," cried Prelice blushing.

"I have occult powers which enable me to read hearts," said Madame Marie coldly, "believe, or disbelieve, as you like."

"I shall believe if you will read my heart now."

"There is no need of my exercising occult powers for that," she replied, waving her beautiful hands; "you wish to learn the truth about the murders so that Miss Chent's name may be cleared and Felix thwarted."

"Yes," said Prelice coolly; "you are right. And you can help me to clear Miss Chent's name, to discover the truth, as I can help you to marry Jadby."

"How can you do that?"

"By marrying Miss Chent myself."

Madame Marie nodded, and thought, pressing her hands to her head. "I can help you by the power of the herb," she said rapidly. "Listen. I shall go into a trance, induced by the herb. Do whatever I say, but do not attempt to waken me. Simply listen to what I say, and then leave the room. I shall send my spirit to seek out the truth; but first," she said, slipping down on to the cushion again, "tell me how much you know."

Prelice saw no objection in being thus clear. Even if Madame Marie wished to work against him—and seeing that her love for Jadby was at stake, he did not think that she would—all that he told her would do little to harm his own schemes. He therefore made no demur, but detailed everything from the time Lady Sophia had first drawn him into the case by sending him to the New Bailey. Madame Marie listened intently, nodding at intervals.

"It is useless for Felix to strive," she said when he ended, and with an air of triumph; "the fate of yourself is mingled with that of the girl. You love so speedily now, because you loved before, in previous incarnations. Her Karma is your Karma. Felix can never marry her, nor can Mr. Shepworth marry her, even if he did not love Mrs. Rover."

"Pardon me," cried Prelice quickly; "I made no mention of Mrs. Rover beyond the fact that she wore the green domino and the scarlet-embroidered dress. And she, as I explained, is innocent. You have no right to talk of Mr. Shepworth's love for a married woman."

"Lord Prelice," said Madame Marie quietly, and moved towards the wall, "my knowledge of these affairs is greater than you imagine. Mrs. Rover has consulted me, and Felix learned—how it matters not—that she loved Mr. Shepworth. However, we can talk of these things another time. I will go into a trance, and search in Alexander Mansions for what I can find, only, as I said, after I have spoken and have become silent, leave this room at once. In due time I shall come out of the trance, when the power of the herb is exhausted."

Prelice nodded in silence, and Madame Marie, drawing aside a portion of the black hangings, revealed a small recess. From this she took some purple leaves, and moving towards the tripod, threw them on the perfumed fire. "Lie down on your face," she commended, "else the fumes will send you into a trance. Quick! The smoke rises."

It certainly did, in a thick white cloud. Madame Marie stood over it, letting the odour flow into her nostrils. Not wishing to experience the power of the herb, as he had witnessed its results before, Prelice lay full length on the red carpet. The smoke was circling so high up that he could not breathe it, although a sickly whiff of tuberose perfume came to his nostrils. Perhaps the draught sweeping from under the door neutralised the powerful scent at this lower level; but be this as it may, Prelice lay perfectly flat, and, as in a dream, heard Madame Marie speak after the manner of the tranced in an unemotional voice, and very distinctly.

"I leave this room," she said in her mellow tones. "I rise high. I pass across London; the streets are under me. I see the Park, and now I poise above Alexander Mansions. I sink; I pass through the roof; I am in Mrs. Rover's flat."

"Search for the dress," commanded Prelice softly.

There was a pause, and then the calm voice sounded again. "I search in Mrs. Rover's room. The dress she wore is there in a wardrobe together with a green domino."

"Search for another dress," said Prelice, risking the chance; "another dress of the same style."

Again there came a pause. "I am searching!" said the voice, and a silence ensued. For quite two minutes it endured; then Madame spoke again, still with the same awful calmness. "A man's dressing-room—in the flat across the landing. I see a cupboard, in which many clothes are hanging up. Men's clothes they are. Behind them is a green domino with a scarlet-embroidered dress sewn to it."

"Who wore it?" asked Prelice, his heart beating.

"I cannot tell. It is not permitted by the Powers."

Then came a long silence.

CHAPTER XIX.

CIRCUMSTANTIAL EVIDENCE.

It was with extraordinary feelings that Lord Prelice emerged from that mystic room into the everyday world of Bond Street. After the refusal to declare the name of the person who had worn the dress Madame Marie had become silent, and Prelice raised his head, to see her standing rigid and white between the painted windows. The white smoke had disappeared into thin air, and save that the strong tuberose scent still lingered behind, there was nothing to show what had placed her in the trance. Obedient to instructions, the young man left the still figure in the lonely room, and passed through the outer apartment on his way down the stairs. The boy, cross-legged in the corner, looked up anxiously as he went out.

"You have said nothing?" he breathed apprehensively.

"Nothing," answered Prelice softly, and descended the stairs. When he stood in the street again he removed his hat, and drew a long breath of the smoky London air. Impure as it was, it dispelled the slight dizziness which the odour of the Sacred Herb had produced. Then the young man chartered a hansom to reach his rooms in Half-Moon Street; but not until he was in his very own den, and seated in an armchair with a brandy and soda within reach, did he find time to reflect. His reflections were considerably aided by a first-class cigar.

"A queer adventure," thought Prelice meditatively. "What am I to do next, I should like to know?"

Of course, the answer to this was obvious. He should go at once to Alexander Mansions, and learn if what Madame Marie said was correct. A very difficult errand to go upon, Prelice thought, as it would be hard to induce Mrs. Rover to explore her husband's dressing-room in search of evidence which might bring him into trouble. And what excuse could he make, without telling the whole truth? Then, again, Mrs. Rover might scoff at Madame Marie's astounding statement, made under such astounding conditions. Yet, on reflection, Prelice did not think that she would scoff, considering that she had consulted the fortune-teller herself, and believed in the occult. There was a considerable vein of what the vulgar call superstition in Constance Rover.

That the dress was there, Prelice had not the least doubt. Of course, on the face of it, an ordinary mortal would laugh at the idea of evidence being procured in such a way. But Prelice had travelled too widely, and he had seen too much to make him a sceptic. In Cairo, in the West Indies, in South America, and in the South Seas, he had witnessed occult ceremonies and doings, which proved clearly the existence of that Unseen World at which many people laugh, and of which all people are afraid. Drink, drugs, music, rapid movement, and even absolute stillness, are all aids to open the psychic senses, as Prelice knew very well. Madame Marie had used the fumes of the Sacred Herb to rend the spirit from the body, and he quite believed that she had gone to Alexander Mansions to make the strange discovery. When she woke from the trance she would be—according to psychic laws—quite unconscious of what she had said.

But here Lord Prelice began to doubt. Madame Marie had admitted that she knew more than Prelice imagined. Seeing that she had been at the Grange during the tragedy, and was closely connected with Jadby, it seemed very probable that she was aware of much which it was necessary to learn before the actual truth could be made manifest. So far as Prelice could judge—and he was a shrewd reader of character—the fortune-teller was entirely honest in her dealings with him. If she wished to gain Jadby as her husband it was necessary that she should be so, since only by the marriage of Lord Prelice could the girl whom the buccaneer loved be removed from her path. It was not worth her while to play Prelice false, since his aims and hers were identical. Prelice desired to marry Mona, and Madame Marie wished this also. She was anxious to make the sailor her husband, and Prelice was quite willing that this should be so, since it would put an end to Jadby's troubling, and might perhaps take him out of England. Therefore Prelice believed in Madame Marie Eppingrave.

He credited her powers also, for she had the true eyes of one who can see into the Astral World; but he could not be certain if she had used her occult powers on this occasion. She may have known beforehand of the dress, and might merely have used the trance as a means of communicating it without arousing Jadby's wrath. If the dress was found, and evidence therefrom was forthcoming likely to solve the mystery of Agstone's death, the captain, wishing to keep Mona in uneasy terror for her reputation, would be much annoyed. But then Madame Marie could explain that she had only gone into a trance for Prelice, as an ordinary client, and was unaware of what she said. Under these circumstances the buccaneer could say nothing.

"Well," said Prelice, stretching himself, and talking aloud, a habit which he had contracted when travelling in silent places, "it's rum business altogether. If the dress is in Dolly Rover's wardrobe, what then? I can't accuse him, as he certainly had no reason to kill Agstone. Humph! I wonder if this is what Horace meant when he said that I would be sorry if I searched further into the case? I certainly don't want Dolly to be hanged; but if he were, I am quite sure that Ned would console the widow. Ugh!" Prelice shivered, "what a horrible thought. Rover is a bounder and a blighter and a cad, but I honestly don't think that he is a criminal of this sort. I don't believe that he has the pluck, for one thing; and for another, he had no motive. Hum!" he reflected, "I'd best get along and see Constance."

On glancing at his watch Prelice learned that it was half-past five, and concluded that probably Mrs. Rover would be at home sipping tea, after the manner of women, worn out with shopping. He decided to give her half-an-hour, and then catch the seven train from Charing Cross to Hythe. Come what might, the young man intended to get back to Hythe that night in order to walk over and see Mona. He assured himself that she would be anxious, and would wish to learn how he had sped. But he might as well have confessed the truth to himself—namely, that he pined hungrily for a sight of her face, and that every moment passed away from her side was spent in the outer darkness. "Where there is wailing and gnashing of teeth," said Prelice to himself, quite ready to wail and gnash if he missed his train.

As fate would have it, Mrs. Rover was at home, and came forward to greet her friend in a wonderful tea-gown, which suited her queenly figure. The rose-hued blinds were down, and the room looked like the grotto of the Venusberg; but in spite of these softening aids, Mrs. Rover appeared somewhat haggard. Nor was her greeting of Prelice very friendly. Indeed, it was so harsh that he congratulated himself on finding her alone. But then had anyone else been present, she would have been all smiles and gentle words.

"How dare you come and see me after leaving as you did last time," was Mrs.

Rover's polite salutation; "and I know why you went too. Yes, you may look and look, Lord Prelice, but I know. I explained your conduct to Ned, and he told me how he had described the dress to you."

"Which means!" asked Prelice calmly and unflinchingly.

"Means!" she cried in stormy tones. "It means that you believed me to be the woman who came in and waved the bronze cup under Ned's nose."

"I did believe it for one minute," confessed her friend, making a clean breast of it in view of what was coming, "but, of course, on reflection I saw how ridiculous it was to suspect you."

"It was—it was—it was!" retorted Mrs. Rover, sitting down and tapping her foot. "I have not many friends, Lord Prelice, but I did think that Dorry was one of them."

"Dorry is," he assured her.

"A fair-weather friend. Pooh! To suspect Me," she went on angrily. "Me of all people. As if I would have hurt Ned. Had it been that Chent girl, you might have had some cause."

"Speak gently about Miss Chent," said Prelice quietly.

"I sha'n't. Why should I?"

"Because I am engaged to her."

"You!" Mrs. Rover started to her feet in delighted amazement. "But Ned?"

"Ned's engagement was merely an official one to prevent Jadby——"

"Oh yes, yes! I know all about that; but I didn't believe that Ned was speaking the truth. I thought that he was throwing me over for that horrid girl. No, no! Don't look at me like that. She isn't a horrid girl now that she is engaged to you. I shall love Lady Prelice much more than I loved Mona Chent. Engaged—engaged!" Mrs. Rover made a ball of her handkerchief, and tossed it in the air. "What a rage Lady Sophia will be in."

"She is in it already," said Prelice dryly. "I don't care."

"Of course you don't. You're a man—a man. Oh, how I love a man. Not that my married life gives me any experience," she ended bitterly.

"Constance," said Prelice seriously, "sit down, and let us talk quietly about your married life."

"I don't wish to talk of it," she retorted, but nevertheless took the seat he pointed to.

"You must. I am your friend, as you very truly say——"

"I admit it, now that you are engaged to Mona. But I say, Dorry—yes, I'll call you Dorry now—I say, isn't it rather sudden? You have only known her a week or two."

"It was a case of love at first sight," said the young man very earnestly.

"Pooh! pooh! I don't believe in such a thing."

"I didn't either until I experienced the sensation; but I really did love Mona from the moment I saw her in the dock, and it was only honour which held me back from speaking even earlier."

"Honour! What honour?" asked Mrs. Rover contemptuously.

"She was supposed to be engaged to Ned, you know. Only when I learned that the engagement meant nothing was I able to speak out."

"You have very many scruples," said Mrs. Rover, with a shrug, "and evidently forget that all is fair in love and war."

"That's a purely feminine view, Constance. Had Ned really been in love with Mona, and really engaged to her, I should have left England without saying a word."

"So like a man," retorted Constance scornfully. "Why, if a dozen women loved Ned, I shouldn't give him up."

"Constance, you forget that you are married."

"I don't; Dolly never gives me a chance of forgetting."

"Constance," Prelice spoke sharply, "you are a foolish, headstrong woman. Do you want to be disgraced?"

"There is no chance of that," cried Mrs. Rover in a fury. "How dare you talk to me like that?"

"Because I see you going headlong to ruin."

"You see nothing of the sort. I am a loyal wife, to Dolly. Ned knows that I love him now as I loved him before my marriage, and you know, Dorry, as he does, how my marriage came about."

"I know, but you ought to make the best of it."

"I am making the best of it," cried Constance, rising to stamp her foot in a royal rage. "There is not a breath of scandal against my name. No one can couple my name and Ned's together. We scarcely ever meet; but we can't prevent our feelings."

"Still," urged Prelice, in rather a futile manner, "since you have elected to become Mrs. Rover, you must consider your husband."

"Let him consider me first. I made a bargain with him, and he accepted, knowing that I loved Ned, and not him. He has broken that bargain in the meanest manner, and my father died of sheer worry through the breaking of it. Now I have to stifle my deep love for Ned, and act the part of a loving wife. I feel like a hypocrite."

"I don't think you need, Constance. People say that you treat Rover badly. It is as well that you should know."

"I do know. I have heard that before. But Dolly himself put that story about. I don't love him, and I don't pretend to; but I am as obedient and kind as I can be. I told you that I treated him like a dog. So I do, like a pet dog, a dog that is fed up and smoothed and cosseted and given cream and meat and all the things poodle dogs like; but Dolly goes about posing as a husband that is badly treated. He does not dare to say that I have deceived him, however," she added, drawing a deep breath; "he would suffer for it if he did. Miserable as I am, I abide by the bargain which he broke."

"But what is to be the end of it?"

"I don't know. I don't know," wailed Mrs. Rover, pacing the room, and holding her hands to her head. "I really believe that Dolly wants to see me disgraced. He took these flats above Ned's in spite of my protestations. I want him to go away, but he won't."

"Oh," said Prelice thoughtfully, "so Mr. Rover took these flats above Ned's, did he? Purposely?"

"I don't know." Constance paused, looking startled. "Why do you ask?"

Lord Prelice considered. "Constance, I want you to do me a favour."

"Yes." Mrs. Rover spoke softly and with an effort.

"Do you think that your husband wishes to get Ned into trouble?"

Constance put her hand to her head. "He hates Ned," she said at last in a strained voice, "because he knows that Ned loves me, and I do Ned. But for all his jealous watching, he cannot find anything wrong between Ned and myself. Because," she added, drawing herself up to her full height, "there is nothing wrong, and never will be."

"You have not answered my question," repeated Prelice quietly. "Do you think that Rover wishes to get Ned into trouble?

"Yes; I believe that he would be glad to see him dead."

"Well then, Constance, answer me another question. Would you like to see your husband get into trouble?"

"No," she said, with a startled air. "Dolly is a fool, and cruel, and I can scarcely endure him; all the same, I don't wish him any harm."

"That is all right," said Prelice, rising. "Then I can trust you to hold your tongue?"

"About what? Why are you so mysterious?"

"My poor girl, I would rather hold my peace than tell you what I am about to tell; but it is necessary that you should know. If I do not move in the matter someone less friendly to you and Rover may do so, and then only God knows what would happen."

"Dorry," Constance caught his hand, and passed her tongue over her dry lips slowly, "what do you mean? I have gone through so much that I'm quite able to face the worst."

"You won't scream?"

"No; I'm not a fool. Oh, what is it?" she blazed out, with a stamp, clenching her hands, and clenching her teeth also.

Prelice raised his hand. "I must tell you as I best can," he said in a peremptory tone, which quietened her. "After all, I may be mistaken. Is that dress you wore at your ball in your room?"

For answer Constance pressed the bell-button, and when the footman appeared, gave an order. "Tell my maid to bring me the frock and domino I wore at the ball—at the masked ball," she said; then faced Prelice when the man went out. "Are you about to accuse me?"

"No. Don't ask questions, Constance. I am sorry to keep you in suspense, but I can't help it. The whole thing is so extraordinary."

"What thing? What thing?"

But Prelice, perhaps mistakenly, would not tell her. The maid entered with the domino and dress, which Prelice at once recognised as the masked ball costume. He simply cast one glance at it, and then, "You can tell her to take it away again," he remarked.

Mrs. Rover did so wonderingly, and waited to hear what he had to say next.

"Take me to your husband's dressing-room in the other flat."

"What for?" she asked. "And how do you know that Dolly's dressing-room is in the other flat?"

"Never mind; take me there," said Prelice impatiently. He wished to get the things over as speedily as possible, as he saw how strung up she was; and yet until he was certain how could he accuse Rover? In his heart of hearts, Lord Prelice wished that he might be spared the disagreeable task of accusing Rover at all. But if he did not do so, it was not improbable that Jadby—to further his own ends—might intervene. And it was much better that Jadby, at all costs, should be kept out of the business, since he was not likely to spare either Constance or her husband. "Come, come," cried Prelice impatiently, and seeing that she did not move, "take me to your husband's dressing-room." And Constance led him thither like a woman in a dream.

They left one flat, and crossed the landing to the other. When in the dressing-room, which was luxuriously furnished, Mrs. Rover remained silent and observant at the door, while her friend examined the sanctum of her husband. So mysterious were his words and movements that she began to wish that she had not admitted him, since she did not desire to harm Dolly, objectionable as she found him. But if she could not trust Dorry in all ways, who could she trust?

Meanwhile Prelice peered into a wardrobe, and shook out the many suits it contained; he searched a large wooden press, wherein shirts and underlinen and handkerchiefs and collars were neatly laid out. But in each case he failed to find that for which he hunted, and drew a long breath of relief. Perhaps, after all, Madame Marie was wrong, in spite of the magical powers to which she laid claim. When at his wits' end, Prelice turned to Constance. "Isn't there a cupboard?" he asked.

"Over there," she said, pointing to the hither side of the fireplace. "You must be blind not to see it. Oh, it is unlocked," she added, noting that he hesitated. "Dolly has no secrets. There is nothing in it but old clothes and rubbish, which Trimmer"—this was Mr. Rover's valet—"stows there. Look into the cupboard by all means."

The young man made no reply to the sarcasm, but opened the cupboard of Bluebeard. It was deep and wide, with many pegs at the back and round the sides, upon which hung many clothes, out of date and slightly worn. On the floor was a heterogeneous pile of shabby slippers, discarded boots, sundry medicine bottles, tin boxes of polish, and many odds and ends, showing that this was a bag-o'-rags receptacle for sheer rubbish.

Prelice speedily pulled out all the clothes, and threw them on the floor, while Mrs. Rover shrugged and stared at his zeal. Suddenly he came upon a green silk domino, inside which was sewn the front of a white dress, streaked with thin lines of red velvet. The whole made one garment, easy to slip on and off, which, when worn, would look both like a dress and a domino. This very ingenious garb was hidden behind the discarded clothes, which apparently had not been disturbed for some considerable time, and only by removing all, as Prelice had done, could the domino and its clever fixings have been discovered.

"There," said the young man, holding it up for Mrs. Rover's inspection.

With staring eyes Mrs. Rover drew near, and handled the fabric. "An imitation of the frock and domino I wore at my ball," she gasped; then added after a pause: "A woman never wore this."

"Ned said that the person who waved the bronze cup under his nose to make him insensible was a woman," said Prelice significantly.

"Oh," gasped Constance, taking his meaning at once. "Dolly? It's a lie!"

CHAPTER XX.

MR. ROVER EXPLAINS.

"It's a lie," repeated Constance, seeing that Prelice did not say a word. "Dolly is a little cruel fool, who tyrannises to the full extent of his weak powers. But I don't believe that he killed Agstone."

"Well," drawled Prelice reflectively, "on the face of it, there appears to be no reason, and yet this sham frock is in this rubbish cupboard."

"Dolly can explain," breathed Mrs. Rover hopefully.

"Can he explain why he entered Ned's flat to——"

"He didn't, he didn't—it's impossible, I tell you."

"Constance," declared the other seriously, "you said yourself that Mr. Rover would be glad to see Ned dead, out of sheer jealousy. I quite believe that, and I believe also that he had not the pluck to kill him. But he did his best to get Ned into trouble——"

"By killing Agstone? What rubbish," cried Mrs. Rover feverishly. "If he killed the one he would have murdered the other, and would have chosen Ned in preference."

"Humph! Perhaps with a refinement of cruelty, Rover wished Ned to be hanged, and so slaughtered Agstone, in the hope that Ned would be accused. And accused Ned would have been," cried Prelice decisively, "but that I brought in your guests to see him helpless."

Mrs. Rover twisted her hands in her hair. "It's impossible, I tell you," she lamented, hoping against hope. "Dolly is a fool, he never would be a murderer. He hasn't the pluck. Heaven knows that I have no cause to love him, and that he stands in the way of my happiness. But I tell you, Dorry, that I would have cut off my right hand sooner than have brought you in here to spy out his shame."

"I am glad to hear you say that, Constance," returned Prelice quietly, "for it shows that you have honour if not love, and that, even to secure your happiness with Ned, you will not stoop to injure the man who is your husband. But think, my dear girl, is it not better that I should find this than Jadby?"

"Jadby—the man who loves Mona! What has he got to do with it?"

"Everything," said Prelice tersely; "he wishes to secure Mona as his wife, and will stop at nothing. You may wonder how I came to guess that your husband's dressing-room was in this flat, and how I came to know that this sham dress was hidden behind these clothes. I can explain very shortly. I consulted Madame Marie Eppingrave."

"That fortune-teller," gasped Constance, staring. "I have consulted her myself, and she told me a lot of rubbish. Surely you do not believe what she says in that shoddy room of hers?"

"I am bound to believe," said Prelice dryly, "seeing that the domino with the attached frock-front is here, as she stated. But she may not have told me so by means of occult power, in spite of her claim to exercise the same. In some earthly way—I know not how—she knew where this," he touched the domino, "was to be found. She will tell Captain Jadby, to whom she is much attached, and then he will come here to make what trouble he can. Therefore you can understand that it is better for Rover that I should be the discoverer."

"Yes; I see, I see," murmured Constance, and tottered towards a chair, to fall into it. "Oh, horrible, horrible! But there must be some explanation, Dorry. Think of one—think of one."

Women, as Prelice reflected at the moment, were most extraordinary. Here was a wife who avowedly hated a husband of the tricky effeminate sort, yet when chance placed a weapon against him in her hand, she refused to use it, despite the temptation of thus ridding herself for ever of a marital incubus.

Rover had practically killed her father, he had cheated her into a match which she loathed, and he was doing his best to make her unhappy. In the face of it all, his deceived wife defended him. And this against the strong desire which she had for the man who truly loved her. Truly, women were strange. However, it was not Prelice's business to analyse Mrs. Rover's feelings. What he had to do was to learn the meaning of Rover's hiding the domino in his cupboard, and this he proceeded to do.

"Was Jadby at your ball?" he asked abruptly.

"I never asked him; I don't know him," she replied, clasping her hands tightly; "but you know that owing to the masks, many people—shady people too—were there. Captain Jadby might have come also."

"He did come," said Prelice quickly, "for he was one of the first to unmask when seeing Ned insensible, and to blame me. Certainly he may have come up the stairs opportunely, but since he wore a domino and mask, I am sure that he was at the ball."

"What colour was the domino?"

"Blue. Light blue," rejoined Prelice promptly.

"There were many blue dominos," murmured Constance. "I wonder why this man came to my ball?"

"Ah, that is what we have to find out. But another question." Prelice cleared his throat. "Presuming, as we must, that your husband wore this made-up thing, did he know what you would wear?"

"Yes," assented Mrs. Rover; then started up with a cry and a very pale face. "Oh, Dorry, Dorry, are you going to say that my dress was imitated by him, so that I might be accused?"

"It looks like it," said Prelice reluctantly. "What else could he say?"

"But I can't believe that Dolly would be so wicked," said the poor wife anxiously, "and yet the dress is the same. There is only a front, to be sure. But when worn, anyone would have mistaken him for me. A man always looks taller in women's clothes."

"These are hardly women's clothes."

"Sufficiently like them to deceive anyone. But you said that you spoke to someone wearing a dress like mine. It was not me, Dorry. I should have remembered. Was it Dolly?"

"I never spoke to you or to anyone dressed like you," said Prelice quickly; "I only told you that to get at the truth. But I never expected to hear you say that you had worn the dress. One thing I may tell you," he added, "that the green domino seemed to be ubiquitous. I saw him—presuming your husband is the person—talking and drinking and dancing all over the place."

"I was dancing also," said Constance, "and if Dolly wore a similar dress, it is natural that you should see the frock and domino often. Dolly received my guests unmasked, you know."

"I remember; but later he vanished, and then might have——" Prelice touched the domino significantly. "Still, there is one thing to be said," he added, "how did your husband enter Ned's flat?"

"Don't you remember?" she said, raising her head. "Agstone brought in the lady—Dolly, I suppose—when Ned was in that cataleptic state."

"I forgot that. But who admitted Agstone? What is the matter?"

He asked this because Constance rose suddenly to her feet with a cry of astonishment. "Mr. Haken was at the ball," she said, alarmed.

"I know. I saw him—that is, I recognised him by his chuckle. Well?"

Mrs. Rover sat down again. "You know that Mr. Haken is my godfather," she remarked; and when Prelice nodded, went on. "He was much distressed over my preference for Ned, seeing that I was married, and came to remonstrate with me on the night of the ball."

"Humph," said Prelice coolly, "I wondered why he was at the ball. A most unusual festivity for a dry-as-dust old man like Uncle Simon to beat."

"I gave him the key," said Constance in a low voice.

"The key! What key?"

"The key of Ned's flat."

"Constance, how did you become possessed of the key?"

With a bent head and a hurried low voice, she explained. "Dolly was very cruel to me at times. He even struck me, and I could not strike back at a little rat like that. I told Ned, who was furious, and wanted to frighten Dolly. I prevented him, so that there might be no scandal. Ned then gave me the key of his flat—he had an extra key—and told me if Dolly ever struck me again to come to him. I should not have thought of doing so, but to quieten Ned I consented to take the key."

"What an injudicious thing to do," breathed Prelice, alarmed; "if your husband knew, he might do a lot of damage. But how did Uncle Simon get the key out of you?"

"I told him about it the night of the ball. He got me into a quiet corner to remonstrate, so I explained everything. Mr. Haken was angry at Ned for having given me the key——"

"He was quite right," interposed Prelice. "Ned ought to have had more sense than to do such a mad thing. Go on."

"Mr. Haken insisted upon having the key, and then said that he would go down and see Ned."

Prelice turned suddenly pale. Was this what Horace had warned him against when he advised him to leave the case alone? "Did Uncle Simon go?" he asked in a stifled voice.

"I don't know. He certainly said that he would go down and give Ned back the key, and talk to him about his folly in letting me have it."

Prelice felt very uncomfortable, and his thoughts flew to his aunt with her merry ways. It would be terrible for Lady Sophia if Haken were involved in this dreadful case, and indeed if he were—as seemed apparent from Constance's story—Prelice wished that he had taken the doctor's advice, and had left it well alone. While he was puzzling over this new problem, and trying to find reasons against his uncle's complicity, he heard Constance cry out, and looked up, to see Rover standing in the doorway.

The little stockbroker, dressed to perfection, and overdressed at that, looked more dapper and neat than ever. His face was more colourless, his eyes more plaintive and blue, than they had been in the artificial light in which he had received his wife's guests. Such a mean-looking, bloodless man could scarcely get into a rage; yet a venomous look crept into his eyes as he surveyed his wife and her visitor.

"What is the meaning of this?" he demanded, trying to assume the dignity of an injured husband, which sat very badly on him.

Before Constance could speak, Lord Prelice stepped forward with the domino over his arm, and spread it out. "This is the meaning of my being in your dressing-room, Mr. Rover," he said sharply and perfectly cool. "I found this behind some clothes in yonder cupboard."

"How dare you search into my private affairs?" cried Dolly, standing on tiptoe, and growing red.

"Is it not better that I should do so than the police, Mr. Rover?"

The little man looked genuinely puzzled. "The police? What do you mean by mentioning the police?"

"This dress, this domino, both are an imitation of the dress and domino which your wife wore at the ball. And the lady who was introduced by Agstone to make Shepworth insensible—if you remember the case—was arrayed in this way."

Instead of turning pale, Dolly became redder than ever, and turned like a snake on his wife. "You!" he said savagely, "you entered Shepworth's flat. You dared to——"

"I never was near the flat," said Constance, coming very close to him, and looking down contemptuously from her great height; "and if you dare to hint at such a thing I shall leave you for ever. I have put up with enough from you. Don't drive me too far."

"Mr. Rover has enough to do to defend himself without troubling you, Constance," said Prelice quietly.

Dolly started. "What do you mean?" he asked nervously.

"This sham dress was hidden in your cupboard."

"I never saw it before; I didn't know it was there." Dolly gasped, for he was beginning to scent danger.

"The presumed woman introduced by Agstone was dressed in this," went on Lord Prelice mercilessly. "You hated Shepworth, you wished to get him into trouble, and so——" Prelice stopped. "I leave you to draw your own inferences," he ended.

Dolly trembled, as well he might, for the visitor had drawn up a very good case against him. "I tell you I never saw the dress before," he quavered. "And how did you find it?"

"That is neither here nor there," said Prelice, wishing to shield Constance from the mean wrath of the little man. "Later on the police can explain."

"The police—the police!" Dolly grew as white as a sheet.

Constance laid her hand on his shoulder. "Don't be afraid, Dolly; I do not believe that you killed that man Agstone."

Dolly brushed her hand away, with the snarl of a terrified cat. "Keep yourself to yourself," he snapped, showing his teeth. "You hate me, so you need not defend me."

"I don't love you," answered Constance bitterly. "I have small cause to, considering the way in which you tricked me. All the same, I do not wish to see you get into trouble over a crime which I truly believe you had not pluck enough to commit."

"You are quite right," retorted her husband shamelessly. "I never did have pluck enough to kill a fly, much less a human being. I should have stabbed your lover long ago if I had."

"Shepworth is not Mrs. Rover's lover," said Prelice, quietly.

"He is. She is always howling after him," taunted the venomous little man; "but she sold herself to me, and——"

"And you did not pay the price," said Constance, scornful and still.

"No," Dolly chuckled. "I got the better of you there. But you are my wife now, and I'll make you pay. Shepworth can marry that criminal girl whenever he likes. I hope he will, so as to torment you."

Mrs. Rover's eyes flashed. "Ned shall never marry——" she began, when Prelice made a sign to her to keep the secret of the new engagement, and spoke himself, coldly and sternly.

"Miss Chent's character has been perfectly cleared by her acquittal, Mr. Rover, and if you dare to say a word against her I shall throw you out of the window."

"How brave you are in defending Shepworth's bride," said Dolly, wincing at the flash in Prelice's blue eyes.

"I am," replied the other, not contradicting the mistake under which he saw Dolly laboured; "but as yet you have not proved your innocence."

"There is no need to prove it." Rover's voice whimpered unsteadily. "It is ridiculous to accuse me."

"This dress was hidden in your cupboard," insisted Prelice.

"What of that? This room was used as a place for the coats and hats of the men who came to the ball. Any one of them might have hidden the domino and frock there. I did not. I received my guests unmasked, and afterwards put on a black silk domino."

"Ah!" Prelice took a step forward, "then it was you who appeared in Shepworth's dining-room, and who gave the alarm."

"Yes; it was me. I came down to see Shepworth, and to make it plain to him that he was not to make love any longer to my wife."

"He never did make love since our marriage," flashed out Constance with scorn. "Ned has been true to honour, as I have been."

Prelice raised a hand to stop a promising quarrel between the ill-matched couple.

"Only you, Rover, knew what kind of a dress your wife was to wear at the ball," he said judicially; "only you could have had a similar one made—so as to get her into trouble, I expect."

"Another person knew," cried Dolly, with a flash of triumph in his china-blue eyes. "Yes. I asked Haken to come to the ball to remonstrate with Constance about her love for Shepworth. He is godfather to Constance, as you know. I was aware that Constance would try to dodge Haken, as she didn't want to be scolded, so I described her dress to him that there might be no mistake. Haken was at the ball, Lord Prelice. Why don't you accuse him?"

The young man sneered, although he felt distinctly nervous at the many proofs accumulating against his uncle. "Haken had no reason to get Shepworth into trouble; you had."

"Nothing would have pleased me better; but I should have stopped short of putting my neck into a noose, and I did. I tell you again that I don't know how that domino-frock thing came to be in my cupboard; that I never entered Shepworth's flat, as I certainly could not do so, without a key; and that I was the man in the black silk domino who gave the alarm. And when I entered the flat then, you had left the door open."

All this explanation was perfectly natural, and Dolly gave it with such an air of truth that Prelice was reluctantly obliged to believe him. The young man threw the domino over his shoulder, and moved to the door. "I shall take this with me," he said curtly.

"And see the police?" asked Rover, with twinkling eyes.

"No. Not at present."

"Not at any time, if you value your uncle's liberty."

"What do you mean?" Prelice faced round sharply.

"I mean nothing, as I know nothing. But there is as much evidence against Haken as against me, and if you accuse me I shall accuse him. How will Lady Sophia like a scandal of that sort? Eh?"

Prelice turned away without vouchsafing a reply. "I shall see you again, Constance," he said coldly.

"You shall not see her until Shepworth marries Mona Chent," snapped the venomous little husband; "and I shall move heaven and earth to bring that about."

"You will need to," retorted Prelice, remembering his engagement and thinking how angry Dolly would be when he learned the truth. "And let me tell you, Rover, that if you ill-treat your wife I shall make it my business to thrash you."

Dolly drew back, and snarled, but seemed distinctly afraid. Prelice, with a nod to the unhappy wife, passed from the room, and out of the flat. He felt distinctly nervous about Simon Haken.

CHAPTER XXI.

A POSSIBLE SCANDAL.

After all, Lord Prelice did not return to Hythe on that night, much as he desired to. In view of this new complication, which threatened the domestic peace of Lady Sophia Haken, her nephew decided to remain in London, and give all his energies towards solving the problem. He could not think that Haken had anything to do with the murder of Agstone. In the first place, he had no reason to kill the man; in the second, he did not possess any leaves of the Sacred Herb with which to make Shepworth unconscious. Certainly it was Agstone who had kindled the leaves in the bronze cup, but he must have obtained them from Mr. Haken—presuming he was the disguised lady— since he could have obtained them in no other way. Sir Oliver had possessed a portion of the plant, but had used it in the library when he was murdered, so the old sailor could not have procured the leaves in that direction. Prelice began to wonder if Haken had got the leaves from Madame Marie Eppingrave to execute his purpose.

But then, so far as Prelice knew, his uncle was not acquainted with the Bond Street fortune-teller. And again, he was well acquainted with Dr. Horace, who admitted to possession of the leaves, and, more than this, had actually burnt the Sacred Herb in the New Bailey. Lord Prelice decided first to call upon his uncle in the city, and lay the facts discovered before him, and then to interview Dr. Horace. In these two several ways he might get at the truth. Also, somewhat later, he decided to again speak with Madame Marie, and if possible see her in the presence of Captain Jadby. When that buccaneer learned that Mona was engaged to another man, and that she had inherited the property, he might bow to fate and leave things alone. Finally, Prelice knew that he had a powerful ally in the fortune-teller. From what he had seen of her strong-willed character he guessed that she would stick at nothing to secure as her husband the man with whom she was infatuated.

Bearing all these circumstances in mind, Prelice sent a wire to Mona stating that business detained him in London, and also went to his club to write his first love letter. In this he carefully refrained from mentioning the case, and merely poured out his heart in a passionate dithyramb in honour of his goddess. Mona, for the moment, felt some disappointment when she noted the absence of information regarding Madame Marie, but later confessed that her lover was right. It would never have done for the first letter which had passed between them to be soiled by the sordid tragedy in which she had been implicated. All the same, much as she appreciated Prelice's slightly turgid prose, her heart hungered to learn of his doings relative to the case. She felt that she would not know a happy moment until the truth were made manifest. Then she could become Lady Prelice with a light heart.

The next day Prelice went into the city to see his uncle, and learned that Mr. Haken had gone to Paris for a few days. He was expected back on the morrow, as he already had been absent for some time, so all that his eager nephew could do was to possess his soul in patience. Prelice returned to his club rather disappointed, and there found a telegram waiting for him. It had been sent to his Hythe hotel, and had been repeated on to his club, since it was marked "Urgent." It proved to be from Horace, and asked Prelice to come up at once. "Be at my house at three in the afternoon. Important," said the wire.

"I wonder what this means?" Prelice asked himself uneasily, and fretted over the matter until the time came for him to go to Rutland Square.

There was no getting over the fact that the mystery of this case was telling on Prelice's strong nerves.

Nor was his uneasiness diminished when he found that Dr. Horace was not alone. With him were Captain Jadby and Madame Marie Eppingrave, both of whom appeared to be on very good terms with their host. As usual, the room was untidy with its litter of curiosities, but Prelice managed to find a seat with his back to the light. This he did so as to keep his face well in the shade, as he had a premonition that there was about to be a duel of words. Indeed, the first whispered remark of Horace hinted at a storm about to break.

"You silly ass," grumbled the doctor in his beard as he went forward to welcome his guest, "why couldn't you leave things alone as I told you to? Now all the fat is on the fire with a vengeance."

Prelice shrugged his shoulders with a carelessness which he was far from feeling, and saluted Madame Marie with a bow. Of Captain Jadby, who stood fidgeting by the window, he took no notice. The buccaneer noticed the omission, and resented it. "English manners, I suppose," sneered the half-caste pointedly.

Prelice sat down calmly, and took up the challenge. "Considering our last meeting, when you treacherously fired on my friend, you can hardly expect me to behave courteously."

"I wish I had killed him," flashed out Jadby viciously.

"I quite believe that; but you did not harm him in the least," retorted Prelice, lying bravely to defend Ned, and to annoy the captain.

"I wounded him in the arm," snarled Jadby. "Didn't I, Marie?"

"I certainly saw that Mr. Shepworth was slightly hurt," replied the fortune-teller; "in a trance, of course."

"Ah!" replied Prelice negligently, "your trances are not always reliable, Madame."

"I think you have found that one is, at least," she replied in her turn, and very significantly.

"What does Captain Jadby think?" asked Prelice genially. He felt sure that the woman had not dared to risk the buccaneer's rage by explaining what she had said.

"Madame Marie told me that she went into a trance on your account," said Jadby, taking a chair, sullenly, "but, of course, she did not remember what she said, and could not explain to me."

"Since Madame is certain that this especial trance is reliable," was Prelice's retort, "she must remember something."

"Oh, the deuce take your chatter," shouted Horace ruffling his shaggy red hair, in a high state of irritation. "I didn't ask you here to waste my time in drivel."

"In that case, as my time is also valuable, I had better go."

"No, no, confound you," said Horace crossly, and seeing that Prelice knew well how to treat his humours. "Madame here, and Jadby, wish to speak to you seriously."

"I fail to see upon what subject."

"Upon the subject of Miss Chent," cried the buccaneer savagely.

"I decline to discuss an absent lady," said Prelice coolly.

"You are engaged to her."

"Am I indeed?"

"But you sha'n't marry her."

"Won't I! See here!" Prelice rose, very tall and very straight and very cool-headed, "if you persist in going like this, Captain Jadby, I shall be compelled to twist your neck."

"English manners," sneered the half-caste again.

"Not at all. Colonial manners, South Sea manners if you will, and very necessary manners for dealing with a ruffian such as you are."

"I'll kill you for this," muttered Jadby, sinking back into his chair.

"With your little gun?" taunted Prelice pleasantly. "I hope you'll shoot straighter. I never saw so rotten a shot."

"I can do more than shoot."

"Yes—you can bark."

"And bite too. See here, I asked you here to tell you, in the presence of Horace, that if you don't stop meddling with things which do not concern you, I'll disgrace your uncle."

Prelice never winced. He had a kind of idea that something of this sort was forthcoming, and merely laughed aggravatingly. "Which uncle?" said he, calmly. "I have two or three."

"Mr. Simon Haken."

"Oh indeed." Prelice turned to Horace. "Are you on my side, or on the side of these blackmailers?" he demanded.

Madame Marie arose furiously. "I am not a blackmailer," she cried, and her deep-toned voice became shrill with anger. "I did not want to say anything, and if Felix does not swear to give up this girl, I shall refuse to speak out."

"No," snapped Jadby, with a fierce glance; at which, strange to say, the courageous woman looked cowed. "You shall speak as I direct."

"Are you on my side or on theirs?" Prelice asked Horace again.

"On yours, hang you," snarled the ugly little man. "And if I were not, you would find yourself in Queer Street, I can tell you."

Prelice took no notice of this outburst, but turned to the woman. "Are you against me?" he demanded.

"I am neutral," she retorted uneasily.

"I see; and Jadby there is an open enemy. Well, now that I understand the situation, perhaps you will let me know how Mr. Haken can be disgraced by you two, or you three."

"We can accuse him of murder," said Jadby, choking with anger at the exasperating coolness of the young aristocrat.

"Good. Go on."

"Of two murders?" spat out the half-caste.

"Better and better. Ha! I understand then that you, Captain Jadby, and you, Madame Marie, accuse Mr. Haken of killing Sir Oliver Lanwin and Steve Agstone?"

"Yes," snapped the captain; and "Yes," breathed the woman, very pale.

Prelice looked quietly at them. "Prove these charges," he said.

"One moment," said Dr. Horace, getting out his German pipe. "Remember, Prelice, that this business is none of my bringing about. I warned you against meddling in the case, and you would not take my warning. You have only yourself to thank for what is coming."

"I am perfectly ready to take the responsibility of my actions," was the stiff retort of the young man; and he turned to Jadby. "Go on!"

The captain, bursting with venom, was only too pleased to relieve himself in a torrent of words. "Before my father, Sir Oliver, died, he frequently talked to me about the estate—sought my counsel, in fact. I thus learned that Mr. Haken, although supposed to be a wealthy man, was in difficulties owing to disastrous speculation. He asked Sir Oliver to lend him fifty thousand pounds to tide over a crisis, and this my father refused to do. Naturally Mr. Haken was very angry——"

"Probably!" put in Prelice coolly; "but what you say does not prove that Mr. Haken killed Sir Oliver."

"Let me speak now," said Horace rapidly. "I was the sole possessor of the Sacred Herb, which, if you remember, Prelice, I brought from Easter Island. I gave some to Haken, who desired to get the same for Sir Oliver. You see," pursued the traveller, "Haken knew that Lanwin was much interested in occult studies, so thought to tempt him to lend the necessary fifty thousand pounds by getting him this rare herb, which, as you know, produces a trance."

"I see." Prelice nodded. "Then Mr. Haken confessed to you that he desired the loan of this money?"

"He did, saying that his affairs were in a bad way. With the gift of the Sacred Herb he hoped to soften Sir Oliver's heart, which was somewhat hard where money matters were concerned."

"I never knew that Mr. Haken was aware of Lanwin's inclination to the occult," said Prelice quietly.

"He was in a way," said Madame Marie suddenly, and taking up the story; "but, of course, I told him more, being very friendly with Sir Oliver, as you know. Mr. Haken was superstitious himself—as the saying goes—and frequently consulted me about stocks and shares."

"What?" Prelice looked incredulous. "Do you mean to tell me that a hard-headed man like Mr. Haken consulted you?"

"He did; and I was enabled to serve him by my powers. I understood, Lord Prelice, that you believed in the Occult World."

"I do," rejoined the young man dryly, "because I have had considerable experience and possess imagination. But Mr. Haken——"

"He believed also," interrupted the fortune-teller quickly, "and came to me for advice. It was I who recommended him to apply to his old friend, Sir Oliver, for the fifty thousand pounds. When Sir Oliver refused, I told Mr. Haken that he should get some of the Sacred Herb from Dr. Horace, and give it to Sir Oliver, in the hope that the gift would make Sir Oliver hand over the money."

"How did you know that Dr. Horace had the herb?" asked Prelice sharply.

"Madame Marie and I were acquainted in Samoa," put in the traveller, "and when we met in London I told her that I had succeeded in getting the famous trance herb of Easter Island. She asked me for some leaves to use in her business, and I declined."

"Why, when you gave the same to Sir Oliver?" inquired Prelice.

"Because I wished to keep the herb to myself," said Horace, his rugged face growing dark; "but when Haken asked me for it to get money out of Lanwin I gave it readily. I hated Lanwin. He thwarted me in Tahiti—it matters not how —and he treated my brother Steve like a dog. I knew that Haken would lose the fifty thousand, and wished Lanwin to see the last of the cash. I would have ruined Lanwin if I could."

"This is quite a new light on your character, Horace," said Prelice, with uplifted eyebrows. "However, I understand that for your own purposes, which you have so kindly set forth, you gave the herb to Lanwin."

"Not personally," retorted the doctor, scowling; "I gave it to Haken, and he passed it to Madame Marie."

"And it was I who presented the herb to Sir Oliver, after retaining some leaves for my own use," said the woman coolly. "It was on the night of the murder that Mr. Haken came down to see Sir Oliver."

"Can you swear to that?" demanded Prelice, watching her.

"I can," she assured him emphatically. "Mr. Haken knew that I was to give the herb to Sir Oliver on that night, and came down so as to strike the iron while it was hot, by explaining how he had procured the herb from Dr. Horace. Mr. Haken came in quietly by the window when I was conversing with Sir Oliver in the library. That was about nine o'clock. Agstone entered to close the windows—they were not shuttered, remember—and also saw Mr. Haken. At five minutes after nine—if you recollect the evidence I gave in Court—I went to bed, leaving Mr. Haken alone with Sir Oliver——" She paused.

"And then?" questioned Prelice.

"There is nothing more to say," she replied coldly. "Mr. Haken was in the library with a man from whom he desired to get money. It was, I believe, refused; and then Mr. Haken murdered Sir Oliver, afterwards burning the Sacred Herb, about the time Miss Chent entered the room. Needless to say, before she entered, Mr. Haken had gone."

"A very pretty story," said Prelice, quite unmoved. "That is one crime no doubt; but the other?"

"I can explain," said Jadby, enraged at the young man's coolness. "From Madame Marie I learned that Mr. Haken was going to Mrs. Rover's ball to see his goddaughter and Shepworth, and——"

"How did you know that?" asked Prelice, turning to the woman.

"Mrs. Rover consulted me occultly about her marriage, and confessed amongst other things that Mr. Haken was her godfather. I saw that Mrs. Rover was in that reckless state which might lead to a scandal, and I told everything to Mr. Haken. He resolved to go to the masked ball and remonstrate with Mrs. Rover, and afterwards with Mr. Shepworth. I told Captain Jadby."

"And I went there," said the captain quickly, "because I knew that Haken had killed Sir Oliver, and wished to see him, in order to get some money."

"To blackmail him, in fact," said Prelice coolly. "So you were the Continental individual whom my uncle was to meet."

"Yes. But he was too clever for me. He came in an ordinary domino, and afterwards changed to a green one with a dress similar to that of Mrs. Rover's."

"How can you be sure?"

"Because I was hunting for Mr. Haken, and heard him chuckle. For the moment I fancied that he was Mrs. Rover owing to the dress, but when he chuckled I guessed it was Mr. Haken. He eluded me, however, but not before I had smelt the perfume of the tuberose, which the Sacred Herb gives out. When you discovered the crime, Lord Prelice, I guessed that Mr. Haken, disguised as Mrs. Rover, so as to implicate her with Shepworth, should there be trouble, had gone down and murdered Agstone."

"How did Agstone come there? How did Mr. Haken know he would be there?"

Jadby leaned back coolly. "I cannot answer either of those questions," he said calmly; "perhaps Mr. Haken can."

There was a few moments of silence, which Prelice broke. "Well," he asked, rising, "and what are your terms for silence?"

"You must give up Miss Chent to me," said the captain, with a glance of gratification, for he fancied that Prelice was yielding. "I shall marry her, and then we shall live at the Grange."

"Ah, but you see it will not be your property," said Prelice politely.

Jadby sprang to his feet. "Not my property?"

"No. I fear that Dr. Horace has not informed you that Agstone brought the will, leaving everything to Miss Chent, to him, and that he has restored it to the lady. You are a pauper, Captain Jadby. Miss Chent has the money, and shortly she will have me as her husband."

Jadby took scarcely any notice of Prelice, important as was the matter he talked about. "Horace," he cried, glaring viciously, "you have played me false."

"I never intended to play you true," said Horace contemptuously.

"Then I shall ruin Haken," cried Jadby, at his wits' end with sheer rage.

"Do so," said Prelice, walking to the door. "I decline to be blackmailed. Good-day." And he walked out.

After him came Madame Marie before he could descend the stairs. She gripped him by the arm earnestly, and looked into his face. Prelice could hear the captain and Horace quarrelling desperately in the room he had left, but waited patiently until the woman spoke.

"Swear to me," panted Madame Marie, "that Jadby will never, never marry that girl, and I will help you."

"In what way?"

"For one thing, I shall stop Felix from denouncing your uncle."

"Pooh! That's bluff!"

"Indeed, indeed it isn't," said the woman passionately. "What I have told you is perfectly true. Your uncle will be in great danger if Felix speaks. But swear to save him from that girl, and I shall stop all trouble about Mr. Haken."

"I swear," said Prelice quietly; "especially as it is the dearest wish of my life to make Miss Chent my wife."

"Beware—oh, be careful!" implored Madame Marie, clinging to Prelice. "I know that Felix is desperate; he is dangerous."

"I am not afraid of him. He cannot hurt me."

"But he may hurt her," cried Madame Marie. "If anything goes wrong, come to me. I can help you."

"I shall do so; but why do you work against the man you love?"

"Because I can secure him in no other way. I want him to leave England to marry me. While he stops here, and is infatuated with Miss Chent, there is no hope. Hark! Felix is calling. Remember, we are outwardly enemies, but inwardly friends. You promise." On this she produced a small golden crucifix.

Considering the exigencies of the case, Prelice was willing to promise anything, even to a doubtfully good woman, such as Madame Marie appeared to be. But the production of the crucifix took him aback.

"I give you my word," he said, stiffly.

"I want your oath," she retorted. "Swear on this, to aid me to marry Felix, or I do nothing."

There was no help for it, and Prelice had to make allowance for Madame Marie's flamboyant, foreign way of exaggeration. "I swear to help you," he said, and kissed the crucifix.

CHAPTER XXII.

THE UNEXPECTED.

"Don't talk nonsense to me," cried Lady Sophia, rapping the dinner-table with her lorgnette. "The idea is too ridiculous for words. To marry a girl out of gaol? Monstrous! Your father would turn in his grave, and *he* wasn't very particular."

Lord Prelice was dining with his lively relative, when this speech was made at the tail-end of a very excellent meal. Haken had duly returned from Paris on the day after the interview of Prelice with Dr. Horace and his two friends. On finding a note from his nephew stating that he desired to speak on an important subject, Mr. Haken had responded with a wire inviting the young man to dinner. Lady Sophia had also arrived in town from Folkstone, and explained to Prelice, when he appeared, that she would do nothing for Mona. This remark led to a request for explanations, which Lady Sophia was only too anxious to afford, and the presence of footmen and butler at the dinner-table alone kept her from raging at Prelice all the time he was eating. Haken, looking more dried-up than ever, sat at the foot of the table—his wife invariably took the top—and chuckled at intervals. He had not yet heard what Prelice wished to speak about, and was waiting until Lady Sophia retired to the drawing-room, a thing she seemed disinclined to do at present, so rabid was she against her nephew.

Having made the above remark, she waited for a reply; but as Prelice merely crumbled what was left of his bread, and said nothing, she launched out again with a peremptory question. "Do you, or do you not, wish your father to turn in his grave?"

"My dear aunt," replied Prelice very distinctly, "I wish the corpse to take the position it finds the most comfortable."

"Oh!" cried Lady Sophia, outraged in her deepest feelings, "oh, that I should live to hear my late brother called an 'it.' Have you no reverence, Prelice?"

"Not so much reverence, as I have patience," he replied, very bored.

"Ah." Lady Sophia hugged herself. "I might have expected that. You never, never will face the truth."

"What is the truth?" asked Haken, his eyes twinkling, and putting the question of Pilate.

"The truth," said his wife majestically, "is that Prelice must have been changed at nurse. He has not the feelings of his ancestors."

"I have their gout, however," said Prelice humorously. "What possible objection can you have to my marrying. Aunt Sophia?"

"It's not the marriage itself I object to, Prelice, but to the bride you choose. You know that well."

"There won't be a prettier bride in the Three Kingdoms than Mona."

"I am quite sure there won't," said his aunt spitefully, "if she only gets as far as the altar."

"The communion-rails, you mean. I'll do my best to bring her there."

"Not in my presence, Prelice."

"All right. We'll have a quiet wedding."

"A quiet wedding," raged Lady Sophia, "and with such a notorious girl as the bride. Why, all the——"

"Aunt Sophia," interrupted Prelice, growing restive under these insults, "permit me to remind you that Miss Chent is to be my wife, and that I am quite capable of managing my own affairs."

Lady Sophia rose, and swept to the door. "I'm sorry for you. I am truly sorry for you," said she with scorn, and throwing back her head.

"Thank you," replied her nephew meekly, and politely holding open the door; "the same to you, and many of them."

"Oh, Prelice, how I should love to box your ears!" And unable to say anything worse, Lady Sophia disappeared in a royal rage. Prelice did not feel very amiable himself for having been baited unnecessarily, and closed the door with a bang, which said volumes. Then he returned to the disordered dinner-table, poured himself out a glass of port, caught his uncle's twinkling eyes, and laughed in spite of his irritation. Haken nodded approvingly.

"That's better than banging the door," he said, stretching his legs in a genial fashion. "Have a cigar?"

Prelice accepted one of the best, and lighted up, while his host followed his example. When the blue smoke was curling round the old head and the young, and the glasses were full, they dismissed the trouble of Lady Sophia by common consent. Haken looked interrogatively at the young man. "Well," he demanded quietly, "and what have you to say to me? If I know anything of young men, you wish to borrow money." And ended with a chuckle at his joke, knowing the wealth of his nephew.

"And if I know anything of old men," said Prelice coolly, "I should advise them to borrow from their relatives instead of from strangers."

Haken was somewhat startled by this speech, which was as rude a one as Prelice could well have made. But he felt irritable, and wished to smash, rather than break the ice. "What are you talking about?" asked the elder man cautiously.

"About fifty thousand pounds."

"A very tidy little sum," said Haken, quite composed. "I required that precise sum myself a month or so ago, to tide over a crisis."

"Did you get it?"

"Not from Oliver Lanwin," retorted the city man dryly.

Prelice jumped up from his chair, and let his cigar fall. He was far from expecting that Haken would own up so quickly. Leaning forward, he placed his hands on the table, and looked straight into the withered face before him. "What do you mean?"

"Don't burn the carpet with your cigar," said Haken irrelevantly; and when Prelice stooped to pick it up he continued. "I should rather ask you that, my boy. You know something, or else you wouldn't talk of my borrowing, and of the exact sum which I required."

"I know a great deal," said the young man, and sat down.

Haken settled himself luxuriously in his chair. "Let us hear all about it, my boy," said he. "Is your glass filled; your cigar all right? Good. Fire away. I am in a mood for listening."

"Are you in the mood to face danger?" questioned the other man, astonished at this coolness.

Haken wrinkled his brows as a monkey does. "Danger?" he repeated. "And from whom?"

"From Madame Marie, from Captain Jadby, and from Dr. Horace."

"I agree as to the first two," said Haken, perfectly calm, "but I am sure that the last-named will not harm me in any way."

Prelice reflected. "You are right," he said thoughtfully. "Horace is your friend and mine. But the others——"

"Yes. I know all about the others," interrupted Haken in a level voice. "They have their own fish to fry, and are not particular how big a blaze they make to fry them. Of course, I expected you would find out."

"Did you? And why?"

"Why," Haken pushed back his chair, and rose with a chuckle, "didn't Sophia inveigle you into helping young Shepworth and the girl he was engaged to? You could scarcely do that and not cross my trail."

"Why didn't you confess to me?" asked Prelice, much vexed.

"Confess what? That I murdered Lanwin?"

"And that you stabbed Agstone."

"The deuce." Haken started at this last remark. "They accuse me of that, do they? I didn't know that they would go so far. Well," he looked very straightly at his nephew, and with very bright eyes, "you have no doubt heard what these people have had to say, and no doubt they have manufactured good fiction out of certain facts. My character, I take it, is as black as a crow."

"Blacker, if anything."

"No doubt. Well, and what do you say?"

"I say that Jadby and Madame Marie, and possibly Horace, are liars."

Haken walked round the table, and placed his hand on his nephew's shoulder. "Do you believe that I am guilty?"

"Certainly not."

"Why. On what grounds?"

Prelice laughed. He had always doubted the guilt of his uncle, ever since the telling of it in Rutland Square. Now he was sure that, however cleverly the story had been put together, Simon Haken would be quite capable of reconstructing it so as to prove his innocence. He therefore answered, with a laugh: "On the grounds that you are much too clever a man to commit a murder without making things much safer than they appear to be in this instance."

"Thank you," said Haken simply, and after a friendly squeeze of Prelice's shoulder he returned to his seat. A weaker man would have required a more emotional denial, but Haken was too strong and too business-like to trouble about sentiment. "You see," he remarked, when again in his chair, "it would not have suited me to murder Lanwin."

"No," assented Prelice, tickled by the remark; "murder in this country is attended with certain disadvantages."

Haken chuckled, and drank a second glass of port. In spite of his nonchalance, he was more nervous than he chose to admit. "Now tell me how our friends bring home the crime to me, and why they told you about the business."

"I shall tell you the whole case from the beginning," said Prelice after a pause. "My connection with it began when Aunt Sophia came to bully me into doing something."

Haken nodded sympathetically. "When your aunt interferes there is generally trouble. Well?"

Prelice settled himself to work, and recounted the whole story, ending with his parting from Madame Marie on the stairs of Horace's house, and the oath upon the crucifix. Haken smoked quietly while the narrative proceeded, merely raising his eyebrows when he heard how ingeniously the fortune-teller and Jadby proved his guilt. When Prelice concluded Haken chuckled, and passed the port. "Have another glass, my boy," he said quietly; "you must be dry over that talking."

All the same, Prelice noted that the perspiration was beading the old man's brow, and that he was exercising considerable will power to keep himself in hand. While Prelice sipped his fresh glass of wine, Haken walked up and down the length of the dining-room, keeping silent. After quite five minutes he began to talk, still walking steadily.

"I should have come to you for that money," he said in a conversational tone, "only that I don't like taking advantage of my wife's relatives. I needed fifty thousand pounds badly, and when Lanwin refused to lend the money, I scarcely knew what to do. However, the cash turned up unexpectedly, although I had to make a sacrifice to get it. I calculate that I shall have to pay cent, per cent, for that money. However, it is worth it. The worst is over, and everything is going swimmingly. I shall have no further trouble, so don't look glum, Prelice."

"Oh, I'm not afraid of your finances," said the young man quickly, "as I know your head for figures, and know also that the soundest men in the city have their money troubles on occasions. But I am thinking of your being in the power of these wretches. That is," added Prelice, correcting himself, "in the power of Jadby. I don't think that Madame Marie is so bad, and Horace is gruff, but honest."

"Oh, Horace is all right, but Marie is as bad as they make them."

"Nonsense! She wants to help me."

"Selfishly. In order to secure Jadby she must make use of you, otherwise you could go hang. But I must tell you that portions of her story, and Jadby's story, and that of Horace are correct. I got the herb in the way you heard, and I did go down to Hythe to see Lanwin."

"Were you in the library when Madame Marie went to bed?"

"I was," admitted Haken coolly; "but by that time Lanwin had not commenced his hanky-panky with the herb. I asked him straight out to lend the money. He refused, with a word or two of abuse; so I walked away, and back to Folkstone, where I was stopping. There was no row, as I disdained to reply to Lanwin's coarse language. Madame Marie left the library at five minutes after nine; by fifteen minutes past I left it also, and by the window, on my way to Folkstone. What happened after I left I cannot say."

"What was Lanwin doing when you left?"

"Fiddling with his herbs. He came and shut the window after I had gone, and shouted out a word or two as I departed."

"Do you suspect anyone of the crime?"

Haken shrugged his shoulders. "Unless it was Jadby—no," he replied thoughtfully. "Jadby was in London, and did not return until later. You heard his evidence in Court."

"Then Agstone must be guilty."

"Agstone certainly hated his master," said Haken.

"Why," Prelice looked astonished, "I understood that Agstone was devoted to Sir Oliver."

"So Lanwin said, and everyone believed. But the fact is—as I learned from Madame Marie—that Agstone was Lanwin's slave. Sir Oliver knew something about him, which he used as a threat, and so kept him in bondage. Lanwin was not a pleasant character," ended the city man, twirling his cigar.

"Oh," Prelice sunk his chin in his breast, and thought. He knew well enough that so far as the evidence of the knife was concerned, Agstone could not possibly be guilty. Nevertheless, since Agstone had brought the missing will to his brother—and the assassin could only have procured that will—it would seem that the old sailor, after all, had struck the blow. But why had he tried to put the blame on Mona both by placing the knife in her hand and by accusing her? "Did Madame Marie say that Agstone hated Mona?" asked Prelice, raising his head.

"No! On the contrary, I understand that Agstone liked Miss Chent because she was kind to him. Sir Oliver, however, was of a jealous disposition, and Agstone was afraid to display his liking."

"Do you suppose that Madame Marie herself killed Lanwin?"

"Certainly not; she had nothing to gain by doing so, and, moreover, lost a valuable client by Lanwin's death. Marie is fond of money too. She wants to make all she can, so as to marry Jadby. She is strangely infatuated with that rascal."

"Jadby is good-looking in a way," replied Prelice. "Humph! It seems to me that we are as far as ever from learning the truth."

"No doubt," assented his uncle; "still, one thing is certain, that I did not kill Lanwin. As to Agstone——" he hesitated.

"You are not going to confess that you killed him?" said Prelice, with a wry smile.

Haken chuckled. "No; I never tell unnecessary lies. But I certainly saw him dead and Shepworth insensible."

"Oh!" Prelice was quite unmoved, "so you did make use of that key?"

"No," said Haken again, and unexpectedly; "there was no need to. I went down, intending to remonstrate with Shepworth on behalf of Rover, and found that the door was unfastened. I entered, and saw—what you saw—so at once I came upstairs, reclosing the door as I had found it."

"Why didn't you give the alarm?"

"What, with Jadby hanging about, already intending to blackmail me for Lanwin's death? I should have given myself into the hands of the Philistines with a vengeance had I raised the alarm."

"I see. So Jadby was the Continental swell whom you told me that you were to meet?"

"Yes. He insisted upon seeing me at the ball. Why he chose such a place I don't know, and how he got to the ball I can't imagine."

"Oh, that was easy. Remember the masks. Jadby had only to assume a mask and domino, and could slip in easily. But this dress——"

"I didn't wear it," interrupted Haken quickly; "woman's disguise is the last thing I should think of assuming, with my figure and face, to say nothing of my age. It's my opinion——" He paused.

"Well, well?" questioned Prelice impatiently.

"That Madame Marie wore the dress herself."

"But how could she come to the ball? Constance never invited her."

"You answered that question yourself a few minutes ago with reference to Jadby. Madame Marie could easily have slipped on a mask and domino, and have come to the ball to meet Jadby. Probably she wore that dress to implicate Constance, and concealed it in Rover's dressing-room to bring him into the matter. Remember, Madame Marie herself told you where the sham dress was to be found."

"Yes!" assented Lord Prelice thoughtfully; "but how did Madame Marie learn what kind of a costume Constance would wear?"

"Rover told her. Yes! he came to me about Constance's love for Shepworth, and told me that in his efforts to gain his wife's love he had gone to see if Madame Marie could give him a philter of sorts. Infernally silly to act in that way now-a-days. Madame Marie told him to learn the exact costume which Constance would wear at the ball—you see, Constance was keeping her style of dress a secret even from her husband—so that Rover could watch if she went down to see Shepworth. Rover learned about the dress from Constance's dressmaker, and told me, and also told Madame Marie. It was easy then for Madame Marie to get the frock imitated and slip down to Shepworth's flat. By doing that she managed to kill Agstone, to implicate young Shepworth, and to throw the blame on Constance. A confoundedly clever woman is Marie Eppingrave," ended Haken, chuckling.

Lord Prelice rose thoughtfully. "The further we go into this case the more complicated does it become," he remarked. "Certainly Agstone, knowing Madame Marie, would bring her into the room; while not knowing Constance, he would not. Then again, Madame Marie knew about the herb, and Constance did not. It would seem——" He stopped, and walked abruptly to the door. "I must sleep on this," he said wearily.

"But you know that I am innocent now that I have explained," said the old man, following, and speaking anxiously. He liked Prelice, and did not wish him to have a bad opinion of his uncle by marriage.

Prelice grasped Haken's hand. "I believed in your innocence before you gave the explanation," he replied. "Wish my aunt good-night for me, Uncle Simon. I am going home to think over things."

"Your aunt will be annoyed."

"Not so much as I will be, if I listen to her scolding. Good-night."

Haken grumbled a trifle at being left to explain to Lady Sophia, but on going to the drawing-room he found that his wife had gone to a concert in Park Lane. Thus he was saved the trouble of making things smooth, and went to bed very thankfully. Haken was not a young man, and the interview with Prelice had shaken him greatly.

Meanwhile Prelice himself had driven straight to his rooms, and had gone immediately to bed, thinking that he could better argue out the case as it stood when lying down than when sitting or standing. But he was so weary with talk and with the strain of the last few days that he fell sound asleep before he could arrive at any conclusion regarding the guilt or innocence of Madame Marie. It seemed to him that he had only been resting for five minutes when his valet woke him in the morning at nine o'clock; woke him also in a most unpleasant manner by presenting a telegram. Prelice, half awake, tore open the orange-hued envelope, but he was wide awake when he finished reading the news it contained. The wire proved to be from Mrs. Blexey.

"Miss Mona has disappeared."

That was all the wire said, but it was quite enough.

CHAPTER XXIII.

HELPLESS.

At Lanwin Grange all was confusion. About twelve o'clock on the previous day Mona had left the house with the intention of going to Folkstone to interview Lady Sophia. She was unaware that this formidable personage had returned to London, and wished to explain how much she loved Lord Prelice, so that Lady Sophia might offer no opposition to the marriage. From the time that she had left the Grange she had not been seen. Mrs. Blexey was not alarmed until her young mistress failed to return to dinner, as she had promised. Then the housekeeper had sent a groom with a dog-cart over to the Folkstone hotel at which Lady Sophia was supposed to be stopping. The man had returned with the information that Miss Chent had not been seen at the hotel, and that Lady Sophia Haken had gone back to London. It was then that Mrs. Blexey grew terrified.

"Whatever will his lordship and Mr. Shepworth say?" she wailed. "They will be fit to take the skin off me."

The butler advised an immediate wire to both the young gentlemen; but Mrs. Blexey, hoping to save the situation, refused to listen, alleging that perhaps Miss Mona, walking across the Downs towards Folkstone, had lost herself. But when the night passed, and still the girl did not put in an appearance, the housekeeper was compelled to send telegrams to Prelice and the barrister. The two friends, oddly enough, met at Charing-Cross Station to go down by the same train. Naturally they secured a first-class carriage in order to talk over the disappearance of Miss Chent.

"What do you think about it?" asked Shepworth anxiously.

"It is a new move on the part of that blackguard Jadby," replied the other between his teeth.

"But would he dare?"

"He would dare anything to gain his ends. He tried to shoot you, and now he has kidnapped Mona."

"Are you sure of that, Dorry?"

"What other explanation can there be, Ned? Mona has not returned, and she never went near the Piccadilly Hotel in Folkstone, where my aunt has been staying. I expect after our meeting at Horace's this scoundrel came down, and watched for an opportunity to get Mona by herself. Then he kidnapped her."

"But he could not do that alone and in England."

"No doubt he had help of some sort, and the Downs are lonely. Besides, he threatened at Horace's to do me an injury, and what greater one could he inflict than to carry off Mona? Also, Madame Marie hinted that Jadby would strike at me through the girl I love. By the way, I have sent a special messenger to bring that lady down to Hythe."

"For what reason Dorry?"

"Madame Marie," said Prelice quietly, "may be a bad woman; Uncle Simon says that she is. All the same, she loves that Jadby beast, and will move heaven and earth to secure him. If he has carried off Mona—as I suspect— Madame Marie will help me."

"How can she?"

"She can go into a trance, and see where Mona is hidden."

Shepworth raised his eyebrows. "Dorry, do you really believe in these magical things?"

"There is no magic about them," retorted Lord Prelice bluntly, "save to people who can't see farther than their noses. Everything works under well-defined laws both in the seen and in the unseen worlds. It only needs a person to learn and understand these laws to work what the unthinking call miracles."

"And you believe that this woman——"

"Yes, I do," interrupted Prelice impatiently; "you have only to look into Madame Marie's eyes to see that she has the Sight. She may be a bad lot, as Uncle Simon says, but there are Black Magicians as well as White ones. But there," he ended abruptly, "I am only talking in High Dutch to you."

"I confess that I am not superstitious," said Shepworth thoughtfully.

"Occult powers have nothing to do with superstition," said Prelice in a calm and decisive way. "Everything is law, as I tell you, and when the law is known, certain things can be done. By means of the Sacred Herb, the spirit— that is the astral body—can part from the flesh and go where it will. When Madame Marie arrives at the Grange, I shall make her help me in that way. She will be quite willing, if only to thwart Jadby. But there," Prelice again brushed away his words with a gesture, "I have explained enough to a sceptic such as you are. Let us talk of other matters. What do you intend to do about Constance?"

Shepworth coloured, and looked out of the window at the landscape, which was flying past, dream-fashion. "I do not like to discuss Mrs. Rover even to you, Prelice," he said stiffly.

"Ned," answered his friend, "don't be a fool If you had confided in me when we first met in Geddy's Restaurant a great deal of trouble might have been avoided. Besides, you told Mona, why should you not tell me?" And Prelice waited for a reply.

"I only told Mona that I loved Constance," said Shepworth, after an uneasy pause; "naturally I didn't like to say too much."

"I quite understand. But the fact remains that you love Constance, and that Constance loves you. She is a married woman."

"Unfortunately for me," said Shepworth bitterly.

"And unfortunately for her also, seeing that she is tied to a man who hates her more than he loves her. Rover's pride is wounded, Ned, by his wife's preference for you, and he'll make trouble."

"I see that, and I wish to avoid trouble for Constance's sake. But what can I do?"

"You can move from Alexander Mansions for one thing, and take a trip to the

176

Colonies for another. Rover may die."

"There is no chance."

"Pooh!" said Prelice contemptuously, "the man's a bloodless little rat. And look at those dilated eyes of his—like those of a fierce rabbit, if there is such a thing in nature. I shouldn't be at all surprised if Rover pegged out unexpectedly. He doesn't motor, nor golf, nor bicycle, nor shoot—in fact, he avoids all excitements. So Aunt Sophia told me. That shows how weak his heart is. Depend upon it——"

"No, no!" said Shepworth impatiently; "even for Constance. I do not want to build my future happiness on a man's death. I shall take your advice, and go to Australia for a few years. It will be better for me and for Constance, since here we can only look at one another, and dare not meet, much less speak, save in the presence of others. But there has been no scandal since Rover's marriage, and so far as I'm concerned there shall be no scandal. There, we have talked enough."

"Poor old chap," said Prelice, leaning forward to shake Shepworth's hand, "you're having a deuce of a time. Your Karma——"

"Oh, hang your theosophy!"

"Very good. One wastes words in speaking to the deaf. Besides, the matter of Mona's rescue is more important than anything else. Hang it, how slow this beastly train is!"

This was hard on the engine driver, who was doing his best, and actually was sending along the train at top speed. But had Prelice been mounted on a flying bombshell he would have found its speed too slow, since his thoughts, outstripping all other means of locomotion, had flown long since to the house in the hollow.

However, the longest rivers get to the sea in the end, and the young men found themselves on Hythe platform. A motor car—ordered in advance by wire—waited them, and they were soon buzzing upward to Lanwin Grange. On arriving at the great mansion they were met by Mrs. Blexey, all tears and lamentation. But Prelice, in his stiff military manner, soon reduced her to common-sense talk, and learned that although every inquiry had been made, and every possible place searched, as yet Mona had not been found. She had disappeared as completely as a dewdrop does in the ocean. Even the local police could do nothing.

"Which is just like the local police," growled Prelice. "I say, Ned, you take the car and scout over the Downs. Somewhere about there Jadby may hold her prisoner."

"Oh, sir," wailed Mrs. Blexey, "do you think that such a nasty man has run away with Miss Mona?"

"It is the sole solution of her disappearance that I can think of, Mrs. Blexey. There, there! Don't talk any more. Ned, you go round the Downs, and use the car for speed. I'll wait until the arrival of Madame Marie, and then search Folkstone. Humph!" Prelice looked sharply at Ned. "Do you know if Jadby has a boat, or a yacht, or a steamer of any sort?"

"Yes," said Shepworth, starting to his feet; "now you mention it, I did hear him say to Sir Oliver that he had a small steamer anchored in the Thames. But I can't give particulars."

"Never mind. I'll set the police to work on this possible clue. If that steamer has been brought round to Folkstone Harbour, you may be sure that Mona is held prisoner on board. But if this is so, and Jadby has gone off to the South Seas—which is just what he would do—I'll borrow Uncle Simon's yacht. Twin screw, triple expansion, and a devil to go. I'll follow Jadby to Polynesia, and to hell if necessary," ended Lord Prelice grimly.

Arrangements being thus made, Shepworth went off in the car with a policeman who knew the neighbourhood, and with the chauffeur, who was a magnificent driver—and driving of the best was needed on the rolling uplands of the Downs. Prelice, left behind, waited for Madame Marie, and in the meantime asked Mrs. Blexey about the herb which Horace had given to the girl.

"Was it a small white parcel?" asked the housekeeper.

"Yes. It contained some roots and leaves."

"Miss Mona took it with her," explained Mrs. Blexey; "she asked me to make a linen bag, and then sewed it inside her dress."

"Good," said Prelice; adding to himself: "If she has the herb and can make use of it, she may render Jadby insensible, and escape."

The reflection that Mona had this means of protection quietened him somewhat; but his anxiety rose again to fever heat when Madame Marie appeared. On this woman and on her occult powers depended the chance of saving Mona; but had Prelice told this to the police he would have been jeered at. However, he had his own methods of going about things, and it was not needful for him to expose himself to ridicule. He watched anxiously for the fortune-teller, and was amazed when she arrived in the unexpected company of Mr. Dolly Rover.

"What the devil are you doing here?" asked Prelice rudely.

"I shall tell you," said the little man very deliberately, and looking at the other with his dilated blue eyes. "This morning I went to see Madame Marie about my wife. She loves Shepworth, and I want Shepworth removed out of her path and mine."

"Did you propose murder to Madame?" asked Prelice coolly.

"No," replied Rover, with a shudder, while the fortune-teller sat down; "but I wished Captain Jadby to marry Miss Chent——"

"The deuce you did——"

"To Shepworth. That is, I fancied that Jadby could manage the business, and I offered—through Madame Marie here—a sum of money if the marriage could be brought about."

"Oh, indeed. And did Madame Marie tell you——"

"I told him nothing," interrupted the woman in her deep voice. "I never intended to, without your permission, as I said that I was your friend. Your wire came while Mr. Rover and myself were talking—that is, your messenger came—so I brought Mr. Rover down with me."

"And I came to help to find Miss Chent," said Rover hurriedly. "I want her to be found and married to Shepworth. Any money I can offer to help in the search——"

"I have ample money to deal with the matter," said Prelice, pleased to find that the fortune-teller had respected his confidence about the new engagement. "But I don't see why you need have applied to Jadby to bring about this marriage."

"Because I know that Jadby loves Miss Chent and wants to marry her, Lord Prelice. As you know, that would not remove Shepworth beyond my wife's reach. I wished to bribe Jadby into letting Shepworth marry Miss Chent as was arranged. Then my wife——"

"All right, all right," cried Lord Prelice irritably; "don't worry your head, Rover. I'll see to this. And you had better clear off, back to London. Jadby is a rough customer, and if we get involved in a row it will be bad for your heart."

"My dear Lord Prelice!"

"Yes. Anyone can see—oh, pooh! don't worry me."

"My heart is weak," said Rover with dignity, "and my wife's behaviour is not likely to make it strong. Nevertheless, I shall wait and help in the search for Miss Chent, and bribe Jadby as I said. He must not marry this young lady."

"He won't," Madame assured him coolly; "he shall marry me."

Prelice turned to the fortune-teller. "Will you go into a trance and see where Mona is?"

"I have already been in a trance before leaving Bond Street."

"Then you know——"

Madame looked at him unflinchingly. "I could see nothing but clouds, and clouds, and clouds," she responded. "Only one thing I am certain of, and that is that Miss Chent is hidden somewhere amongst these Downs."

Prelice shrugged his shoulders. "Much good that information does. I quite believe it; but where?"

"I can't say. But," added Madame Marie with animation, "I can tell you that the steamer which Felix owns is coming round to Folkstone Harbour this afternoon. Felix asked me two days ago to tell his captain to take the boat round. I didn't know why he wished that. I can understand now."

"So can I," rejoined Lord Prelice quickly. "Jadby intends to take Miss Chent to the steamer at nightfall, and do a bunk."

"Yes," replied the fortune-teller, breathing hard; "leaving me in the lurch. But he sha'n't—he sha'n't. I'll kill him first."

The young man looked at her curiously, and wished to ask her if she had killed Agstone. But he did not think that it was wise to irritate her at so critical a moment, so merely asked: "What is the name of the steamer?"

"The *Kanaro*. That is the name of one of the Easter Island statues which are worshipped by the natives."

"Jadby seems to be very closely connected with Easter Island. He certainly has made good use of the Sacred Herb."

"What do you mean?" asked Madame Marie angrily.

"Nothing," replied Prelice, wondering why she should grow so angry. "But I think that we have talked enough. Mr. Shepworth is exploring the Downs in a motor car, so you and Mr. Rover here can go also if you like."

"Yes, yes!" said the fortune-teller eagerly, and with very bright eyes, "we can do that; but I would rather go alone."

"No," said Dolly, piping out his decision. "I wish to aid in finding Miss Chent. I must get her married to Shepworth."

"Very good," said Prelice, with a short laugh; "go and hunt. I shall go into Folkstone and see after the *Kanaro*. Describe her, Madame."

The woman did so at once, and Prelice left the house an hour later with a full knowledge of what kind of a boat Jadby owned. Walking to Hythe, he took the train to Sandgate, and then used the funicular to reach the Leas. Here he swept the horizon and the harbour with his marine-glass to seek for the steamer in which Jadby intended to fly with Mona Chent; but he could see no sign of the boat.

Had Prelice been absolutely wise he would have gone to the police station to engage a couple of constables to board the vessel; but he preferred to trust in his own strong arm and in his own wits, which had hitherto served him excellently. Also, unless the constables had a warrant, they could not board the yacht if refused permission. It was better, thought the young man, to go alone and interview the captain. If Jadby was not open to argument, the captain might be, and an intimation that the law would be put in force if Miss Chent was kidnapped might prevent the commander of the *Kanaro* from risking his own liberty and the liberty of his crew. So Prelice went down to the harbour, and watched for the coming of the steamer. To his surprise, he found that she had arrived an hour since, and was anchored some distance away from the land. There was no doubt that this was the *Kanaro*, as not only did she correspond to the description given by the fortune-teller, but by means of the glass he saw the name on her stern.

Lord Prelice acted promptly, and engaged a boat to be rowed on board the steamer. When he climbed up the rope ladder hanging over the side he was greeted unceremoniously by a rough-looking man in a nondescript sort of uniform. In reply, Prelice handed his card, upon which the officer's manner changed to one of courtesy. He conducted Lord Prelice to a richly furnished cabin, and removed his cap with an explanation.

"I know your name, my lord," he said politely. "Madame Marie mentioned it to me. I am Captain Brisson, in command of this yacht."

"It belongs to Captain Jadby?"

Brisson shrugged his heavy shoulders. "So he says, my lord; but I think that it is the property of Madame Marie herself. Still as Captain Jadby is to marry her, they can both own it."

"Captain Jadby wants to marry a young lady whom he is kidnapping," was Prelice's sharp reply, "and if you aid him to do so, the law——"

"Stop, sir," said Brisson, rising. "My first mate said something of this to-day. I'll bring him in." And he tramped heavily out.

Prelice waited, but the man did not return. Then he tried the door of the cabin, and found it locked. It flashed across him at once that he had been trapped.

CHAPTER XXIV.

THE BEGINNING OF THE END.

After a strong word or two, Prelice sat down philosophically to consider his position. A weaker man might have raged aimlessly, and have wasted his strength in battering at the closed door; but Lord Prelice was too wise to kick against the pricks. He had been trapped sure enough, and he did not see any way out of the trap. No one knew where he was save the boatman who had brought him, and even as this thought came into his mind he heard the raucous voice of Brisson telling the man that his passenger would remain on board; more than this, Brisson paid the waterman, and sent him away. Until the hue and cry was raised the owner of the boat would say nothing, so it was absolutely certain that Prelice would have to remain in durance vile, without hope of immediate rescue.

The situation, however, was not devoid of certain consolations. Without doubt Jadby's plan was to bring Mona on board the *Kanaro*, and steam away with her to Polynesia. Prelice, at all events, would be on the same boat as the girl, and if it came to fighting with Jadby he felt certain that he could hold his own. Moreover, if, as Brisson declared, the yacht belonged to Madame Marie, he, as her captain, owed fealty to her rather than to Jadby; and the fortune-teller certainly would not allow her steamer to carry Mona Chent to the South Seas to be the bride of her precious Felix. No! Things, on reflection, were not so bad after all. In any case, Prelice felt that he was in the thick of the whole villainous business, and soon would be within arm's length of Mona. When she was dragged on board by her scoundrelly kidnapper, it would then be the time to act. Prelice lovingly fingered a revolver which he had strapped behind him, and wondered if it would be necessary to use it. The weapon formed a strange addition to the very civilised suit of tweeds which he wore, and was out of place in sober, law-abiding England. But then danger and murder and sudden death had entered into his life, and it was necessary to prepare for emergencies.

"I am not a bloodthirsty man," said Prelice, while seeing that his gun was well loaded and worked without a hitch, "but I should like one clean shot at Felix

Jadby!" And it may be mentioned that if the shooting took place Prelice would probably hit the bull's eyes, represented by the buccaneer. He was a clean shot, and very quick with his weapon, as those who inhabited uncivilised parts knew from experience.

The afternoon wore on to six o'clock, and still Prelice was left alone in his floating dungeon. Probably Brisson did not desire a personal explanation, knowing that he could not make any very pertinent reply to this breaking of the law. And it was possible that he preferred to leave the explanation to Jadby when he arrived with his prey. Personally, Prelice cared very little. He knew that Mona was safe, though in the power of a scoundrel; for she was a brave girl, and a religious girl, who firmly believed in God. So did Prelice, and he was quite content to think that God, who was slightly stronger than Felix Jadby, would look after his angel. This being so, and the young man knowing that God would bring everything to pass for the best in His own good time, Prelice quietly smoked cigarette after cigarette throughout that weary afternoon. Then he stretched himself on the divan, and went to sleep, wondering how Ned was getting on with his search, and what Madame Marie and Rover were doing.

He was awakened about eight o'clock by a bright light, and a sense that someone was looking steadily at him. With a yawn he opened his eyes, and saw that a steward was lighting the swing lamp over the central table, and that Captain Brisson was looking down upon him. The sailor had a rugged but somewhat good-natured face, and possessed an extraordinary athletic figure, which promised well for fighting purposes.

"Well," said Prelice, swinging his legs on to the floor, "are you going to starve me?"

Brisson burst into a horse-laugh, while his unwilling guest blinked and rubbed his eyes. "You're a plucky chap, my lord," said he approvingly.

"Thanks awfully; but I prefer food to compliments."

"I'm just about to eat myself. Hurry up, steward!" Then, when the man had gone out, Brisson threw his cap on a chair, and resumed. "You wonder maybe why I keep you here?"

"No," said Prelice, stretching himself; "it's all in the game."

"What game?" asked Brisson abruptly.

"The very dangerous one you are playing along with Jadby and your mistress. With Dr. Horace too, for all I know."

"I never met Horace, whoever he may be," retorted Brisson gruffly; "but all I know of the game is that I have to obey orders——"

"If you break owners," finished Prelice, remembering the saying, "and you will break them before you've done."

"None of your larks, my lord. I've got a gun."

"So have I," answered Prelice, "loaded in all six chambers. But you need make no mistake, Brisson. I intend to stop here, and see the game out to the end. Captain Jadby and I have to settle accounts."

"What sort of accounts?"

"Well, Jadby is kidnapping the lady to whom I am engaged. You can't expect me to stand that?"

"I guess not," assented Brisson agreeably. "I'm hitched up with a girl of spirit myself, and if anyone dare to——" He clenched his huge fist, looking pistols and daggers and Maxim guns.

"That's the proper spirit, Brisson. By the way," Prelice got out a cigarette, "you might tell me how much you know of this business."

"Very little, I reckon," answered the captain, more and more puzzled by the young man's coolness. "Jadby and Madame came to London some months ago, and she started the fortune-telling racket, while he went to see his uncle. I anchored the boat in Thames River, and went a loaf round the coast at times to keep the barky in trim. Then the other day Madame sends a message that I'm to bring the *Kanaro* round here, which I have done. Now I'm waiting for further orders."

"When Jadby comes on board with Miss Chent?"

Brisson nodded. "But I don't take any orders from any son of a sea-cook, you can bet your boots. Madame's owner, and she wants to run in double harness with Jadby, rum though her taste may be. If he's skipping with a girl, that's Madame's lookout. I don't sail until she gives the office."

Prelice nodded his approval. "In that case, Jadby will get left," he remarked coolly, "for he's trying to play low down on Madame Marie. By the way, if you know so little of the game, why detain me?"

"Well," said Brisson, scratching his head, "Madame visited the yacht at times when we were swinging off Gravesend. She told me there was some trouble over these murders——"

"You know about them?"

"Only what I read in the papers. But Madame said that you were taking a hand in the meddling way, and that she'd like to keep you out of the whole business. As I like Madame—who is a dandy fine woman with a temper—I put you in quod the moment I heard your name. You must stop here, my lord, until Madame comes on board."

"You have acted in a somewhat high-handed manner, and without any instructions to go upon," said Prelice calmly. "If I wanted to make a row I could."

"Not in this ship," growled Brisson.

"Oh, I think so. Yonder is the port-hole, and there isn't very much distance between this boat and the shore. Also, there are other steamers lying at anchor close at hand. Not to speak of my boatman having been in a position to be spoken to from the port-hole. I could fire a shot or two and rouse the harbour, and I could have hailed my boatman before you sent him away. I did none of these things. And why? Because I am in the very position I wish to be in. Jadby is coming on board, and I want to meet Jadby."

"And to rescue the girl."

"To rescue the young lady," corrected Prelice coldly. "If you attempt to clear out with Miss Chent, I'll make it hot for you."

"What can you do?"

"What I said. I have my revolver. See!" Prelice whipped out his weapon before Brisson could move. "I have you covered. What is to prevent me from shooting you and racing on deck to swim ashore?"

The captain did not move a muscle. "You can put the gun down, my lord," said he, with a note of admiration in his voice. "I promise you that I won't steam for the Southern Cross until Madame gives the word."

"Madame won't come on board."

"Then I wait until she does," retorted Brisson. "Will you put that gun down, or am I to be shot?"

"You are more use to me alive than dead," said Prelice, and slipped his derringer behind him, handy for the grip; "but I see the tea is on the table. I'm infernally hungry."

Brisson smacked his great thigh, and looked at Prelice with much admiration. "Guess you'll come home on the winner," said he as they sat at table, "and I should just love to see you get the bulge on that son of a sea-cook."

"Meaning Jadby?"

"Meaning Jadby," assented Brisson gravely. "Have some salt tack."

The hungry guest assented very readily, and ate a decent meal of extremely bad sea food. Prelice was not fastidious when in the wilds, and passed over the table like a prairie fire. At the conclusion of the meal Brisson mixed him a tot of rum, and handed along a box of very good cigars, which had never paid duty. Then to pass the time until Jadby arrived, they chatted. Amongst other things, Prelice learned that Brisson had met Sir Oliver Lanwin, and did not like him. The baronet had a bad record in the South Seas.

"I was in his service once," growled Brisson, cutting up tobacco with a clasp-knife; "but he gave me the chuck 'cause I wouldn't pile up a schooner, which he'd insured for wrecking. Agstone did it, though." And he filled a dirty little pipe with the rank tobacco.

"Humph! You knew Agstone?"

Brisson nodded. "He was a fairy-tale pirate, was Agstone," said he. "Lord, I could put in the night yarning about his doings. Murder amongst 'em too." And he spat. "Sir Oliver knew of that, and got the hang of Aggy. No wonder Aggy got square with him."

"Do you mean to say that he murdered Sir Oliver?"

"You can hold on to that, my lord. Sir Oliver treated Aggy like the old devil treats a holy man. Course I wouldn't swear to Aggy's knifing him in a Court o' Law; but it sounds like Aggy. Wonderfully quick with his sticker, was Aggy."

"And who do you think murdered Agstone?"

Brisson leered. "You've got me there," he confessed. "I can't lay my hand on the son of a gun that did that."

Prelice nodded. Possibly Agstone had turned on his tyrant to send him below; but it was impossible to say who had sent Agstone to join the baronet. "About Madame Marie, now. Is that her real name?" he inquired.

"Oh yes. Marie Eppingrave. She's the daughter of a Tahiti merchant and a French lady. There's no half-caste rubbish about Madame, you bet. She's got cash too—this yacht, and a slap-up island all to herself. Why she wants to collect Jadby into her life, I dunno; but there, you can't understand womenfolk."

"You like Madame Marie?"

"Seeing she nursed me through a yellow fever bout and gave me this command, I do," said the man of the sea. "A good sort is Madame, with a temper of sorts, of course, as every woman should have. She'd knife a man as soon as look at him, and nurse him square after her temper had busted. Wish she'd knife Jadby. He's a rotten beach-comber."

"Humph!" Prelice thought for the space of half a cigar. "And Madame Marie's fortune-telling?"

"Well, I guess there's no explanation of that, my lord. She's got piles of cash; but maybe her heart's in them hocus-pocus things. I've seen her do some rum business on occasions. When she looks at you, you feel cold water freezing your spine. Can't say I'd like to have her to be Mrs. Brisson, even if I put my old gal into her wooden overcoat. But Madame Marie's a dandy fine woman. No mistake about that."

In suchlike conversation did the two wile away the time until ten o'clock, then they went on deck. Brisson was quite willing to allow Prelice to accompany him, as he had grown to like the young man, and, moreover, was ready to take his word that he would not try to escape. But Prelice warned him that he would make trouble to save Mona if needful, and Brisson being on the side of Madame Marie was agreeable that it should be so. Besides, he had a sneaking liking for Prelice's somewhat stormy wooing, and wished to help him. Perhaps a strong dislike for Jadby had something to do with Brisson's attitude.

It was a perfect night, lighted by a brilliant moon and countless stars. A warm wind was blowing from the land, and far up on the heights twinkled the innumerable lights of Folkstone. The *Kanaro* rocked at anchor a stone's throw from the shore, and many other vessels of a less piratical nature were anchored in the harbour. The water shone like a sheet of silver, and the green and red riding-lights of the ships glittered in the sheeny depths. Prelice leaned over the side of the boat, and strained his eyes to see if any craft was approaching the *Kanaro*, but for quite half-an-hour he beheld nothing. However, he was tolerably certain that Jadby would come carrying Mona with him, and felt if his revolver was ready in his hip-pocket. If need be, he was resolved to shoot the buccaneer; and who can blame him, considering how basely Jadby had acted?

It was when the clock from the church tower boomed out eleven that the trouble came. Brisson laid his big hand on Prelice's arm, and pointed to a boat which was putting off from a somewhat deserted part of the shore. Three figures were in it, two rowing and one seated holding the tiller-ropes. The rowers were labouring hard to reach the *Kanaro*, and Prelice saw through his glass that other figures on the land were launching another boat to follow.

"There's going to be a holy show," swore Brisson under his breath. "I wish ——" He fingered his revolver, but did not dare to use it. The place was too civilised.

The first boat came on swiftly, and Prelice discerned that Jadby was rowing with the other man, and that Madame Marie was seated in the stern. He could see nothing of Mona, and his heart thrilled, as he thought from the presence of the second boat, which had now put off, that the girl had been saved, and that her kidnapper was now being pursued. Brisson watched the race between the two boats, and then ran on to the bridge. Prelice heard him shout to the engineer to start the engines—for the boat had steam up—and a minute later he heard the steady throbbing of the screw, while a rush of men hastily pulled up the anchor. Apparently Brisson saw that the only chance of safety for Madame Marie and Jadby was to have the boat ready to start, and risked the engines going before the anchor was up. Indeed, this latter took so much time, and time was so precious, that he shouted out to let the anchor slip, and the roar of the chain showed that his orders had been obeyed. Meanwhile many people were rushing to and fro on the shore. It was apparent that everyone knew something untowards was going on, and that there was intense excitement. Already other boats were putting off, and Brisson was cursing, like the old salt he was, at the danger of his beloved mistress.

The first boat swung near the side of the yacht, and Brisson raced from the bridge to the side to shake out the rope ladder. Madame Marie rose to grip the rope; but in a moment Jadby was on his feet, and catching her round the waist, had thrown her into the sea. Brisson gave a cry of wrath, and as Jadby placed his hand on the ladder, he leaned over, fumbling behind with his hand. The next moment there was a clear, sharp crack of a revolver, and Jadby, with a wild cry, fell off the ladder into the sea. The boatman cowered in his craft; and Prelice could see the head of Madame Marie appear some distance away, as she came to the surface and drifted with the tide. On witnessing the sudden catastrophe, the second boat rowed towards the drowning woman.

Brisson uttered a shout of rage as Madame Marie was pulled into the boat, and ran up again on to the bridge.

"Damn it, they've got her," he yelled, and twirled the dial to "Full speed ahead." Then he sprang to the wheel, and wrenched it out of the steersman's hands.

Prelice soon saw what he meant. The *Kanaro* bore straight down on to the boat. Brisson was evidently prepared to kill his mistress rather than let her fall into the hands of her enemies. A shout of dismay arose from the boat as the great bulk of the yacht swung forward. In a flash Prelice took his choice, and poised his revolver at the mad captain. There was a crack of the revolver, a cry from Brisson, and he went down like a shot, while the boat swung helplessly in the harbour, the engines working powerfully, but the wheel swinging idly.

Two or three sailors seeing that Prelice had shot the skipper, came towards him with a rush. The young man did not lose time. He jumped on the taffrail, and dived straight into the silver tide. As he rose to the surface the crew flung belaying-pins and spars, and bits of coal lying on the deck, at him. One man, with a straighter aim than the others, hit Prelice with a lump of hard coal. The young man uttered a gasping cry, and flinging up his hands, went down. His last look was at the yacht, and he saw that she swung round, and was heading full speed for the entrance to the harbour.

CHAPTER XXV.

EXPLANATIONS.

When Lord Prelice recovered his senses, he opened his eyes in a comfortable room on a comfortable bed, and saw as in a dream that Ned was seated beside him. His head felt confused and sore, but he regained sufficient command of his wits to recognise his friend.

"Where am I, Ned?" he asked in a feeble voice, and put up a weak hand to his head, which was bandaged.

"At Lanwin Grange," replied Shepworth quietly, thinking it best to explain reasonably, and glad to think that Prelice was sane. The knock on his head had been a nasty one.

"Who pulled me out of the water?"

"One of the boats that followed us picked you up when you rose for the second time. You have had a narrow escape from death, Dorry."

"Mona?" asked Prelice, closing his eyes.

"She is all right, but somewhat shaken after her experiences."

"With that blackguard Jadby. What of him?"

"Dead—shot through the heart. His body was found, and now lies at Folkstone, awaiting the inquest."

"And Brisson, the man who shot him?"

"Oh, Brisson did that, did he," said Shepworth. "He's got a good eye, and saved us a lot of trouble. Well, Brisson and the *Kanaro* have gone into the wide world. I expect he's on the high seas, making for Polynesia, and won't be caught. I hope not, for after all he only saved Jadby from the hangman."

"Why? What did Jadby do?"

"He murdered Dolly Rover."

"Ned, do you mean to say——"

"I mean to say nothing just now. Try and go to sleep. Here, drink this first; you are still weak. Hang it, Dorry, you have been unconscious for twenty-four hours, and heaps has happened."

"One last question, and then I'll sleep," said Prelice, who felt that he was weak from loss of blood. "Madame Marie?"

"Dead. She killed herself, after confessing."

"Confessing what?"

"Many things. Go to sleep, Dorry, I tell you."

Prelice did not answer, but closed his eyes with a groan, feeling very stiff and sore and wonderfully weary. But sleep, the great healer, soothed his too restless brain, and mended his broken body, so that he woke again, after hours of slumber, feeling hungry and refreshed, and eager to learn all that had taken place. It was candle-light when he closed his eyes, but the sun was shining into the room when he opened them again. And beside his bed, Ned had been replaced by Mona. She was hanging over him like a mother over her first-born, and uttered a coo of satisfaction when he looked at her and smiled.

"Mona—darling," said the sick man, thrusting out one weak hand.

She kissed it, and tucked it again under the clothes. "Go to sleep!"

Prelice, feeling ever so much stronger, objected to being treated like an infant, sweet though it was when Mona was the nurse. "I have had enough sleep," he said, yawning; "one can overdo laziness, my dear girl. Besides, I am hungry."

"Ah!" Mona laughed, "you can't live on love."

"No," said Prelice ruefully. "I am too earthly. Now breakfast——"

"Is waiting. Come, let me place this pillow behind you, and smooth the clothes so, and——"

"And kiss me, so," said the invalid, suiting the action to the word.

The future Lady Prelice tapped his cheek in pretended displeasure, and went to the door. In another minute she returned, followed by Mrs. Blexey bearing a tray, which she placed before the hungry young man.

"Coffee and cream, two lightly biled eggs, thin bread and butter, and honey from our own bees," said Mrs. Blexey, arranging the tray. "I hope that your lordship is better."

"My lordship is starving, Mrs. Blexey."

"And no wonder," sighed the housekeeper, placing one fat hand on her ample breast; "you ain't had anything for hours and hours, my dear, if you'll excuse my boldness in calling you so. And to think of all the terrible things that had happened, while you were lying there, as pretty and neat as though you were in your coffin, and——"

"Blexey, you're a ghoul. Go away," said Mona imperiously.

"I'm a United Inhabitant of the Celestial Regions," said Mrs. Blexey with dignity; "but I see that you want to feed him, my dear lady. May the dear Lord bless your marriage, and happy I am that I should have lived to see this day."

She waited for a reply, but Mona was too busy assisting Prelice with his breakfast to answer, and the young man was too busy admiring Mona to worry about the stout housekeeper. So she heaved a sigh, and retired in a flood of tears, as she thought how happy they would be. It was an odd way of showing her joy; but Mrs. Blexey, after the manner of her class, wept indiscriminately for a wedding or for a funeral.

"Mona, dearest and best," said Prelice when half way through his second egg, "I am a selfish beast. You are looking tired, and here I am letting you feed me."

"I am not tired at all," denied the girl vigorously, "but my nerves are a trifle out of order after what I have undergone. Hush! eat your breakfast, you tiresome boy."

"Will you give me a kiss if I drink another cup of coffee?"

"No. I'll give you a cigarette. Then you can sleep, and get up at midday. Mr. Shepworth and Mr. Martaban want to see you on business."

"Why do you speak of Ned so stiffly, Mona?"

"I am engaged to you now," she replied demurely.

"That doesn't mean poor Ned is to be left out in the cold."

"He won't. I expect that he'll marry Mrs. Rover after her months of mourning are over."

"Ah, yes. Ned mentioned that Jadby had murdered Dolly. How did it happen, Mona, my dear?"

The girl shuddered, and took away the tray. "I don't think Captain Jadby meant to kill him," she said in a low voice. "Madame Marie denies that he did. But Mr. Rover's heart was weak, and so——"

"Give me that cigarette, and tell me all about it from the beginning, dear," said Prelice coaxingly.

Mona did as she was asked, as he really now looked much the better for the food and the night's rest. In fact, Prelice was in such good spirits that he apologised for his untidy appearance. "I must look a regular Bill Sikes with this rough chin," he said, passing his hand over his face. "Oh, how delicious this cigarette is. Well?"

"I'll tell you all as quickly as I can," said Miss Chent, sitting beside him, and allowing him to hold her hand, on the principle that sick people must be humoured. "You know that Captain Jadby carried me off in a motor car."

"Infernal insolence——"

"Hush, George; the poor wretch is dead, so I forgive him everything."

"All right. I'll try and be a Christian such as you are, although it is not easy. Fire ahead."

"I started to walk to Hythe to catch the train to Folkstone in order to see Lady Sophia," explained Mona slowly. "I did not know that she had returned to London. Just as I got into the belt of woods between Hythe and the Downs a motor car met me, coming up. Captain Jadby was driving it."

"Didn't know he could drive," growled Prelice restlessly.

"Oh yes. Uncle Oliver talked of having a motor, and asked his son to learn driving, so that he might take him about with him. And, in fact, I think that Uncle Oliver presented this motor to Captain Jadby when he learned how to handle the machine."

"Didn't your uncle tell you that he did?"

"No, and yes. That is, he let slip a word or two. But what does it matter? Captain Jadby had this motor, and a very good one it was—at least Ned says so."

"Ned, and not Mr. Shepworth. That's right, darling." And Prelice patted her hand. "Go on, sweetest."

"I can't if you keep interrupting," said Mona severely. "Well then, Captain Jadby got out, and said that he was coming up to see me, and while he was speaking to me he lighted a cigarette."

"Hang him—confound him."

"But it wasn't a cigarette after all, as I found," went on Miss Chent hurriedly. "He had twisted up a leaf or two of the herb into the form of a cigarette, and when it was lighted he suddenly seized me, and held it smoking under my nose. I screamed, but no one was near to hear me, and then I became rigid and helpless. Owing to the scantiness of the smoke, I did not become quite insensible, but fell into a cataleptic state, as Mr. Shepworth did."

"And as you did in the library."

"No; for then I became quite insensible. Of course, had not Captain Jadby tricked me by twisting the leaves into a sham cigarette, I should have run away. As it was, the smoke seized me before I could do anything. I became cataleptic, as I said, and could move neither hand nor foot, although I was quite conscious all the time. Captain Jadby put me into the car, and arranged the rug round me. Then he"—Mona hesitated, and coloured, "he—he kissed me."

"Damn him—hang him—curse him!" raged Prelice, banging on his pillow. "I wish he was alive that I could horsewhip him. The beast! The——"

"Hush! hush!" Mona placed a cool hand over her lover's mouth. "He is now dead. Leave his punishment to God. But you can fancy my feelings when, owing to the herb, I had to suffer his kiss. Faugh!" She passed a handkerchief across her mouth; then, while Prelice swore under his breath, she continued quickly, so as to prevent another outbreak of anger. "Captain Jadby drove the motor up the hill and over the Downs. As I was conscious, though helpless, I carefully noted the way, so that I might return if I escaped."

"Did you see anyone on the road or on the Downs?"

"Not a soul," she replied. "We went far inland, and then turned to one side. Captain Jadby drove the car off the road and across the grass for over a mile. It swayed and bumped; but he is a wonderful driver, and managed to prevent the car from overturning. At last we came to a small hut in a hollow, quite concealed from the surrounding country. No one would have noted it, for the side and chimney were built of turf, and the roof was thatched with green rushes. It looked quite like a part of the hollow itself, and great grey stones were lying about on all sides. Captain Jadby drove the car into some bushes, and carried me into the hut. He then sat me down, and talked."

"What did he say?" asked Prelice, frightfully pale, and grinding his teeth.

"I am bound to acknowledge," said Mona quietly, "that after the one kiss he behaved like a gentleman. He told me that he would keep me here until the next evening, when he intended to take me on board Madame Marie's yacht, and steam for the South Seas. I heard all he said, but could not reply until the effects of the drug had worn off. Captain Jadby had evidently prepared the place for my prison. The door was strong, and the one window was barred; and then there was a girl to wait on me."

"A girl?" Prelice stared in great surprise.

"Yes. I was astonished and thankful to see one of my own sex. After Captain Jadby had explained that he intended to carry me off in the *Kanaro* he went out, and brought in the girl. She was a native of the South Seas, very handsome and dark, called Vavi, but could speak very little English. Captain Jadby told me that the girl was Madame Marie's maid, and that he had brought her here to be my companion. Then he went away, and I never saw him again until eight o'clock the next evening—at least," added Mona, correcting herself, "I fancy it was eight o'clock. But it might have been six or seven; I lost all count of time. So that was how I was kidnapped."

"It was cleverly done," said Prelice caustically. "Go on."

"In about an hour I came out of the cataleptic state, and tried to escape; but the girl showed me a knife, and intimated in her broken English that she would stab me if I did. I tried to bribe her, but she would not be bribed. I had therefore to make the best of it, as I was alone midst those lonely hills, with a half-savage woman for a companion. All the same, George, I was not afraid. I knew that you would look for me, and that God was watching over me."

"Dear, I thought the same." Prelice kissed her hand.

"Then I remembered the Sacred Herb which Dr. Horace had given me. I got it ready, and when Captain Jadby came the next evening with the car to take me on board the *Kanaro*, which he told me was at Folkstone, I waited my opportunity. Vavi had been cooking—there was plenty of good food—" said Mona, in parenthesis, "and the fire had smouldered to red ashes. When Captain Jadby entered he sent Vavi away. Where she went I do not know; but Captain Jadby sat by the fire, and made me sit also. We had two stools. Then he talked a lot of rubbish about loving me and of the necessity of getting away from Madame Marie. He said that she was an old fool, who loved him, but that he intended to make use of her yacht, and run away with me. He finally said that by the time Madame Marie found him again in the South Seas I would be his wife. After that he called you names, and——"

"I can guess the stuff he spouted," said Prelice contemptuously. "What about the herb? Did you make use of it?"

"Yes. When Captain Jadby was not looking at me, but bending over the fire stirring it with his cane, I dropped all the leaves on to the ashes. A thick, white smoke arose. I got up quickly, and sprang on Captain Jadby's shoulders to hold his nose over the smoke. It caught him in a second, and he received the full volume in his face. I felt dizzy myself, but managed to pull him back out of the fire, and ran to the door. It was not locked since Vavi went out, so I escaped into the open. It was growing dark, and I ran up the hill, to get out of the hollow as quickly as I could."

"And Vavi with her knife?" asked Prelice excitedly.

"I never saw her. I don't know where she went. I ran without a hat or cloak up the hills and over the Downs. Then I saw the road, and struck out for that. It was very late when I reached the Grange, and I fainted in Mrs. Blexey's arms."

"No wonder," muttered Prelice, "but thank God you tricked the beast, and with the Sacred Herb too." Prelice chuckled. "You paid him out in his own coin. But what happened next?"

"I can't tell you myself. I can only repeat what Ned told me. He gathered a lot from Madame Marie when she confessed."

"What did she say?"

"Wait, and I'll tell you in an orderly manner, George. After I ran away, Vavi came back to the hut. She found that I was gone, and Captain Jadby insensible with the smoke. Instead of hunting for me—very luckily—she set to work to revive him."

"But could she, seeing that the herb——"

"Vavi," said Mona quickly, "came from Easter Island, and knew all about the herb. The priests there have a way of reviving those who go into such trances. How Vavi did it I don't know, but she managed in an hour to bring Captain Jadby to his senses. As soon as he got them, he rushed out, still half dizzy, to search for me. Just as he left the hut he came upon Madame Marie and Mr. Rover, who had been searching on the Downs for me."

"Yes! Yes! I remember they started out. Well?"

"Captain Jadby thought in his dizziness and in the twilight that Mr. Rover was you, and seized him by the throat, saying he would kill you rather than let you marry me. Madame Marie tried to pull him off, but Captain Jadby held on tight. Then Vavi helped, by Madame's command, and they released Mr. Rover. He was dead."

Prelice nodded. "I quite understand. The poor devil had a weak heart, and should not have mixed himself up in this business. I told him that Jadby was a rough customer. Strange how Jadby has been the means of removing an obstacle from Ned's path. Well then, what happened?"

"Madame gave Captain Jadby something to revive him entirely—some drug —some antidote. He became quite himself, and was terrified when he saw what he had done. Madame insisted that he should fly with her from England, lest he should be hanged for the murder of Mr. Rover, and made him get the car. It was ready to take me to the *Kanaro*, if you remember, but instead it took Madame Marie and Vavi and Captain Jadby. When they reached the road, they met the car with Mr. Shepworth, who had been searching for me, and were recognised."

"Perhaps Ned took Vavi for you?"

"Perhaps he did in the twilight," assented Mona; "at all events Ned's chauffeur followed, and then there was a race to Folkstone Harbour. Captain Jadby's car was the best, and he gained about ten minutes. In the harbour he and Madame seized a boat, and leaving Vavi on the shore, they offered the boatman twenty pounds to row them to the *Kanaro*. He did; and then—well, you know."

"Yes," said Prelice slowly, and with a sigh. "Jadby tried to kill that poor woman, who loved him too well, and Brisson shot him. I shot Brisson when he tried to run down the boat in which Ned was following, and into which he had pulled Madame Marie. I wish I had killed Brisson, but unfortunately I only winged him," ended Prelice regretfully. "I daresay he's all right now, and sailing for the Southern Cross. Oh, my dear, dear angel!" he cried, gathering Mona into his arms, "what an escape."

"Let us thank God, darling," she said reverently; and they both did with full hearts. It was a very excellent beginning to the new life.

CHAPTER XXVI.

A CONFESSION.

That afternoon Prelice was up and dressed, and seated in the drawing-room, talking earnestly to Martaban and Ned Shepworth. His head was perfectly clear, although still a trifle sore, and he wore a picturesque bandage round it, which added to his pale and interesting looks. But the colour was gradually creeping back to his cheeks, and he was well enough to hear further what had taken place since he had been rendered unconscious.

Shepworth was lounging in the window-seat under one of the painted windows, and it might have been the rosy light which came through this which made him look so happy and healthy. On the other hand, it might have been the consciousness that fate had opened the way to his marrying the woman he loved, and who loved him. He could not find it in his heart to regret Rover's timely death. The man had always behaved badly to his wife, and had done his best to make her life a martyrdom. Now, poor victim of a family sacrifice, she would have a chance of being happy for the rest of her life.

Mr. Martaban, seated at the table with a few sheets of foolscap before him, also looked happy. And no wonder. His beloved client, Miss Mona Chent, had inherited the lovely old house and ten thousand a year, and shortly was to become Lady Prelice. A great change this from the time, not so long ago, when she had stood in the New Bailey dock accused of murder. And again, the sheets of foolscap with which the lawyer fiddled contained a confession by Madame Marie Eppingrave which entirely cleansed the name of Miss Chent from the stain of crime.

"This is not the original document," explained the delighted Mr. Martaban to the anxious Lord Prelice. "Inspector Bruge has the original, which was signed by Marie Eppingrave in his presence."

"How did she come to make the confession?"

"I think it was because Captain Jadby was dead," put in Shepworth from his end of the room. "She held up, until it was proved beyond all doubt that he had been shot through the heart. Then—I suppose—she saw that life was not worth living without him, and so decided to put an end to herself."

"How did she manage it, seeing that she was in custody?"

"Oh, she had some phial filled with poison about her. I expect she had everything prepared to make away with herself should Jadby have succeeded in kidnapping Mona to the South Seas. However, we stopped that, thank Heaven, and Madame Marie confessed."

"I wonder she did," said Prelice reflectively.

"I think it was because she had a sneaking regard for you, Dorry," said the barrister after a pause. "To the last she declared that she was your friend, and hoped that you would be happy. However, she did confess, and yonder is the copy of her confession."

"What does it say?" questioned the other man.

"I am about to read it to you," said Martaban, gathering up the sheets skilfully; "or else, if you prefer it, I can give you a shorter account in the form of a story."

"I should prefer that," said Prelice gravely. "I haven't patience to wait to the end of that long screed to know the exact truth. Who murdered Sir Oliver? Tell me at once."

"Steve Agstone, inspired and coerced by Madame Marie."

"Humph! So Brisson was right after all," commented Prelice. "And who got rid of Agstone?"

"Captain Jadby."

"The deuce!" Prelice raised himself on his couch. "Did he wear that sham frock?"

"He did," said Shepworth quickly; "and being, as you know, slimly built, I quite mistook him for a woman, seeing how clever was the disguise——"

Martaban waved his hand impatiently, as Shepworth drew breath to continue his speech. "Let me speak," he said, leaning back in his chair. "Lord Prelice, you know, of course, that Madame Marie Eppingrave was deeply in love with this man Jadby."

"Yes. Brisson told me so, and so did Madame herself."

"To make a long story short," said Martaban, gathering up the papers, and speaking with much deliberation, "this woman wished to marry Jadby, and as she was rich, he was willing to do so. Then he decided to go to England, and see if Sir Oliver—his father, remember—was keeping to his promise of leaving the money to his natural son. Madame Marie supplied the cash for Jadby to live in London, and brought him there in her yacht—the *Kanaro*—commanded by Captain Brisson."

"And the yacht was anchored in the Thames until Madame sent it round at Jadby's request to Folkstone for the kidnapping," said Prelice. "I know all that, Mr. Martaban. Continue."

The lawyer did so very willingly. "For some reason—I know not why, seeing that she was wealthy—Madame Marie took to telling fortunes in the Bond Street establishment. Jadby, on the other hand, came down to see his father in this house, and here fell in love with Miss Chent. He kept this secret from Madame Marie, naturally fearing what she would say; but she suspected something, and insisted upon coming down to see Sir Oliver, whom she had known in the South Seas. Madame learned that Lanwin was in favour of the match, and therefore set herself to work to thwart it by every means in her power. She implored Sir Oliver to allow Miss Chent to marry Shepworth here ——"

"Thinking that we loved one another because of the sham engagement," said the barrister quickly.

"Quite so, quite so," said Mr. Martaban, annoyed by the interruption; "I hinted at that before. However, Sir Oliver was bent upon his natural son inheriting the property and marrying his cousin—as Miss Chent truly was. Miss Chent refused, and Sir Oliver drew out a new will, of which Madame Marie knew. It confirmed the will made in Jadby's favour."

"But what was the need of that?" asked Prelice, surprised. "Wasn't the first will good enough?"

"Oh yes, but as it had been made in the South Seas, Sir Oliver thought—very wrongly, in point of fact—that there might be some flaw. Now, Lord Prelice, you can see that if Jadby married Miss Chent, the elder woman would lose him——"

"Madame Marie, you mean?"

"Yes, yes. I speak plainly, do I not? Well then, if Jadby inherited the property Madame Marie lost him all the same, as while he had money he would never marry her. She therefore decided to destroy the third will, which had not been signed, and—to have Sir Oliver murdered."

"Why didn't she stick him herself?" asked Prelice.

"A strange woman," said the solicitor meditatively; "she would do much to gain her ends, even employing a third person to commit a crime. But for some feminine reason she would not stain her own hands with blood."

"Rather a quibble."

"It is, my lord, it is. However, to continue. As Mr. Haken wished to borrow money from Sir Oliver, and consulted Madame Marie about the same, she used his confidence as a lever by which to obtain the leaves of the Sacred Herb from Dr. Horace. Before that time he had refused her, but he gave the herb to Mr. Haken. I don't know why."

"I do," said Prelice below his breath, and thinking of the openly expressed hatred which Horace had proclaimed towards the dead man.

Martaban took no notice of the interruption. "Mr. Haken got the herb, and gave it to Madame Marie, who handed it to Sir Oliver on the day of the murder. As you know, Jadby and Shepworth quarrelled on that day."

"Yes," said Shepworth vigorously. "Jadby learned about my love for a certain lady—through Madame Marie, I believe—and threatened to make himself disagreeable. I gave him a black eye, and myself a sprained ankle. Then the murder took place."

"Yes," said Martaban; "and Mr. Haken was in the library, when——"

"I know," interrupted Prelice sharply; "my uncle told me. But how did Madame Marie induce Steve to murder his master?"

"It seems that she knew how Agstone was wanted for certain other murders in the South Seas," said Martaban, glancing at the papers, "so she threatened to have him extradited unless he did her bidding. He was, I regret to say, quite willing to do so, as he hated Sir Oliver, who treated him like a slave."

"That," said Prelice emphatically, "I also know from Brisson. And then?"

"Then when Mr. Haken retired, Sir Oliver burned the herb in a shallow bronze cup—the same as Mr. Shepworth saw in his flat—and went into a trance. Madame Marie had arranged with Agstone that he should watch at the window until Sir Oliver was insensible, and then kill him. The man did so with the jade-handled paper-knife."

"Why wasn't Agstone stifled with the smoke fumes?"

"Because the smoke had died away. When Sir Oliver was dead, Agstone heard a step, and, after setting fire to some more leaves, he ran out of the window, not the one opened by Miss Chent, but another one. He watched, and saw Miss Chent enter; saw also how she fainted with the acrid smoke. He entered, and placed her in the armchair where she was found. It was then that Madame Marie came downstairs and into the room. She snatched up the third will, at which Sir Oliver had been looking, before manipulating the herb, and tearing it up, flung it into the fire. Then she gave the will leaving everything to Miss Chent—which Lanwin had also been looking at to destroy, I presume —to Agstone, and told him to take it up to his brother, Dr. Horace."

"What for?" asked Prelice, surprised.

"Madame Marie said she had no grudge against Miss Chent," explained Martaban, "and wanted the will placed safely out of Jadby's way, so that Miss Chent might inherit, and that Jadby might be kept poor."

"One for Mona and two for herself," said Prelice grimly. "But who placed the knife in Mona's hand?"

"Agstone, who hated her, did. A step was heard—that was Shepworth coming down—so Madame Marie ran out of the window, and got back to her room by another door, which Agstone had left open. The man waited to smear Miss Chent's dressing-gown with blood and to place the knife in her hand. Then Mr. Shepworth—so he says—secured the knife, and——"

"I know all that," said Prelice, "and understand the why and the wherefore of the first crime. But the second?"

"That arose out of Jadby's hatred for Shepworth and his love for Miss Chent. Jadby learned the truth about the crime from Agstone, whom he found hiding in London, under the protection of Madame Marie. He threatened to denounce him to the police to save Miss Chent, and then resolved to make use of him to incriminate Shepworth, and, at the same time, to kill him, so that he might not come forward to give evidence against Miss Chent, which Agstone wanted to do."

"But surely he would not have accused Mona of a crime which he had committed himself?" said Prelice indignantly.

"Yes, he would," said Ned quickly; "he hated Mona, and Sir Oliver, and Madame Marie, and Jadby, and everyone. The man was a Caliban; and to tell you the truth," added Shepworth candidly, "I don't think that his brother is much better."

"Ah!" said Prelice suddenly, "did Agstone confess the truth to Horace?"

"No; he did not. He simply came and handed over the will, as Madame Marie had instructed him, and then cleared out. He had to do what he was told, or else he would have been hanged."

"Well, I see. Now the Alexander Mansions crime."

Martaban went on again, glancing at the sheets. "Madame Marie learned about Mrs. Rover's dress, and told Captain Jadby, so that he could get a double made, which he did."

"Was she in favour of this second crime?"

"Oh no; for then Miss Chent would be set free to marry Jadby. She liked Miss Chent in a way, but did not intend her to be an obstacle."

"I don't believe that she liked Mona at all," snapped Prelice irritably; "she saved the second will so that Jadby might be made penniless, and would have stopped the second crime from being committed so that Mona might be condemned on Agstone's evidence. A wicked woman."

"She was all that," assented Martaban. "But allow me to proceed. Madame Marie merely thought that Jadby wished to be disguised to meet Haken, and told him about the dress, knowing that Haken intended to remonstrate with Shepworth about his conduct."

"Which was perfectly correct," cried Ned indignantly.

"But why in a dress like Mrs. Rover's?" asked Prelice, puzzled.

Martaban scratched his head. "I am not quite clear on that point," he declared; "all I know is that Madame Marie wished to mix up things. I believe that she had some clearly defined scheme in her head; but what it was she did not explain. Nevertheless, you can see how Jadby came to the ball disguised."

"Yes. But how did Agstone enter?"

"I can tell you that," said Shepworth, rising with a yawn. "Jadby, as you know, called to see me early in the evening. I opened the door to him, as the servants were out. He entered, and I preceded him into the drawing-room. He went back for his handkerchief, which he said he had dropped in the hall, and then must have set the door ajar. While I talked to him Agstone entered, and concealed himself under the dining-table. Then Jadby went to the ball in his disguise. Agstone set the herb burning, and stifled me, and afterwards admitted Jadby in his disguise. I was incriminated, you see; and Jadby, to make me quite insensible, lest I should see too much, waved the bronze cup under my nose. When I was completely insensible he stabbed Agstone with the knife, which Agstone—having taken it from my desk—had intended to use on me. Finally, Jadby returned to the ball, and concealed his dress in the cupboard in Rover's dressing-room, which was used on that night as a cloakroom. Afterwards he came down in a plain blue domino to clinch the fact that I had murdered Agstone. But you had bowled him out by then, Dorry."

There was a silence. "A strange story," said Prelice thoughtfully. "Does Inspector Bruge know it?"

"Yes; and a carefully prepared account, suppressing certain facts, has been sent to the newspapers," said Martaban, folding up the sheets. "You can be certain now, Lord Prelice, that in two days all London will learn the truth, and that Miss Chent will be looked upon as a martyr."

"Quite so; but I trust in a month or so she will be looked upon as my very dear and loving wife."

"Loud cheers!" cried Ned, adopting Prelice's favourite expression.

CHAPTER XXVII.

ALL'S WELL THAT ENDS WELL.

The title of Shakespeare's comedy quite suited the present state of affairs at the Grange, seeing that the worst was over. Within a week everything was put straight. The inquests on Madame Marie, on Dolly Rover, and on Felix Jadby lead to a disclosure of the whole strange story in the newspapers. Luckily, owing to strong influence being brought to bear, the painful love story of Shepworth and Mrs. Rover was suppressed, and it was supposed that merely the desire to save Miss Chent had led Dolly to that lonely hut, where he met with his death. Indeed, the little man became somewhat of a hero, and—as the saying goes—"nothing in life became him better than his manner of leaving it." The public followed his body to the grave with eulogistic comments, and Dolly's spirit must have smiled at the irony of the semi-public funeral. Jadby and the miserable woman, who had loved him so dearly, were buried quietly in the Folkstone cemetery. As to Brisson, he disappeared into the unknown, and nothing was ever heard of him again. Which was just as well, as Prelice had punished him in a measure by shooting him in the shoulder.

But the whole affair was a nine days' wonder, and those connected with it were glad when the excitement began to simmer down. It was annoying to have photographs of the Grange appearing in numberless illustrated papers; and still more annoying when the said pictures sent trippers across the Downs to the lonely hollow. They came in shoals, in char-a-bancs, in motor cars, in traps and carts, and riding on bicycles. But Martaban, who was taking charge of everything until his dear client became Lady Prelice, instructed the police to keep the sight-seers out of the grounds. Therefore these could only stare from the smooth heights of the Downs into the woody hollow.

And that was unpleasant enough to a couple of ardent lovers, who found their wanderings in the enchanted gardens overlooked by kodak fiends, though Heaven knows what kind of a picture these creatures hoped to obtain at such a distance. However, unless Mona and Prelice took refuge in the woods or in the house, they had nowhere to go, for the lawns, girdled by trees, were quite open to the gazers from above.

"I feel like a Christian martyr in the Colosseum," said Prelice, when the sight of three bicycles, with three dismounting riders, sent them hastily into the drawing-room. "What an infernal nuisance it is to be kodaked to make a British holiday."

"Never mind, darling," said Mona, taking his arm to lead him to a most comfortable window-seat; "let us sit here and talk. I have something to show you. Mrs. Rover sent it down. Look!"

Prelice glanced at the near table, and saw a shallow bronze cup of a somewhat graceful shape. "Is that THE cup?" he asked, examining it.

"Yes. Mrs. Rover found it in the cupboard. I expect Captain Jadby left it there along with the dress. It is rudely made, but pretty."

It was indeed quaint, being of rough bronze, carved with hideous heads twined round with wreaths of some strange plant. Prelice examined it closely. "By Jove, Mona," he said, "I believe these faces are wreathed with imitations of the Sacred Herb. See, the same spear-shaped leaves with the serrated edges. I wish we had some of the herb to compare."

"I have," said Mona, going to a cabinet and pulling out a drawer; "I have just one leaf left!" And she brought forward the purple withered leaf which, as Prelice had pointed out, exactly resembled the chasings of the cup. "It must have come from Easter Island," said Mona, while the two bent their heads over it.

"I never wish to hear of Easter Island again," said Prelice, putting down the cup; "it has brought such misery."

"Do you call me misery?" said Mona reproachfully. "Hasn't it brought me to you?"

"Yes, in a way; but Lady Sophia is really responsible. Jerusalem! Just fancy, Mona, dearest, she sent me to the New Bailey to find an interest in life, and ——"

"And you have," said Mona, blushing and smiling.

Prelice said nothing, but kissed her twice, with a look which spoke volumes. "But I wish Aunt Sophia would be agreeable to the match," sighed the young man. "I am fond of Aunt Sophia, although she is such a worry. Besides, I want her to present you at Court after our marriage."

"Do you indeed," said a complacent voice at the door, and the two looked up in great amazement to behold Lady Sophia standing there in the best of spirits, and the most perfect of summer dresses. "I have stolen a march on you," said the lady, coming forward, "and waited for a dramatic moment upon which to enter. Your speech, my dear Prelice, was a happy one; but I am *not* a worry."

"Aunt Sophia, how did you come here?"

"In a motor car along with Dr. Horace, who will soon be in. We left the car at the lodge-keeper's, because the creature would insist that we were trippers wanting to see the house. Do I look like a tripper?" And Lady Sophia spun round for inspection.

"You are a——" Prelice stopped, and glared. "I sha'n't say what you are until you tell me if you come in peace or war."

For answer Lady Sophia turned to Mona, and took her to her breast. "My dearest girl," she said, smiling, "when you marry George Prelice you must really try and put some sense into his head."

"Do you wish me to marry him?" asked Mona rather scared.

"Of course I do," cried Lady Sophia with asperity. "What else am I here for, you dear, silly, pretty, sweet, angelic darling?"

"Hurrah, Aunt Sophia! I endorse all the unnecessary adjectives save the second!"

"You can take that to yourself, Prelice. Now what am I?"

"A weathercock," said her graceless nephew promptly, although she quite expected him to say something else. "You bully-ragged me about my marriage, and now you—— Oh, I say," ended Prelice in dismay, for Lady Sophia had burst into tears, "whatever is the matter?"

"I'm so wicked," sobbed the old lady, clinging to Mona. "Simon has told me all, and how very nearly he was being accused of murder. It was so lucky that his connection with this horrid herb thing was kept out of the papers, or else I never, never, never should have held up my head again. Oh, that I might have lived to see my husband in a nasty dock."

"Don't trouble," whispered Mona, leading the old lady to the sofa; "it is all right. Mr. Haken is in no danger."

"And that being so," cried Prelice indignantly, "he might have held his confounded tongue, and not worried you."

"My dear George," said Lady Sophia, wiping her eyes, "he did it for your sake. I was raging against the marriage, and he told me how nearly he had been an Old Bailey thing, or a New Bailey creature. I forget which. I saw then how very easily one can be accused of things they hadn't the slightest intention of doing. And so—I am here. Kiss me, my love," cried Lady Sophia, again embracing Mona. "You are much, oh, ever so much, too good for Prelice."

"And I was too good for her some time ago," laughed Prelice. "Aunt Sophia, you are a weathercock; but," he added, shaking hands, "I am glad that a kind wind has blown you round to being pleased. You are an angel."

"I've been very horrid," said Lady Sophia penitently, "but I have made it up with everyone—even with Constance, poor thing, although she did behave badly with that silly poodle creature."

"He is dead, so let him rest, Aunt Sophia; and Constance has been punished, so don't blame her any more."

"I am not blaming her. How silly you are, Prelice. Don't I tell you that I've called to see her? She looks so well in her mourning, and so very happy. Mr. Shepworth is keeping away from her for a time; but they quite understand each other, and marry in a year. It will be a good match for Mr. Shepworth, for Constance will have all that poor thing's money. She won't have any bridesmaids, though, being a widow."

Lady Sophia's discontented chatter was ended by the entrance of Dr. Horace, still gruff and untidy and aggressive. "Oh, here you are," said Lady Sophia, "looking more like a man out of the Stone Age than ever. I take him about as an illustration of the time when people lived in sweet little caves, and wore sables all the year round."

"'Day, Prelice," said Horace, taking no notice of Lady Sophia's babble. "How are you, Miss Chent? I have come to say good-bye. I can't stand this London rot, so I'm off again to the other side of the world."

"Go to Polynesia, and ask Brisson how his arm is," said Prelice. "But, I say, you treated me rather badly over this case."

"Bosh! Pickles and fal-de-lal," snorted the traveller. "Why, I gave you back the will, and did my best for Haken's sake to keep you from going into the case."

"Yes, yes!" said Mona, jumping up to take Horace's hand. "I won't have him scolded."

Horace grunted, and disengaged his arm, in no wise impressed by the beauty of Mona. "Such a dear, delightful cave bear," sighed Lady Sophia on seeing this.

But Dr. Horace's eyes were fixed greedily upon the bronze cup. "I see that you have the Sacred Herb Burner of Easter Island," said he, fingering the bronze lovingly.

"How do you know?"

"I saw it there. I expect Jadby stole it. This cup," said Horace, raising it aloft, "is thousands and thousands of years old. It is a remnant of Lemurian civilisation. See how like these heads are to the heads of the Easter Island statues. And the leaves of the herb are indicated. Give me this, Prelice, and I'll take it back to those poor priests on the island. They will be delighted to see it again. It is used in their sacred ceremonies."

Prelice glanced at Mona. "What do you say?" he asked. "Mrs. Rover sent it to you, my darling."

"Take it away, take it away," cried the girl, shuddering, and spreading out her hands. "I never wish to see or hear anything of the Sacred Herb again. It has been a terrible time all through, but," she added, looking tenderly at Prelice, "it has led to happiness."

"I should like to see the herb," said Lady Sophia, coming forward, with her lorgnette raised. "Dr. Horace, can you show it to me?"

"No; I can't," growled the doctor. "I gave all I had to your husband."

"There is one leaf left," said Mona, picking up the same. "Give me the cup. Dorry, have you a match?"

"Don't send us into trances," said Prelice jokingly.

"I should love it above all things," said Lady Sophia.

Mona laid the leaf on the bronze cup, and lighted it. A thin stream of white smoke curled into the air, and, while the two women and the two men stood back to avoid the fumes, a sickly scent of tuberoses spread through the room.

The leaf frizzled into nothing, and Dr. Horace slipped the still warm cup into his capacious pocket. "That's the last of the Sacred Herb in England," said he; and without saying farewell, trotted towards the door. There he stopped to wave a friendly hand, and departed, *en route* to Polynesia and to Easter Island.

Lady Sophia fell back on to the sofa. "I declare this smell makes me quite giddy," she said, sniffing; "it's like funerals and coffins. I don't wonder people go into trances with it and see things." She bent forward, with her lorgnette to her eyes, and laughed. "I am in a trance now," she said gaily. "I see—I see—the prettiest bride in the Three Kingdoms."

"And the happiest bridegroom," said Prelice, slipping his arm round Mona's waist.

"And I see—I see——"

"You see this," said Mona; and laying her arms about her lover's neck, she kissed him fairly on the mouth.

"I think trances are quite improper," said Lady Sophia, rising. "My dear, if you will ask me to remain to dinner, I'll stop and talk over your wedding-dress."

THE END.

Lightning Source UK Ltd.
Milton Keynes UK
UKHW041041100820
367987UK00004B/865